STALKER

Other books by Bill Coulton

THE LABYRINTH TRILOGY
THE RELIC
THE SEA SIREN
THE MINOTAUR

ESCAPE TO LISBON

For Sue
My dear friend
With love
Bill

FIRST EDITION, JANUARY 2012

Copyright © 2006 by Bill Coulton
All rights reserved. Printed in the United States by CreateSpace.

ISBN: 1-4699-4110-4
ISBN-13: 978-1-4699-4110-3

This is a work of fiction. Names, characters, places, and incidents either are the product of the author's imagination or are used fictitiously. Any resemblance to actual persons, living or dead, events or locales is entirely coincidental. The reader should also be aware that the novel is set at a time when stalking laws were few or did not exist, cell phones were quite limited, and portable computers were still in their infancy. Nevertheless, there were sophisticated electronic technologies available in 1985 to those savvy enough to know where to acquire them and how to use them to advantage.

Printed by CreateSpace, a part of Amazon. com Group of Companies.

STALKER

A Novel
By
Bill Coulton

Bill Coulton (signature)

To Valerie

For Lucie

Acknowledgements and Special Thanks...

The author is indebted to several critical readers who provided a broad range of comments and suggestions that improved the story. Immense thanks go to Judith Adams, Gail Anderson, MD, Robert Bowers, Valerie Coulton, William Dingas, Esq., Salley Jessee, MD, Jayne Klein, Julie Painter, and Charles Vaughn, Maj., USA Retired.

Thanks to Erica Robb and Yoni Art for the cover design. It was through her efforts that this novel moved from draft form to final published format.

Thanks to David Shedden, Library Director, The Poynter Institute, St. Petersburg, Florida, for providing copies of microfilmed pages from **The St. Petersburg Times** for May 13, 1985 through June 16, 1985. His contribution enabled the author to report accurately weather conditions and news stories related to critical fictional events occurring in the novel.

Thanks also to Walter E. Sippel of Leather Creek Holsters, Gainesville, Georgia, for providing information about guns, ammunition and firing range details used in the novel.

Chapter 1

The stalker believes, almost delusionally, that the person he is obsessed with feels the same attraction, or would, if only they could connect in an intimate way.

–Ann Radcliff, M.D.

Monday, May 13, 1985.

The dark form of Bryan Cutler blended into the shadows of the ornamental plum tree as he crept past the concrete birdbath to Emily's front bedroom window. His saliva turn brass-flavored as he thought of her undressing there. It happened every time he came there, every night he stayed near the window. He enjoyed the flavor and fresh rush of the saliva as he sucked it to the back of his mouth and swallowed, enjoying it again and again. It was better than a reefer, he thought.

Opening the wooden gate at the corner of the house, he passed through and closed the metal latch behind him without a sound. He moved along the fence beneath Emily's back bedroom window and past the two-story playhouse toward the trees at the far corner of the yard. It was there that he could watch the living room, dining room, kitchen, and Emily's father's photography studio without being seen.

Lights were on in the studio. Jack was leaning over his light table. The opaque light on Jack's face made him look ghostly. He studied the tall, somewhat gaunt man. Emily had his nose and mouth.

Cutler turned away and crossed the yard to the trees, glancing back as Jack stopped working and approached the window. The sash flew open. Jack was peering toward the trees. A twig snapped under foot. Bryan's breath caught; he cursed silently and dropped behind a giant live oak He waited several moments before stealing another glance. Jack stood framed in silhouette, rubbing the side of his face with his right hand. No, Cutler thought, Jack hadn't seen him. After some minutes, Jack turned from the screen, went to the light table, and resumed examining what looked like photo prints.

Cutler sat silently, feeling his heart thumping in his chest. He wiped moisture from his forehead. He glanced at his watch. In five minutes, Emily's little fairy friends would be bringing her home from rehearsal. He pulled up his knees and hugged them, feeling satisfaction at being so close to his love. A mockingbird atop the streetlight in front of the house began to sing excitedly as though privy to some great event that was about to happen.

Chapter 2

Monday, May 13, 1985.

Jack Kaufman entered his studio and threw the fat manila envelope on the light table. He studied his desk calendar and counted the weeks. His world as he knew it was coming to an end. In a little over five weeks, on Thursday, June 20, 1985 to be exact, his daughter Emily would graduate from high school. On Monday, June 24th, she would be leaving for a year in Spain. On the same day, Bernice, his wife of twenty years, would be moving out. And to top matters off, his contract job as city photographer might be in jeopardy.

"I want out, too," he muttered. "QT2 looks awfully inviting." He glanced toward the scale model of his racing ketch–the QT2–resting on a file cabinet. He had always wanted to sail her around the tip of Florida and across the Gulf of Mexico to Belize. But this was not an option; he had frequent Air Force Reserve duty to perform at the Space Center. And he was under pressure from the generals to spend more time covering VIP visits from congressional leaders these days; President Reagan was studying ways to cut the space program's budget.

He tried not to think about the new world before him. But he was living on thin edges again, just like he felt when he returned from Nam. It was scary and he had nobody to talk with about it. A nagging depression made it difficult for him to get out of bed in the morning. Bernice's nightly harangues were moving him closer to nutting up. It was one thing for her to drink too much wine and get belligerent every night, but there was no telling where things would end if he started striking back.

Now and then when he thought about everything that was going wrong, the notion of killing himself crept in. The demons still lived and thrived. No. He couldn't let the demons get control again. He couldn't nut up at this time in his life, especially for Emily's sake. It was so important to see her through graduation and be there for her while she was in college. Nutting up was out of the question. Besides, Bernice sure wouldn't be there for her.

Hell, he thought, what would he have done without Em? She had become his reason for being, the person he most cared about in the world. He sat down and rubbed his eyes. There must be some way he could get his life back on track, but he had no idea how. He grinned sardonically and whispered, "Maybe I'll win the lottery." He laughed. Fat chance!

He opened the hasp on the manila envelope and spread the latest grip-and-grin photo proofs across the light table. Somewhere, he thought, there had to be one decent shot of the mayor when he was not posturing. He examined each thumbnail with the loupe. Not a single damn frame was acceptable. He threw the loupe on the table. A whole day wasted. He stood up and stretched, trying to rejuvenate his tired body.

Crossing the room to the window, he raised the sash and peered out. It was a sailing moon tonight. Heady fragrances of jasmine and honeysuckle hung thick in the moist air. Nothing like Florida in spring. The sweet fragrance changed suddenly with memories of Nam, tinged by growing scents of urinals and diesel fuel. Instead of jasmine and honeysuckle, the stink of war and death returned for an instant in his nostrils before relapsing into jasmine and honeysuckle fragrances again. That hadn't happened for a long time. Not good, he thought. He shrugged in an effort to dismiss the notion, but it lingered.

A twig snapped. He turned toward the sound. In the corner near the oak tree. Did he discern movement or was it his imagination? He tried to relax, but Vietnam reflexes would not allow it. Something was out there. He leaned on the sill and listened. Nothing. Probably one of the neighborhood cats. Or a dog. He tried to concentrate on the direction of the sound, waiting for it to reoccur. Nothing. A dog would have made more of a thrashing noise. They are clumsy. It must have been a cat.

The neighborhood mockingbird atop its favorite lamppost in front of the house broke the silence with a burst of melody. It went into a series of calls, catchy phrases, trills, and splendid codas, then stopped as if it had been shot. Here comes Em, he thought. Chuck's Olds bomber would stop any bird from singing. Yup, there was the telltale blast of music and chattering teen-aged voices growing louder by the second. A car door slammed. The front door opened and banged shut. Em's footsteps came down the hall.

"Hi," she said flatly. She dropped her books in the doorway.

"What's wrong?"

"Dad, we need to talk."

Em looked like she was about to tell him something he didn't want to hear. He hoped she wasn't going to say she was on drugs.

Stalker

All through high school she had been so cool, not smoking, drinking, or doing stuff. She was an honor student. No, it was too late for her to spoil it all by saying she had done something very wrong.

"Can't be that bad, honey. Sit down and let's talk about it."

Em sat on the edge of the work stool, her long legs drawn together elbow to knee, chin in hand. Her dark hair obscured her eyes.

"You remember Bryan Cutler?"

He tried to remember, hoping Bryan Cutler hadn't made her pregnant.

"No. Don't believe I do."

She brushed her hair back. Her brown eyes fixed on his.

"Remember? I met him at Ocean State College on that orientation tour in February? Bryan was the guide. He asked me out. I told you. We went to a movie and afterward to Harvey's for coffee and pastries."

He scratched his chin.

"Yeah. Kind of. Bryan Cutler... A big guy, dark, Orson Wells type, all black clothes? Five o'clock shadow?"

"That's him." She brushed her hair back again. "He's been hanging out at night across the street."

"What do you mean hanging out?"

"Hanging out across from our house. I've seen him."

"When?"

"At night. Sometimes in the morning before school."

"How often?"

"Oh, several times."

"And you said nothing about it?"

She shrugged.

"He's been following me around, too."

"Wait a minute." Jack sat down. "You mean this has been going on for weeks and you didn't say a word about it?"

"I didn't see that it was any big deal, Dad...until I got this letter from him today. He says last night he slept out there."

"Oh, great!"

She handed him the letter. The message was printed with ballpoint on lined notebook paper.

Emily:

Please go out with me. Why won't you? We had so much fun last time. I love you. I can't stay away from you. Last night, I had to be close to you, so I stayed all night across from your window. I don't want anything to happen to you. From now on, I will stay close to you. Talk to me. Don't hang up like you did yesterday.

All My Love,
Bryan XXXXXX

"Damn! Tell me what is going on. Start from the beginning. I want to know everything."

Em's eyes filled. A tear trickled down her cheek. She wiped it away and leaned on her knees.

"I just didn't want to bother you with it. You've been so busy lately."

"Not so busy I don't have time for you. You know better than that."

"I know... But Mom said it isn't a big deal. She says some guys are like that. They follow you around for a while until they get the message."

So, her mother knew about it and hadn't told him. What the hell is going on here?

"What message?"

"You know, that you aren't interested in them. Eventually, they'll stop following you."

"Is that what your mother says?"

Em sighed. "Yeah. She says if I keep ignoring him, he'll go away."

He felt a rising heat in his chest. Why would she confide in her? Hell, Bernice had made it perfectly clear she wasn't interested in what happened to Em. "How long has he been following you?"

"Oh, maybe a month, six weeks?"

"Jeez!" His face felt hot. "And by following you, what do you mean?"

"He's at play practice. He's at school when I arrive. He calls me up and tries to make dates. He sends me letters and leaves notes."

"You mean there's more like this one?"

"No. Not like this one. I'll show them to you. Mostly he writes about what music he likes, the movies he's seen, the usual stuff... until this one." She bit her lip.

"How many are there?"

"What do you mean?"

"The letters. How many has he sent you?"

"Oh, five or six. I'll get them."

She went to her bedroom. He reread the letter. He did not know what to say to her. How could she allow this to go on without telling him? It was all he could do to retain his composure. Old emotions were flaring up. He wanted to strangle the bastard with his bare hands.

Chapter 3

Monday, May 13, 1985.

Emily handed him six envelopes. He opened them one by one and read Bryan's scratchy writing. Interesting. He used a blunt pencil for one, a blue ballpoint for another. A couple were written using a fountain pen; splotches of ink here and there. He talked about a rock group called Acid Flavors and some tapes he had bought. Went to see a foreign film at the Art Theater about two gay women. Every letter mentioned how much he enjoyed dating Em and hoped she would go out with him again. He talked about female classmates at college and how he would like to date one of them but was afraid to ask. In one letter, he asked Em's advice about how he might approach a woman named Helen who lived in his apartment building. Weird. Some letters were stamped; others had no postage. No pleading like the latest letter. Many of the envelopes had brightly colored butterfly stickers on them, but no return address."

"How come these two don't have stamps, Em?"
"He hand-delivered them here."
"How?"

"He left them on the screen door. I found them when I came home from school."

"You were never around to see him or talk to him?"

"No."

"May I make copies of these?"

She looked confused. "Okay... What will you do with them?"

"I'm not sure." He gazed at her so she looked away. He pointed to the letter she had received today. "This one is different from the others. I think we've got reason to be afraid of what he might do."

"How so?"

"He sounds like he is obsessed with you, lurking, following you around."

He shoved the letters to one side and studied Em. Her face, what he could see of it behind her mop of dark hair, was tearing up.

"So how come you dated him? How did it happen?"

She pulled her hair away and took a deep breath. "We talked during the tour. I thought he was interesting. When Bryan asked me out to a movie, I kinda checked him out with some friends. He's on a scholarship at Ocean State College, majoring in marine biology. I thought that was cool."

He nodded approval. She brushed a tear aside.

"I remembered him vaguely from when he was a senior in high school. I was in tenth grade. He played chess every day at lunch. I used to see him once in a while last year at Harvey's. He worked there after school. But I didn't know him to talk to until the day he led our tour group."

"I see. So you had no reason to think he would bother you."

"No. Really, when we went out, he seemed an okay guy. And we had a good time together, until he asked me out again."

"And?"

"It was like, he couldn't accept it that I had other plans. Like, I could tell he felt I was rejecting him or something."

"Were you?"

"No. Honest. It was true, I had a date with Chuck for the next weekend. It was nothing personal. But Bryan got this strange look in his eyes and began asking me all kinds of questions."

"What sorts of questions?"

She shrugged. "Oh, like, 'Aren't I sexy enough?' and 'How come you're not attracted to me? Don't I turn you on?' You know, stuff like that. Sort of sexual… I just got this creepy feeling. Especially after only one date."

"Did you kiss him or make out with him?"

"No. Maybe held hands is all."

"This was when you came home from the movie?"

"It was when we stopped at Harvey's for coffee."

"Is there more you want to tell me?"

Em pulled her hair back with both hands. "I can't remember. He just said stuff like, 'Why don't you like me as much as Chuck or Dave?' He seemed to know all about the guys I'd been dating. And then he starts writing me all these letters."

"Did you write him back or call him?"

"No. I didn't encourage him."

"So, you've been putting him off for two months?"

"Yeah. He's too bizarre."

"And your mother is telling you to just ignore him?"

"Yeah."

He felt distance between them unlike at any other time in their lives. How could she tell her mother and not him? He wanted to scold her, but couldn't think of any appropriate words. And to top it off, Bernice was treating this like it was puppy-love. He tried to calm himself and spoke gently.

"Did he call you tonight?"

"No, but he was hanging around Harvey's when Chuck picked me up from school today. He was at play rehearsal when we got there and was there when we left. It's not cool, Dad."

So that explained who had been calling and hanging up when he answered the phone. "Do you know his phone number?"

"No. He lives in Seagate with his mom."

"What about his father?"

"He doesn't have one…"

"What's his mother's name?"

She shook her head. "I don't know."

"What's Bryan's last name?"

"Cutler."

"With a K or a C?"

"C."

Cutler… His head filled with images from Nam. Cropped photos fresh out of the developer. Cut-off bodies. Trimmed heads to fit frames. Snipped-off superfluous people. Cutler. Cutter. Cuts. Bryan Cuts. He shook off the stupid thoughts and tried to show he was not alarmed. But after reading these letters and hearing Em's story, he had the feeling this guy could be nuts. He took her hand and gave it a little squeeze while glancing at the clock. It was a quarter to ten. Any thought about a moonlight walk on the beach was dismissed. He glanced at the open window, wondering if they were being watched. He resisted the temptation to close it.

"About time you got your shower and did your homework. If you don't want this guy hanging around, I can put a stop to it."

"That would be great. But I just don't want it to be a big deal, okay?"

They stood up. He gave her a hug and kissed her forehead.

"Okay. Not to worry," he whispered, "I'll handle it."

"Thanks, Dad. I love you."

"Love you, too. Keep your bedroom blinds closed. Are you sure you want to sleep with open windows? We can turn on the air tonight."

"I prefer the fresh air. The screen is locked. I don't think Bryan would do something really stupid like looking in my window."

"I'll check outside to be sure he isn't around, okay?" The image of Bryan peeping into Em's bedroom brought fresh anger to his chest.

"Thanks. Good night."

"And I want you to tell me every time he calls or you see him tailing you. Okay?"

"Don't worry. I'll let you know."

Chapter 4

Monday Night, May 13.

He grabbed the flashlight from the kitchen cupboard and went outside. The street was silent. A cat furtively dashed across the yard between the houses across the street and disappeared under a shrub. He flashed the light along the side of the house past Em's window and behind the evergreens. Nothing.

He walked across the wet lawn to the crepe myrtle bushes and checked along the fence near Em's old playhouse. Nothing. Across the street, a pool of empty yellow light fell upon the palms. Yet, he sensed the guy's presence. Somewhere close by, he could feel Bryan watching him. He went inside and pondered what to do. Should he call the police? He could count on his friend, Chief Winters. Seek advice from Jim Smith, the former prosecutor? Talk with Em's counselors at school? Maybe he was overreacting when a simple phone call could stop this jerk cold in his tracks.

He entered the kitchen and opened the phone book. As he thumbed through the pages, looking for Cutler, the screen door slammed and Bernice appeared.

"Who are you trying to call?"

Her voice sounded at once challenging and disinterested.

She was wearing too much perfume again. He could barely stand it. Did she spray herself just before she came home so he wouldn't come near her? Perhaps she did it out of spite? Surely, her secret beau wouldn't stand the stench more than two or three dates. You could practically taste its metallic sweetness.

"Has Emily told you about this college student following her around?" he asked casually. Bernice's eyes flickered.

She put her purse on the counter and got a glass from the cupboard. She filled it with water from the tap. At forty-three, she still had a pretty face and nice, trim figure. She wore too much makeup now, masking the natural beauty that he had found so alluring twenty-one years ago. She ran her brightly polished red nails through her dark brown hair as though his question reminded her of another time.

"She's told me the boy's got a crush on her, if that's what you mean." She chuckled. "Bryan Cutler. Follows her around like a puppy."

Bernice drank the water and placed the glass in the sink.

"Well, the guy is sending her letters. Have you read them?"

Bernice wiped fingers across her nose. "No. Emily didn't share them."

"His latest is a beaut. Says he's camping out across the street at night."

"Really? Another Romeo!"

Bernice did not appear shocked at all. Rather, the idea of a guy sleeping all night outside Em's window seemed to delight her. She smiled, showing pretty white teeth and looked at him through half-closed eyes. It was her own version of Barbra Streisand, right down to running her tongue over her teeth.

"I had a boy do that once. Stephen Douglas. We were tenth graders. He was so lovesick my father had to chase him away several times. He'd write me these crazy letters how he could not live without me. How I was the dream of his life. He stayed love-struck for three months or more."

"I don't think this is the same, Bernice. This guy is over eighteen. He knows better."

"He's still a boy, Jack. I wouldn't be uptight unless he gets persistent."

He was already at odds with Bernice. Poles apart. Here she was making light of a very large guy who could be a potential rapist. Bernice reached into the refrigerator and pulled out the half-gallon jug of wine.

"Care for some?"

"No thanks. I'm going to talk to Bryan's mother. Tell her I don't want him anywhere near Emily."

Bernice smirked. She got a chilled wine glass from the freezer and poured it full. It was strange how Bernice could be so blasé when it was her own daughter. She took a swig and sat down at the end of the kitchen table. She folded her hands together. She no longer wore her engagement and wedding rings. Her Streisand pose changed to that of Joan Crawford. Her voice became charged with determination to have her own way no matter what.

"I think you are making too much of this, Jack!" Her lips were pursed in dramatic fashion. "If you ignore him, the boy will stop. The more you make a big deal of it, the more he will persist."

"He's not a boy, Bernice. He's a grown man. He's six feet tall and almost 200 pounds for God's sake!"

"I thought he was very polite when he came to take Emily out. He's smitten is all." She lit a cigarette and pulled an ashtray to her.

"That's your advice?"

Bernice blew smoke across the kitchen.

"I told her not to worry. The boy will stop calling her before long. It's part of growing up. Girls have to learn to be patient. Boys do stupid things until you ignore them long enough. Then, they finally get the message. Grown men are the same way."

He thought she must hate all men. And he didn't know where it came from. She was not always like that. No. Bernie was a loving wife until Em came along. Later, after they split the business and she went into advertising and public relations, she changed even more. She went through the motions of marriage. No feeling. And now, she was seeing some guy. All he knew was that she wanted out after Em graduated. Just a few more weeks. And frankly, he couldn't wait for her to leave.

"Well," he replied, "Em was plenty scared tonight. I don't see how a grown man sleeping outside her bedroom window all night is something to ignore."

"He's exaggerating. No boy would do that, at least not all night. I'd say he's telling white lies to get her attention. Trying to be a modern Lothario."

His recollection of Lothario was that of being a rake who seduced women of all ages, but he didn't want to dispute her knowledge of male characters in plays. They were talking real-world characters here. "Just one more thing we disagree about, Bernice."

"Jack, you're always going off the deep end for no good reason. Why don't you get to know the boy? Become friends. He's bright and on a scholarship. Emily tells me he doesn't have a father. Perhaps he needs a father figure. You two could become big buddies. You've always wanted a son... You might consider taking him sailing."

"Yeah, sure."

He opened the phone book, running his finger down the C column. There was an Adelia Cutler listed in Seagate, a small community adjoining Ocean City. He went to the phone and punched in the number. No answer. Bernice was watching, sipping wine, drawing on her cigarette, and doing her Greta Garbo pose. He didn't know whether it was from watching old movies late at night or thinking she had to be dramatic like her daughter, but lately she was downright comical trying to be somebody she wasn't. Or was it he? Hell, he was not sure of anything anymore. They were on opposite sides of every issue now, large or small, including Em.

He jotted down Adelia Cutler's phone number and address before replacing the book on the shelf. He went back to his studio and checked his calendar: photography assignments all day tomorrow. He put the proof sheets into a manila envelope. Helping the city's public information officer had become almost a full-time job. Anyway, it had gotten him some referrals—and he could use all he could get.

He flipped the calendar pages to the end of the month. Reserve duty. The US Air Force Reserve had been good to him after Nam, he thought. He was closing in on twenty years as a military photojournalist. One more good year for retirement!

He glanced around the walls of the studio. Photos from round the world. He stepped close to the special one—the photograph that still haunted him late in the night sometimes. It showed twelve male members of a patrol just before they went on a so-called routine reconnaissance mission up north of Long Binh. The young faces peered out, some showing a false bravado while others stared in grim defiance of fear and death. All were between the ages of eighteen and twenty-three. Only four of those men were still alive.

Some, they never found enough of their body parts to send stateside for decent burial. Two committed suicide after returning home. Another died of alcohol poisoning. Even though every face in the photograph was etched in his memory, there was seldom a day that he didn't spend a minute or two with them. They were part of an inexplicable puzzle, an emotional puzzle he had never shared with anyone.

He had been doing a special assignment for *Air Force Times* about the grunts and life with Charlie in the jungle. For weeks he had begged the commander to let him go on a patrol. The colonel only agreed when he felt the mission was in a "safe" area. Colonel Johnson could not have been more wrong.

The flight in the Huey was no problem. They landed near a friendly village and intended to walk through the jungle to another village a few miles distant. The path was narrow with high jungle walls on either side when they were suddenly ambushed. It happened so quickly. Sudden bursts of small arms fire in front and then behind them. Lawson, the point man went down, followed by Willard and Peck. A rocket launcher took out the chopper providing cover. Jack crouched, Colt .45 gripped in both hands, firing blindly into the jungle from where Charlie seemed to be shooting. It was his first experience at firing back with something other than a camera. Platoon Sgt. Robbins fell and Jack hunched down behind him, firing the remaining rounds left in his clip. Shrill cries followed the rounds he had clicked off.

As he reloaded, three Hueys came over the hill with guns blazing. Reinforcements were deployed. All ground fire went quiet. Charlie had evaporated.

He helped load Willard and other wounded onto stretchers for airlift. Afterwards, Jack wandered around, staring at the faces of his dead friends. Lance Corporal Gentry was squatted down, holding Robbins' hand and sobbing. DeAngelo, the kid from Fort Stockton, Texas who wanted to be a rodeo star, was vomiting. Four men with machetes chopped through the undergrowth where Jack and Robbins had been firing. They pulled out two Cong, both no older than 14 or 15. The two were wearing only shorts, their bodies ripped and bloody, not old enough to shave yet. Then it was Jack's turn to puke. He retched violently, until there was nothing left. He was convinced he had killed them... and whether or not it was in self-defense, there was still blood on his hands.

He never told anyone what he had done: not his buddies, not the shrinks who tried to calm his war nerves, not Bernice, especially not Em. It was too complicated. For years after he suffered from depression. Sometimes he felt deep shame that would be overcome by anger and occasionally by rage. Sometimes, he wanted to end it all. And other times, he just felt dead inside.

He remembered promising God then and there that if he got out of Vietnam alive, he would never point a weapon at another human being again no matter what the circumstances.

He returned to his chair and considered how lucky he had been. That was his closest call, but even that was not close in the strictest sense—not the kind people talk about where you see white light or your whole life flashes before you—even when he had seen others being blown to bits. He had stood, camera and gun in hand, next to guys whose bodies had literally exploded, showering him with flesh and blood. He remembered how several washings could not remove splashes of Robbins' blood from his fatigues. He finally threw them away.

How is it that one guy is lucky and another is not? Some say God saves you for some important thing when you are spared like that.

Others say the lucky ones are the guys who get zapped; they are put out of their misery early. Lawson used to say that life is just one big crapshoot: you live until your luck runs out. And for him, he was right.

He did not know what to believe. Nothing in his past seemed to outfit him for the new experiences that came his way. Like Bernice being so cold and finding some other man to love. Like Em, suddenly afraid of a guy she barely knows. And here he was, facing separation from the two people he loved the most.

Sure. He had prepared for it. He had carved out his own life away from Bernice. His photography had put him in touch with loads of people. Once in a while he got invited to a party. He and Chief Winters fished on his boat now and then. He had sailing buddies, Reserve buddies, camera buddies, and fishing buddies. Buddies…it was not like having an honest-to-God relationship with a woman you love. Not by any stretch.

Em had prepared her own life, too. Her acting, modeling, dating, going to parties, getting ready to go out into the world on her own were all positives. She had lots of friends. Her trip to Spain this summer would be a great adventure. It would get her away from this Bryan character. Unfortunately, she would be out of her father's life, too, and he would miss her.

Bernice? She had her advertising activities, women friends, a crowd of business people, openings, mixers, parties, and public relations stuff—to say nothing of her future life with Mr. Mystery Man.

Time was, Bernice and he were business partners as well as loving wife and husband. She did the writing and he did the photography. They had a decent freelance business. Now, they were separate and apart except in name and household. Everybody knew how it was, including Em. A warm rush of guilt swept over him.

Was Em inventing all this stuff about Bryan? Could it be, that knowing Bernice and he were going to split up after she graduated, Em was attempting to get their attention by frightening the hell out of him? Maybe she and Bryan were in this together. He's helping her get Dad and Mom thinking about her rather than about themselves? Was that what this is all about? Was it her way of striking back? He dismissed the notion. Em wasn't like that. But her tears could be those of sadness rather than fear. No. Those large brown eyes were frightened tonight...

He went in the bathroom and caught his reflection in the mirror. He studied his image. At five-ten, a hundred-fifty-five pounds, he could still get into his Nam uniform. His shoulders showed upper body strength from years of running, doing thousands and thousands of push-ups, sit-ups, and pull-ups. His dark blond hair was beginning to recede. He stepped closer and touched the lighter tan skin below his right eye with his index finger. It was an old scar across his cheekbone. He felt its smoothness. Bernice once thought it was sexy. A battle scar earned in Nam from a head butt in a touch football game. Ironic. He smiled wryly. Ten stitches. Everybody kidded him about putting in for a Purple Heart. New guys thought he had taken one in the face; they looked at him with awe.

He smoothed his hair and turned toward the window. Was Bryan out there? He retrieved the flashlight and slipped through the rear sliding glass door and crossed the backyard. He stepped carefully around the corner, past Em's playhouse. He moved in silence along the fence, coming through the gate between the crepe myrtle bushes at the corner of Em's bedroom. The gate latch clicked.

"Who's there?"

Em's voice was a frightened whisper, coming from the open window.

"Just me, Em. Go back to sleep."

"Night, Dad. You scared me!"

"Sorry."

Damn! He was scaring Em by playing night watchman. He opened the front screen door. Bernice was sitting in the same place, blowing smoke. She ignored him. She was on her second glass of wine. The strong perfume lingered in the air and mixed with tobacco smoke, creating the smell of a barroom. He hadn't asked where she had been tonight, knowing beforehand what she would say: "A dinner meeting with a client…" or "Had a cocktail party to kick off an ad campaign for So-and-So." It was a standard set of refrains. He headed to his separate bedroom.

Chapter 5

Tuesday, May 14.

The phone rang. Who could be calling at seven forty-five in the morning? Jack picked up the receiver. The sound of heavy metal music assaulted his ear.

"Hello?"

Click. The caller hung up. He hurried into the office and found the note with Adelia Cutler's number written on it. He dialed.

"Hello?"

It was a male voice, hollow and adolescent. The same heavy metal music was blasting in the background.

"Is this Bryan?"

"Yes."

"Bryan, this is Emily Kaufman's father, Jack. Did you just call here?"

A pause.

"No, why?"

"You've been calling and following her around. I've seen the letters you have been sending. The last one concerns me."

"Like, why? I sent it to Emily, not to you."

Stalker

"Your last letter said that you camped out across the street the other night. That's kinda scary, Bryan... I want you to stay away from her."

"It's a free country, man... I'm not mean'n any harm. I love Emily. We're dating you know."

"Yeah, I know, Bryan." He could feel the anger rising in his neck and face. "One date... that is not exactly going steady... You can't push things. You need to ease up and not hang around her all the time. Will you do that?"

"I'm not hurting anybody." His voice caught. "Why are you on my case? Give me a break!"

Between his obstinacy and the heavy metal music blaring, Jack wanted to reach through the phone, grab him by the neck and choke him.

"Can you put your mother on the phone?"

"She's not here. Besides, this is between me and Emily, Mr. Kaufman. Don't get my mom into this. Did Emily ask you to call me?"

"No, but she told me all about you following her around. If you don't want me to speak with your mother, I'd suggest you stay away from Emily. Okay?"

"That's not fair. I love her..."

"That may be, but you've got to understand what I'm telling you. Stay away from her."

"I don't want you call'n my mom. I'll be very upset if you talk to my mom."

"Stay away from Emily and I won't have to, Bryan."

"She works very hard." His voice was shaky. "She doesn't need to hear stuff from you."

"Let me speak more plainly so you get my message... Stay the hell away from my daughter or I will personally take you down. Do you get that?"

Click.

He replaced the receiver. The bastard! Jack was shaking uncontrollably. A sweat had broken out on his forehead. So Bryan was afraid he would call his mother. Damned right. If he didn't stay away, he sure as hell would call her. He wiped his hand across his face and sat down. He made a list of tasks for the day.

Em stood in the doorway, dressed in black, books in one arm, looking pensive.

"Ready, Dad?"

They climbed into the BMW and drove down Seaview Boulevard without a word. Jack scanned the streets and sidewalks for any sign of Cutler. He sensed Em was doing the same. She broke the silence.

"I heard you talking with Bryan. You were scary, Dad."

"Yeah. I lost control. But he was accusing me of making up stuff about him. He's afraid I'll tell his mom."

"Are you going to?"

"Depends on Bryan. He may decide it isn't worth the hassle and stay away."

"I hope so... I don't want this to turn into a full-scale event, you know what I mean?"

"I don't either."

He pulled to a stop in front of Ocean High School. There was no sign of Bryan.

"Have a good day at school, Em."

"You, too, Dad. Love you."

She kissed him on the cheek and was out the door and into the crowd. He drove home.

He checked his schedule, and began loading a medium-sized canvas bag: two cameras, a wide angle lens, a zoom, one 35mm, one 75mm, two flash units, and two loaded film magazines. Bernice's bedroom door was still closed. He called Bryan's house. No answer. He studied the Seagate address for Adelia Cutler, 122 Harlan Street. He hadn't a clue where it was.

He spent the day covering City Hall events, preoccupied with the dark image of Bryan Cutler. As much as he tried, he could not concentrate on getting the quality photographs of the mayor he so desperately needed.

When Em came home from rehearsal, she reported Bryan was nowhere to be seen.

"Good. Maybe you don't have to worry about him anymore, Em."

"I hope not."

She went to her bedroom. Jack sat back in his swivel chair, hoping Bryan Cutler was smart enough to stay away.

Chapter 6

Wednesday, May 15.

"There he is, Dad!"

She pointed across the street. A tall, heavy-set young man in black shirt and pants with unshaved dark stubble was leaning against a lamppost in front of Harvey's Bagel Shack. Behind him was a bicycle with a green knapsack tied to the handlebar. When he saw them watching him, he turned, hopped on the bike, and started pedaling in the opposite direction. Em gathered her books together.

"Don't go anywhere by yourself from now on, Em."

"I won't, Dad. Love ya."

Em hugged Jack and was out the door. He watched her cross the grounds. She disappeared into the crowd. For sure, Bryan was not taking his advice to stay away from her.

He made a U-turn and searched for Bryan. He had disappeared. Jack checked out several side streets and cruised toward Ocean State College, but found no trace of him. He parked a few minutes across the quad at the college, thinking Bryan might show up. A security guard eyed him and casually approached his car.

Stalker

Jack smiled and waved. The guard nodded and walked past. Jack watched in the rear view mirror as the guard glanced at the license plate and walked off, jotting the number on a pad. He waited a few more minutes before heading home.

He called Chief Winters at police headquarters. Florese, his secretary, put him through.

"Hey, guy! How's my favorite photographer?"

He lied. "Terrific, Bill."

"When are we going fishing again? Been too long, ole buddy. I hear the Blues are running."

"Next week, maybe?" He cringed at the thought of getting the boat in condition to sail. He had neglected it for months. "I've got lots of work to do on her before she's ready for guests."

"Hell, I don't count as a guest. You say the word and I'll give you a hand."

"Thanks... I'll let you know."

"Good. So, what's happening?"

"I've got a problem. Maybe you can give me some advice."

"Shoot."

"A young guy's been following my daughter around. A college kid. Shows up at school, at play practice, wherever she is. He hangs around our house at night and sends her letters."

"I take it Emily is afraid of him?"

"Yes."

"Has she been involved with him, like, going out on dates?"

"Once."

"And he won't listen when she says no?"

"Correct."

"My advice is do whatever it takes to keep him away from her."

"I warned him to back off, but he showed up at school this morning."

"Hm. I can scare hell out of him if we catch him loitering around your house at night."

"So can I…"

"How old is he? An adult?"

"Nineteen or twenty."

"A juvenile. That makes it tougher…"

"The problem is catching him."

"You don't want to challenge this bozo."

"No?"

"No. What's his name?"

"Bryan Cutler. Lives with his mother over in Seagate. Goes to Ocean State."

"What's he look like?"

"Tall, dark, heavy set. About six feet, two hundred pounds."

"A big boy. Caucasian?"

"Yes."

"Does he work?"

"I don't think so. He goes to class and follows Em."

"You think he's a stalker?"

"I wouldn't call him a stalker. More like a kid with time on his hands who's infatuated—at least that is what Bernice thinks."

"I'll put an extra cruiser in your neighborhood. How does he spell his name?"

"C-U-T-L-E-R."

"Have an address?"

"122 Harlan Street in Seagate. There's a listing for Adelia Cutler, his mother, in the phone book."

"Adelia… How's that spelled?"

"A-D-E-L-I-A."

"Gotcha... Harlan. That's off East Bay, maybe ten blocks from where you live. Does he own a car?"

"Don't know. I can check with Emily. I saw him this morning on a bicycle."

"When you say he hangs out, does he come onto your property?"

"He claims in his last letter that he stayed across the street all night."

"I wouldn't mess around with this guy, Jack. If he comes on your property, call 911 and we'll nail him."

"I will."

"I oughta tell you these stalker-types are difficult to catch. They seem to know exactly how far they can go without breaking the law."

"I'm not sure Bryan's a stalker, Bill. He's a good student on a scholarship. Bernice says he's just love-struck."

"Well, Jack, listen. If he's following Emily like you say, he's a bona fide stalker. Can you drop off copies of those letters he's sending?"

"Sure."

"I'd like to see what he's saying. There's kind of a pattern all these guys show in their messages and phone conversations."

"Really?"

"Oh, hell yes. Stalkers come in all shapes, sizes and ages, but they all share certain patterns of behavior. I gotta tell you, Jack, in almost every case, they are determined to possess the person they're stalking. They won't let anything get in their way. When their victim refuses to go along, they resort to violence..."

"Yeah?"

"Hey... Let me read something to you. Just a second..."

He heard Bill ask Florese where she had put the book he'd been reading. Paper rustled.

"I just got a new book on predators by Ann Radcliff. You know Ann?"

"No."

"Well, she's a psychiatrist at Dade Regional Psychiatric Center. She's had lots of experience studying these guys–and women, too. It's not limited to males, you know…"

"I've heard…"

"Here's what she says about stalkers: 'The stalker believes, almost delusionally, that the person he is obsessed with feels the same attraction–or would–if only they could connect in an intimate way…' Does that sound a little like this guy?"

He recalled Bryan saying he was in love with Emily after only one date. Said he's determined to see her. "Well, maybe a little…"

"You've got a dangerous situation, my friend."

"Damn!" He felt rage building in his chest.

"Trust me. We both love Emily too much for anything to happen to her. I'd suggest you don't allow her to go anywhere by herself."

Jack's mind was whirling. Bill was making Bryan sound like a criminal. Hell, the kid rides a bike, for crying out loud. He doesn't look violent. "Thanks, Bill. I'll bring you the letters."

"Good. Oh, another thing… It would help if we can track the guy. I'd suggest that you and Emily start a log. Keep a record of Cutler's comings and goings. Each time he's sighted, make a note of the date, time, location, and circumstances. After you've gotten a few notes together, give me a call. I'll check them out."

"We'll do it."

"You should probably notify Sam Oakes over at the high school, too. They can keep an eye on Emily for you. Tell Sam I'll talk to him about it after I gather some background information."

Stalker

"Good. Thanks."

He hung up. He was flabbergasted. He felt angry but had lingering doubts. Was he escalating this, getting Bryan into trouble when there was no good reason? Perhaps he had acted too hastily. Why couldn't he give Bryan a chance to get over this infatuation before calling in the cavalry? He knew Bill Winters well enough to know he would check Bryan out with the Seagate Police Department. They would probably pay a call on Bryan and his mother. Was he jeopardizing Bryan's future career? This also might cause Bryan to retaliate. And who would blame him? He should not have called Bill, at least for a few days.

He grabbed his car keys off the desk and stuffed them in his pocket. Bernice was right. He did not see Bryan being a stalker. At least not the kind Bill was talking about. Hell, he's probably a lovesick kid like Bernice said. Maybe if he could sit down with Bryan over coffee, they could reach an understanding. Certainly, as big as the guy was, he wouldn't be afraid. And he did not intend to hurt Bryan unless he tried to hurt Em.

He slipped the paper with Adelia Cutler's name and address into his shirt pocket. It was a ludicrous joke, he thought. Communicating with Bryan? He couldn't even communicate with his own wife. How could he expect a kid who was into heavy metal music and crazy over his daughter to hear a word he had to say? Still, it wouldn't hurt to make the effort. He would much prefer settling this man-to-man over a cup of coffee. He should not have brought Bill Winters into this. He decided to call Bryan again and see if they could meet some place and talk it out.

Chapter 7

Thursday Morning, May 16.

After dropping Em off at school—with no sign of Bryan–Jack spent the morning covering a meeting of the newly elected mayor with the planning commission, and shooting a tour of the wetlands for the Ocean County environmental committee. Before the tour, he called the high school and set up a two o'clock meeting with the principal and one of the counselors. He made another call to Adelia Cutler. No answer. Strange. He expected that Mrs. Cutler would answer at least once in a while.

At noon, he covered the mayor at a Chamber luncheon and was confident that he had gotten some good shots of him. From being around him a few days, he sensed that Mayor Gottlieb had his own agenda and would definitely make sweeping changes once he felt secure. Gottlieb was one of those tough cookies you could not read. Already, the mayor had surrounded himself with cronies from South Florida as advisors and consultants. "No photos of them, please," he whispered in an aside. "We don't want to cause unnecessary waves." Jack did not question him. He was used

Stalker

to such limitations. The mayor's sidekicks would remain faceless to the community until some scandal made them front page news.

That was one of the more interesting aspects of being a political photographer, he thought. When a VIP like General Selby at the Space Center or Mayor Gottlieb didn't want certain people in a picture, you left them out. And sometimes, one of your bosses would ask you to crop a picture to cut someone out of it, too. Eventually, you discovered the reasons. When you had worked long enough for a boss, you learned who to include and who to leave out.

Jack stopped by the public information office and took Dave Sommers, the director, out for coffee. Dave always had the latest news about city politics. He was a trusted straight shooter.

"Just between us, Jack, the mayor's on a rampage," Dave said in a low whisper. "Wouldn't surprise me if he replaced me with some guy out of Miami none of us has ever heard of."

"Could he fire you outright?"

Dave smirked. "No, but he's clever at making things impossible so you can't do your job. He's already done it to Jim Ayers, the city engineer. Jim resigned yesterday. Said he was trapped into resigning."

"Jim can't take it before the grievance or personnel committees?"

"Nah! Gotlieb has control of them. Wouldn't stand a chance."

Jack considered Jim to be competent besides being a nice guy. And if Dave were to go, Jack's contract with the city wasn't worth a dime. Over the past three years he had given more and more time to city projects. Today, photo assignments for the city made up a majority of his income. Any cutting back would make it tough for him to pay the bills.

What would he do, he mused, if he lost the city contract? As he drove toward the high school, he considered alternatives. There weren't any reliable ones. Could he rent out the house after Em and Bernice left? He could live aboard the ketch. The rent from the house would take care of the mortgage and taxes. He thought he could make it. Perhaps he could develop a portrait business: do families, boat crews, athletes. Yes, Jack, there was a future beyond the city contract. But you better start making plans now, so Gottlieb doesn't surprise you.

He pulled into the visitor's section of the school parking lot. Blaring horns and clarinets playing an off-key rendition of "Pomp and Circumstance" were heard from the direction of the football field. He strode across the foyer to the principal's office. Janet, Sam's secretary, led him to a small meeting room where Sam and another man were waiting.

"Hey, Jack!" Oakes greeted affably, getting to his feet. "Meet one of our counselors, John Sikes. I asked him to sit in with us. You don't mind, do you?"

"Not at all." They shook hands and Jack sat down across from them.

"I appreciate you meeting with me on such short notice. As I mentioned on the phone, Bill Winters suggested I talk to you about a situation involving my daughter Emily."

Sikes leaned in, eyes fixed, looking at Jack from behind steel rimmed glasses. Em had never mentioned him. He had that youthful set of mouth that said he had more aspirations than experience.

Oakes seemed more relaxed, sitting back in his chair, a middle-aged paunch showing beneath white shirt and red tie. Jack had shot sports pictures for him from time to time. Oakes always appreciated his voluntary coverage of school events. Still, both men had that stiff, careful demeanor of educators who sensed that what they said to a parent might be turned against them.

"Yes," said Oakes, "we're all very fond of Emily. We'll miss her when she graduates. I believe you said she's being followed by an over-ardent admirer?"

Jack grinned at Oakes' attempt at humor. He was known for his dry wit. "More than followed," he answered. "One of your graduates from two years ago, Bryan Cutler, is hanging out across from our house at night. He also shows up at play rehearsals, and watches her arrive at school from across the street in front of Harvey's Bagel Shack. He won't leave her alone. He sends her crazy letters, too."

"Oh?" Oakes cleared his throat. "Would you say he's stalking Emily?"

Jack winced. The 'S' word again.

"Well, Chief Winters thinks so. I want to play it on the safe side by taking all the precautions I can. I was hoping you might help me by letting me or Chief Winters know if Cutler tries to bother her."

Oakes shook his head glumly. "We have an open campus, Jack. It makes our job very difficult in terms of protecting individual students. We'll try to help as best we can. I will alert the faculty and staff in the Drama Department. Bryan Cutler... I remember him well, don't you, John?"

Sikes nodded. "Quite well."

"I realize you can't divulge confidential information about former students, but as her father I am concerned about Emily's safety. Is he harmless or not?"

Oakes cleared his throat again. "I can't make that judgment. I can tell you what is public record. Bryan is a very bright young man. He was an 'A' student throughout his four years here. He got a partial scholarship to Ocean State to study marine biology."

"Basically a loner, though," Sikes added.

"He's had a tough life growing up," said Oakes. "No money to speak of. No siblings we know of. And John is right. He had few friends. He's fatherless. His poor mother cleans office buildings at night to keep bread on the table. As I recall, Bryan worked some at the Bagel Shack to earn extra money."

"So, he's conscientious?"

"Oh, yes. Quite industrious, always working odd jobs like delivering newspapers. Curious. An excellent chess player. A math wizard. Quick mind."

"He had no problems here, then?"

Oakes smoothed his tie. "That's confidential information. I can't speak to that." He touched a finger to his mouth. "Off the record, Jack, I can tell you he got into some mischief now and then. Small stuff."

"Like what?"

Oakes broke out in a wry smile and wiped his hand across his mouth. "One time he got creative with spray paint. He changed the color of our dolphin statue out front from gray to pink. Took him several hours to clean it up and repaint it."

They all laughed.

"If anything," said Oakes, "the boy was too serious. He didn't have a sense of humor, except in that one instance. I don't recall that he got into any major difficulties. Do you, John?"

"Except for the fight," Sikes said calmly, dropping his hand away from his chin. "Remember? Out in front of Harvey's?"

41

"Oh, yes," Oakes said, shaking his head. "I'd forgotten. His junior year. It took Coach Ryan and a couple of senior boys to pull him off the fellow. Who was it? Eddie Barnes?"

"Yeah," Sikes replied. "According to witnesses, Eddie started it by calling Bryan some name and next thing he had Eddie down on the pavement."

"Barnes was a troublemaker," Oakes admitted. "Probably deserved it, but we suspended both of them."

"In case you're wondering," said Sikes, removing his glasses and examining the lenses, "this is public record information. The police report, however, is sealed."

"I see."

"It upset his mother something awful," Sikes said, rubbing his hands together, a smirk showing at the corners of his mouth. "Never had another problem with Bryan after that."

"So, you feel that Bryan wouldn't hurt Emily... That he's really a decent young man?"

Both men shook their heads negatively. "We can't say one way or another," said Oakes. "You understand, of course."

"Yeah," Jack nodded, feeling Oakes and Sikes had already gone beyond the legal limits of confidentiality. "I appreciate your candor. From what you've told me, Bryan seems okay."

"He's never had much chance for social life, working nights and weekends, saving for college. Perhaps he just needs some guidance in how to get on with the girls," said Oakes, smiling. "But if you see a problem developing, let us know. An official letter from Chief Winters or the courts is what we'll need to keep Bryan off our campus."

"Thanks for your time."

They stood and shook hands.

As Jack crossed the lawn to his car, he glanced at the statue of the school's mascot, Salty the dolphin. Bryan must have painted it at night. But why? Surely he knew he would get caught. Maybe the kid was starving for attention and didn't know how to get it. He could understand being the kid without money at the candy store window looking in. He was there once. Yeah, he could identify with Bryan.

He crossed the street to Harvey's Bagel Shack. The place was empty. Harvey, the bald-headed, seventy-something proprietor and a young woman were scrubbing the kitchen. Harvey looked up from behind a steel kettle and waved. He came out, wiping his hands on a soiled white apron.

"What can I do for you?"

"I'm Jack Kaufman."

"I know you. You're the city photographer, right?"

"Yes."

"You should take a picture of my shop here. Someday when it's full. Not now, when it's empty. Would you do me that favor, Mr. Kaufman?"

"Sure. Call me Jack. I'll come by one day when business is booming."

Harvey wiped his hand across his white apron again and extended it. "I'm Harvey Gold. You call me Harvey; I call you Jack."

They shook hands.

"Best time for a picture is early in the morning or at lunch between eleven thirty and twelve forty-five. Come by for lunch and I'll treat you to the best bagel sandwich of your life. Whatta-ya-say?"

Jack grinned. "You've got a deal, Harvey."

"Now," said Harvey, looking quite serious. "I suspect you have something besides bagels on your mind. What can I do for you?"

Stalker

"My daughter Emily goes to school over there." He pointed over his shoulder.

"Emily... Emily..." He looked down, shaking his head, then waved a finger. "Beautiful girl, black hair, dark eyes, million dollar smile, right? A senior."

"That's right."

"Sure. She comes in here with the actors. Nice bunch of kids. What about her?"

"It's really about a young man who's infatuated with her. He used to work here."

"And who would this be?"

"Bryan Cutler. He might still be working for you?"

"Bryan Cutler..." Harvey's hand went to the side of his face as he pondered, looking down at the squares of black and white tile floor. "I used to treat him like my son. What can I say? He worked hard for me."

"He doesn't work here any more?"

"No. He's going to college. Is he proposing to your daughter or something that you should be so worried?"

Jack laughed. "Do I look worried?"

"You don't mind I should tell you?"

"No." He gave a forced chuckle.

"Yes. Your eyes tell me you are worried. Now tell me why you should worry about Emily with Bryan."

"Bryan's following Emily. He shows up everywhere. At her play rehearsals, here at school when she arrives or leaves. When she's out with friends, he appears out of thin air. It's like he's stalking her."

"Oy!" Harvey's face darkened. He leaned back against the counter, biting his lip. "That is not so good, then. I understand your worry. Perhaps if you have a little talk with Bryan..."

"I talked to him once on the phone. He didn't heed my warning to stay away. But I do wish I could just sit down with him face-to-face and talk it out."

"Ya?" Harvey shook his head negatively.

"I sense that you know something about Bryan that I ought to know, Harvey."

"Well... Many things... How can I tell you this?" Harvey waved his hands in the air. "Bryan is basically a good boy, and very, very smart. But from childhood neglect, he is like a bagel without sufficient egg and salt. These ingredients missing make Bryan's life difficult. You understand?"

"I'm not sure. Can you explain?"

"Explain... How to explain?" Harvey peered at him through wide eyes, attempting, Jack thought, to gauge his sincerity. "I had to let Bryan go."

"Oh?"

"At first I like the boy as if he was my own son, but Bryan changed. Moody and late for work. I suspect he was experimenting."

"Experimenting?"

"Ya. Perhaps with marijuana or liquor. Whatever, I could not reason with him. He had problems with my staff and customers. So... I gave him many warnings. I finally have to fire him."

Harvey rested an elbow on the counter, shaking his head. "Our relationship is never the same after that. He comes by, but we never talk. I see him often standing outside next to his bicycle, in the mornings and when school is leaving out."

"He's watching for Emily."

Harvey nodded.

"Is that how he gets around? By bicycle?"

"He drove his mother's car a while and then something happen. I see him only on bicycle now."

"Does he show up outside frequently or just now and then?"

"Nearly every day he is here."

Jack felt a growing sense of dread.

"Bryan and I need to talk this out."

"Ya, Have a talk with Bryan. And should I see him, would you like for me to discuss this matter with him?"

"I'd appreciate it very much. I feel like I need all the help I can get. By the way, can you tell me how to reach his mother? I call, but get no answer."

"She's an office maid. Working all night at the Seagate Center. At least she did a year or so back. No education there. And like her boy, some ingredients missing. You know what I mean?" He pointed to his head.

"Yeah, I understand now." He started to get up.

"Would you like coffee or a snack?"

"No, thanks. Another time."

"You won't forget the picture? I can use one for a flyer I want to print."

Jack shook his hand and headed for the door. "Count on it!"

Chapter 8

Thursday Afternoon, May 16.

Dearest Emily:

Why did you get your father into this? Our thing is none of his business. I love you. Please! Please! Please go out with me. I want to be with you. I want to smell your scent. I want to hold your lovely white hand again. I want to kiss those ruby lips. Please say you'll go with me. Acid Flavors is at the amphitheater in Seagate next weekend. I could get us tickets. Please say YES! And keep your father out of this! He won't understand. I will call you before you go to play rehearsal.

Love, Bryan

"When did this arrive?"
"It was stuck in the door when I came home from school."
"So he knows when your mom and I are away. He must have put it there sometime after two, when Bernice leaves, and before four, when you get home."

"I guess so."

Jack looked at Emily, sitting on the desk in his studio.

"Emily... Are you sure you've told me everything? You aren't omitting any details?"

"Like what?"

"Well...I don't know how to say it without saying it. You didn't kiss him or allow him to fondle you or anything, did you?"

The hurt broke across her face like a slap. Tears welled. She dropped her head. "No, Dad. I didn't. And I didn't tease him either. I'm not like what you and Mom think I am."

He suddenly felt hollow and dead inside. "What do we think you are, Emily?"

"A flirt. A tease."

He was struck down. "I've never thought that, Emily. Where'd you ever get that idea?"

"Mom says I am. She said the other night, 'Your father and I think you ask for problems with boys.' That's what she said."

He felt shot by Bernice's insinuation. "No, Emily. I'm not part of that. I've never believed you were a tease. You just happen to be into acting and modeling which naturally attract attention to yourself."

"Then..." She started weeping. "How can you accuse me of having sex with Bryan?"

"Honey..." He held her in his arms. She began sobbing. Her shoulders shook as she cried from deep inside. "I'm sorry, Emily. I didn't mean to hurt you. And I do trust you. It's just that sometimes... a person can get carried away in the moment and do things they wouldn't ordinarily do. I've done it. Did you know that?"

A muffled "No."

"I can tell you, now you're grown, that I once had sex with a girl while I was still in high school. It's so natural a thing to happen when you like somebody a lot. Or you think you're in love with them. And look at me. I'm a result of a teenage pregnancy. My mother just got carried away with emotion one night. It happened with a guy she'd never dated before."

Emily cupped her hands to her face. "I didn't do anything."

"Em, I just needed to be sure I have all the facts."

Emily pulled away and looked around the desk. He reached over and handed her a tissue from the desk drawer. She daubed her red eyes and pulled her hair back. She looked keenly into his eyes, her lips still quivering.

"Why can't you and mom get your act together?"

Her words pierced him with their anger. She began to cry again, this time loudly, holding the tissue to her face.

"You know we can't."

Her bawling got louder and rhythmic like a floodgate had opened and all her sorrows were pouring out. He sat down, feeling helpless.

Here we are, he mused, three people living in the same house with entirely separate lives. She must feel so alone with all the silent anger in the house like Claymore mines that were ready to explode at any moment day or night.

"I feel so bad..."

"I know, honey. Please understand it's not your fault."

"Yes, it is."

"Never think that."

He held her again, pulling her close, feeling her body shaking, gasping for breath.

"I can't help it. It's all my fault."

"No. Your mother and I had our problems before you were born. I just didn't know how wrong we were for one another. None of this was your doing. Kids aren't responsible for the dumb things parents do. You understand that, don't you?"

She pushed him from her. She pulled her hair back to show swollen eyes and wet cheeks. "I want to get out of this house. I hate it. I can't stand being around either of you."

He smoothed her hair, trying not to believe she meant what she was saying. "Soon enough, Em. I know. I'd feel the same way in your shoes. I wish your mother and I had gotten a divorce years ago, but that doesn't matter now, does it? Just a few more weeks. Then, she will find her own place and you'll be off to Spain for summer study. Meanwhile, you've got to concentrate on finishing up school and nailing your role in the play."

"It's all one bad play, Dad. The whole world is one big, lousy play with a crummy ending."

He rested his hand on her shoulder. "You don't really think that, do you?"

"Can I have another tissue, please?"

He handed her one. She blew her nose.

"Remember, Dad, how I used to lay up in my playhouse when you let me sleep up there? I'd look out the window at the stars and think some day I'd meet a man like you and I'd get married and be so happy. I'd live in a little house with windows just like those in my playhouse, with lattice and window boxes with flowers, and I'd be so warm and secure..."

"Yeah?"

"Now, I don't believe that dream anymore. I hate to think about what's ahead for me... I look at you and Mom and realize you're screwed up and out of touch. I see myself ending up the same way."

"It's just that we can't live together anymore."

"No. You're going through the motions. And when I see you, I know it will be the same for me. I'll end up playing out the same stupid role. Only, I'll know what to expect, and that will be the worst of it. It'll be more than I can stand."

She wiped her eyes and glared at him. He didn't know what he could say to calm her. She was venting the same frustrations he felt. Only, she was more truthful than he was.

"Maybe," he said, "that's why you've always wanted to be an actress. Learn new roles. Try new scripts. Not all the plays turn out badly."

"None of them is as bad as real life, though. I feel so awful inside. I wish I could die!"

He embraced her again. "Yesterday, when you came home with Chuck, you were so cheerful. Remember?"

"Um, hm."

"Why was that?"

"He asked me to the prom."

"You were singing that silly song in your room."

She looked at him with sad doe eyes. "Um, hm."

"Remember the day we made it up?"

"Yeah." She wiped tears away, trying to smile.

He began to sing in a soft voice. "Bears eat coats and Schmoos eat boats... and little Rams eat popcorn..."

Em laughed through her tears and finished it. "...A pig'll eat popcorn too, wouldn't you?"

"You weren't more than four or five. And you still remember it."

She reached over and gave him a hug. "I'll never forget it. It's my favorite."

"I love you, Em. I know we're all going through a difficult time, and you probably feel helpless... but your Mom and I do care about you more than anything else."

"I know that, Dad. I really do, deep down. Sometimes, though, it doesn't matter that you guys love me. I still feel so alone."

He wanted to tell her that nobody felt more alone than he did, knowing she and Bernice would be leaving soon. Who knows when he might ever have this closeness with Em again? He stroked her hair.

"You've got a lot of pressure on you. Finals are coming up. The senior play. Getting ready for Spain. Your parents are about to split. And Bryan is like the last straw. No wonder it feels like the end of the world."

"Yeah. It really does."

"Well, love, it's only the beginning." He tried to smile. "A new role. A different play. Believe me."

Emily pulled her hair back and laughed grimly through tears. "I hope so."

"Forgive me?"

She reached out. "Yeah, Dad. I forgive you. I love you so much. I don't know what I'd do if anything happened to you."

He held her and kissed her forehead. He had a feeling that he would not be seeing her very often after she went to Spain. She would be on her own private journey.

"Nothing's going to happen to me. I'll always be here for you. You know that, don't you?"

"Yes." She gave him a big hug.

"When Bryan calls this afternoon, I'll try to talk with him. Maybe I can meet him at Harvey's and talk this thing out. Okay?"

"That'd be good. Have you talked with his mom?"

"No. I haven't been able to reach her."

"I hope she can keep Bryan away. I'd feel a whole lot better knowing he's not hanging around. It's making me paranoid."

"Get some rest. What time's rehearsal?"

"Seven."

"Somebody picking you up?"

"Yeah. David and Chuck. They're bringing me home, too."

"Good. Don't go anywhere alone."

"Gotcha. Anything else?"

He scratched his head, remembering Bill Winter's suggestion about keeping a log. "In fact, I want you to keep a written record."

He shuffled through the photographs, pencils and note pads in the middle desk drawer and found a pocket calendar book and handed it to her. "Jot down every instance he shows up or calls. Date, time, and description of the incident. Okay?"

"Do I hafta do that?"

He didn't want to tell her that he had contacted Bill. Telling her would only increase her fears. "Do it for a few days. Let's see if there's a pattern. Okay? Start with this morning when we saw him across from school. Enter something like, 'eight a.m., in front of Harvey's. Took off on bike when we saw him.' Then make another entry and summarize the contents of this letter; enter the date and time you found it. Can you do that?"

She shrugged. "If you say so."

She went to her room.

Jack reread Bryan's letter. He was pleading for contact with another human being. He thought Bernice could be right; Bryan needed an adult male friend. Although he was not fully convinced, he was willing to at least give it a try.

Chapter 9

Thursday Late Afternoon, May 16.

The phone rang.

"What should I do, Dad?"

He rushed to her room. "If it's Bryan, hand the phone to me."

She picked up the receiver. "Hello?"

"Hold on, just a second..."

She handed Jack the phone. "Hi, Bryan. This is Jack."

A pause.

"I'd like to sit down with you and talk this thing out. What do you say?"

"I'm not sure what you mean. What's there to talk about?"

"I was thinking we could meet for coffee and a bagel at Harvey's. Talk man-to-man."

"What's the catch?"

"No catch. I'd prefer resolving this standoff between us so there are no hard feelings. The only way we can do it is to communicate. Don't you agree?"

"I s'pose... I dunno, I'm pretty busy with college and stuff. I got exams comin' up."

"I'm flexible. You tell me when."

"What would we talk about?"

"Well, you know my concerns… I don't want to see this thing escalate so you get in trouble with the law. It could really mess up your future. I'm as much concerned about you as I am about Emily. What do you say?"

"Hm… I don't know."

"Maybe by sitting down together, we can reach an understanding. Get to know each other a bit. And after we talk about the serious stuff, I'd like to hear about your marine biology studies. I've taken a lot of photographs at the Marine Biology Center at Key West. Maybe you'd like to see some. I've got some great underwater shots. You might find one or two you'd like to have."

"Yeah? That's cool."

"Could we meet tonight or tomorrow morning some time?"

"Hm. What about around eight at Harvey's?"

"Tonight?"

"Yeah. I could do that. Yer sure you aren't trick'n me or nothin'?"

"Positive. No tricks, Bryan. I give you my word."

"See you."

Click. He hung up. Well, it's worth a try, Jack thought as he replaced the receiver.

"Why the change? You seemed ready to beat his brains out the other day. You threatened him. This will only encourage him. He asked me out to a Acid Flavors concert next weekend."

"What I'm trying to do is diffuse an explosive situation. Calm Bryan down. Mr. Oakes and the guidance counselor, Mr. Sikes, think Bryan is basically a good kid. I was over there yesterday after I finished my shooting schedule."

"You were at school?" She looked surprised.

"Yeah. I had a nice meeting with them and afterward went over and spoke with Harvey."

"I don't get it, Dad. Suppose you and Bryan begin to like each other. What happens then? We all become big buddies even though I can't stand being around him?"

"Maybe I'll do some things with him. It was your mother's idea. After I gain his confidence, perhaps I can get it across to him that you don't dislike him; you simply aren't interested in him as a boyfriend. By then... you'll be off to Spain and out of harm's way. The situation will have taken care of itself."

She stretched across the bed, propping one arm against the pillow. "What about me in the meantime?"

"Trust me, Em. I won't let anything bad happen to you. Besides, with your busy schedule, you won't have any time to date. He'll understand that."

She lifted herself into a sitting position and folded her hands in her lap. "I doubt that..." She looked down at her hands. "Mom says you always wanted a son. Was it too disappointing having a daughter?"

His heart felt heavy. Bernice again, saying things she shouldn't. "Honey, I never was disappointed. Don't ever feel I would prefer any person to you. No son could give me the joy I've found in you."

She looked away, seemingly unconvinced. "Boys really are different, aren't they? Mom says they're all stupid."

"Yeah? Your mother says a lot of things. Judge for yourself. Find your own truth. I have my prejudices and your mother has hers. Life is about finding out what you believe based on your own experience. The whole idea is to eliminate your parents' prejudices."

The words sounded hollow. Hell, he had not learned much from his own experience. Em stared out the window. The afternoon light reflected in her eyes. She looked sadly beautiful, reflective, a woman-child.

"The problem with that is," Em replied, "by the time you have experience and discover a truth, it's too late. Isn't that right, Dad?"

He smiled, knowing she was on target. He picked up her favorite ceramic elephant from the bedside table. "The learning is not to repeat the bad experiences, Em. Store up the good ones and repeat them as often as you can. Keep your memory sharp–like these elephants do–and stay away from bad experiences."

"Is that your philosophy?"

He nodded. "I don't always remember to practice it, but that's what I believe."

Her face broke into a contemplative smile, showing her pretty white teeth. "I'll try it. So what you're saying is we can't avoid bad experiences?"

"Nobody can. We can only learn from them. If there weren't bad times, we wouldn't be able to enjoy the good ones."

"That's cool."

He kissed Em on the forehead and left her bedroom. So much for two bit philosophy. Too bad the preacher can't live his sermon, he thought. He was trying, though. God knows he was trying. Lately, it seemed, he was learning more from her than she was from him.

He entered the darkroom, smelling and tasting the chemicals before he could clear them with the fan. That was what happened when you don't learn from experience. You forget to clear the air with the fan after you've been using the lab for several hours. Then, you repeat the bad consequences.

He washed the sinks. It was so difficult to learn the most basic things–even when you had been living for forty years. How on God's earth can he or anybody else expect Emily and Bryan to know the least thing about life?

He set about unloading film and placed the 35mm strips into the developer. He was hopeful that a few candid shots of the mayor would be printable.

He imagined Bryan sitting across from him: dark eyes and day-old black stubble, and pensive, full mouth, set in a round face and framed by long dark hair: a face pregnant with suspicion, fear, and potential fury. What would Bryan say?

Being a father, he believed the tactic should be to listen like a good photojournalist does. Ask short questions and wait for long answers. Keep the conversation flowing. Get to his issues. Find out what makes him tick. Discover what his passions are...if any... besides Emily.

Chapter 10

Thursday Evening, May 16.

Harvey's was nearly empty at ten to eight. Jack chose a table where he could see the entrance. Three teenagers were slumped in the corner booth nursing Cokes. A young couple across from them was holding hands and looking intently at one another like they were getting the hormones heated for some serious making out after they finished their pie and coffee.

In the kitchen, Harvey was singing in Yiddish. His rich baritone voice sounded like a cantor's. He and the young woman Jack had seen yesterday were loading bags of flour into a great stainless steel mixer. Harvey waved and came out. The bib of his white apron was spattered yellow. He pulled the hem of the apron up and wiped his hands as he approached. Jack rose to greet him. "Hi, Harvey."

"You shoulda been here lunch today," he exclaimed, holding out his hand in welcome. They shook hands.

"You woulda had a magnificent picture! A line stretching down the street, we had. Biggest crowd since football season."

"Oh? What was the occasion?"

Stalker

"Dolphin Day! When all the kids come out to celebrate Salty—you know, the school mascot. After the speeches and cheers, a few seniors started to come across the street to have lunch and, guess what?"

"The rest followed?"

"Followed? They raced for places in line. A stampede we have. I normally expect maybe a hundred fifty kids for lunch. Today, I sent out twice for lettuce, tomatoes, cream cheese. Can you believe I ran out of bagels and bread? A hundred fifty kids? Nothing! I serve today nearly five hundred! I send Mary to Winn-Dixie's. We buy all the bagels and bread they can spare, packaged, unpackaged, Deli, whatever. And you with your camera are not here to record such an event!"

He nudged Jack on the chest with his hand.

"Sorry."

"Ach! To be so tired as I am, I decide to prepare my bagels tonight instead of four o'clock in the morning as is my normal custom. Do you not think I am wise to do so?"

"You deserve to sleep in tomorrow."

"What can I get you, my friend? Or are you here on other business?"

"Both."

"Is this business you are here about having to do with Bryan Cutler?"

"He's meeting me here at eight."

Jack glanced at his watch. It was two minutes until eight.

"A funny occurrence, Jack."

"How so?"

"Bryan. He is just here."

"You mean he came in and left again?"

"No. He didn't come in. He stood outside looking in the window. I waved to him to come in, but he turned and walked down to the lamppost where his bicycle was parked. He rode off."

"I see." A sinking feeling started in Jack's chest. Maybe he was still out there, checking to see whether he was alone.

"You are going to have serious discussion about Emily, eh?"

"Well, I decided to try getting to know him. Gain his confidence. I think he might need a male friend."

Harvey's eyes fixed on Jack's.

"Would you mind I sit down while you wait?"

"Not at all."

Harvey sat down and stared at Jack over folded, large, pink hands. "How 'bout some coffee?"

"Yeah, I'd like some. That'd be nice." He sensed Harvey did not think well of his plan to become Bryan's friend.

"Mary," Harvey called over his shoulder. "Two coffees, please, and a cherry blintz."

"Oh, no, Harvey. I don't need any dessert."

"This is no dessert, Jack. Trust me. This is heaven warmed over. It will melt in your mouth like no dessert you've ever had… or would you prefer my New York cheesecake? This cheesecake upon the tongue is like nectar of the gods, I tell you. Would you like some?"

"Please, no, Harvey."

He held up a finger and turned. "Mary! Add a nice slice of cheesecake to Mr. Kaufman's order."

He turned back. "You only live once. And you haven't begun to live until you taste Harvey Gold's blintzes and cheesecake."

Jack smiled at this large, gregarious man. Harvey looked out the window. It was getting dark. The couple holding hands got up and the young man stiffened and grabbed money out of his jeans pocket and dropped it on the table. His girl waited at the door, then went out.

"See you tomorrow, Paul," cried Harvey as the door banged shut. "Nice kids. They've been going steady two years already. Parents hate it, but so what? Good kids. In love! What do they know? What do parents know? Parents! They have no idea what these kids do in the back of a car. But these two are good kids. So why are the parents upset, I ask you? They know. Paul's car has a very comfortable back seat."

Harvey chuckled at his joke, showing strong, square white teeth. Mary brought the coffee and pastries. Jack pulled his coffee over and watched as Harvey slid the dessert plate in front of him. His eyes were lit with expectation, like Picasso showing off a new creation. He pushed a fork to Jack's right hand.

"Taste. You must! One taste of each. Tell me how you like them."

Jack cut into the blintz with his fork, causing a thick mixture of cherries, pastry flakes, juice and cream to ooze. The rich pastry melted in his mouth as the incredible taste of cherries, lemon and butter exploded, tangy, sweet-sour, on his tongue. He had to agree. He'd never tasted the likes of it.

"Now the cheesecake," said Harvey with emotion, pointing to the light textured golden cake edged brown.

Jack tasted it. The cake was as light as whipped cream, tangy with cheese and lemon. It literally dissolved in his mouth before he could swallow it. He wiped his mouth with a napkin.

"Incredible!"

"You see?" Harvey tapped him on the arm with his finger. "You begin living fully from this moment. Everything in your life will change from this time on."

Jack laughed. Harvey sounded like a fortuneteller.

"It's great. Thank you, Harvey."

Jack glanced at his watch. It was ten after eight. Harvey was watching him closely. "He is not coming, you're thinking?"

"I dunno. You know him better than I do. What's your read?"

Harvey looked thoughtfully toward the street and shook his head slowly. "I think like you that he is not coming. He's too afraid. I do not see him coming again here tonight."

Jack surveyed the boulevard and followed the edge of silhouette of Ocean High School. He's out there, probably watching us sitting here, wanting to come in yet wanting to stay hidden. The three teens in the corner booth slid to their feet, put money on the table, and waved at Harvey before leaving. The door slammed. Harvey waved back without looking. His eyes were still fixed on Jack.

"Do you wish to be alone, Jack? Perhaps he is watching and is afraid of my presence at your table."

Jack ate more cheesecake. "That shouldn't make any difference. He knows you and trusts you."

"That is true and not true. Trust is like ice on a pond in winter. It can grow thick and strong or with change in weather grow weak and poof... it is gone forever."

Jack was not sure what he meant. He put the fork down. "I forgot to ask you the other day. Do you remember Bryan being in a fight in front of your shop?"

Harvey's lips flattened. He drummed his fingers lightly on the table. "Of course. A very bad thing to happen. Fortunately, Mr. Ryan was eating here and possibly saved the other... What was his name? I never liked him to come here. More than once I had to run him off. Hm. Never would I believe I can forget his name. A bully. And very, very big."

"Barnes?"

"Ach! Exactly. Eddie Barnes he is. Always starting fights. A reputation for dirty fighting, too. He'd bite, knee you, pull hair, scratch, whatever."

"Vicious, then."

"Most vicious. Except he ran into a person more vicious and totally unafraid." Harvey said it calmly, matter-of-factly.

"Bryan?"

"Ya, Bryan. I saw it happen, just there, near the potted palm." He pointed to a palm in a large terra cotta tub at the corner. "Bryan knocked Eddie Barnes to the ground, kicked him hard in the ribs, then fell on him full-weight and began choking him with both hands."

"My God!"

"He would have killed Barnes if not for Coach Ryan rushing out and pulling him off. Even so, he was unconscious for several minutes. Ryan is just then beginning mouth-to-mouth resuscitation when Barnes shakes his head and opens his eyes. He is blue in the face, nearly purple-black."

"Really?"

Such a contrast to what Oakes and Sikes presented, Jack thought. Neither mentioned Bryan had nearly killed another kid. Which version was correct? Certainly, Harvey had no reason to exaggerate or lie. His gut said he was now hearing the true story.

"I rush out, too," said Harvey. "Bryan is restrained by several boys. I look down to see hand and finger prints still visible on Eddie Barnes' neck. Almost a very terrible event."

"My God." He was appalled. A wave of numbness swept through him. "What happened after?"

"I called paramedics. Barnes was taken to the hospital and released. I think Coach Ryan took Bryan immediately across to the principal's office where he was sent home for three days unexcused absence."

That part matched what Oakes and Sikes said. "Did police get involved?"

"Oh, sure. There was a report made. No arrests. Barnes was given a warning. All the kids who saw what happened said it was Barnes who started it."

"Was Bryan working for you at the time of the fight?"

"Oh, no. He work for me after graduation."

"So why did you hire him later on, knowing he had a temper and could take somebody out?"

Harvey sipped his coffee and set the cup down. His eyes flickered with a strange light. "There is animal in all of us, don't you think, Jack? I liked the strength inside this boy. He was fighting in self-defense after being taunted. He did what all of us dream of doing once in our lives: defeating an enemy with our bare hands. I should be so strong and brave, yes? He did what he thought was right. Only... he went too far. He couldn't stop himself."

"Yeah. The missing ingredients you spoke of."

"Exactly. When he applied with me for busboy job, he came with good recommendations of teachers. How should I say this? I want to help him grow into becoming a good man. I think at the time I can teach him how to harness his powers, make good judgment. Can you understand?"

"Yes."

Harvey's face and arms tensed with emotion at his remembrance. His eyes widened and his arms moved about with open palms. "I feel relationship with him, like how some people feel about heavyweight boxers or bullfighters; a relationship with power and performance they do not have and know they never will have. It is my weakness which makes me feel this way..." He paused. "But I tell you, I wanted to make this boy my son. You know what I'm saying?"

Jack nodded.

Harvey's eyes rimmed with water. "Youthful power. That was Bryan's attraction." He looked off into the darkness. There was husky emotion in his voice, as though speaking of Bryan was opening an old wound. "A power different from religion or sex, or money."

"Yes. I see now."

Jack realized that he also was attracted to Bryan for possibly the same reasons. The boy was young, had brains and brawn. He was twenty and Jack was forty. Bryan had it all out there in front of him, provided he had the judgment to take the right steps, keep his head, and keep going forward without fear. A recipe for champions. Jack Dempsey had it. So did Mohammed Ali. Both surrounded themselves with good trainers and advisors. Everybody else was drawn to them like moths to the flame.

Is that what he was about here? The father trying to do for the potential son what his own father had not done? Instill in the would-be son what he could not be himself? Was this the weakness that Bernice saw when she gazed at him so coldly? Had he lost something in Nam after killing two boys? Was he trying to regain his power vicariously through connecting with a young man? His altruistic feelings were melting as surely as the ice on the pond Harvey spoke of.

"We are alike in that. Yes, Jack?"

"Sorry, I didn't hear..."

"We both want to keep Bryan out of trouble. But as you can see from tonight, it is difficult to reach him. I must tell you I do not give you much hope of becoming his friend. The more you reach out, the more he will run. Bryan could become very dangerous when cornered. I believe that when you pursue him, you will be sufficiently intelligent enough to corner him. However, you cannot corner him without a fight, Jack. And I have seen how vicious he can become."

By now Jack was only half-listening. He did not want to hear any more. He was playing with dynamite and his gut and Harvey knew it.

His watch said eight-forty-five. No chance Bryan would show up. He felt angry and sad. This was about fathers and sons. About the father Bryan never had. About the one Jack never had. When you don't have one, you are missing essential ingredients.

The closest thing to a father was being raised by his Grandpop, Benjamin Kaufman. They had loved one another, but it was not the same as a father-son relationship. Still, it was special because Grandpop was the only father-man in his life. And when he visited him just before he died, it was awful because neither of them could say what they felt.

Grandpop had been staying with Jack's mother in her little white bungalow in a run-down section of Charleston. She'd called to say Grandpop was dying. Jack had taken the next flight up from Fort Lauderdale. He spent the weekend, hoping they could have one good connecting talk. Their relationship had been such a rich one, filled with truths and lies, of deception about Jack's birth father, of love and support after his mother had left home to work in a factory.

All his efforts to connect with Grandpop were in vain. He'd withdrawn from life so he could die. Grandpop was ready. Jack was not. During that weekend, they sat on the glider together, sometimes for hours, barely moving back and forth, barely talking. And when they did talk, it was about rain, flowers, the recent war, Grandmom dying, leaving the old house. They recollected good times at the cabin, deer seasons, and the day Grandpop shot his first buck.

Some would say a talk like that was closure, a gentling of shared memories, a shaking of them down in the mind like how Grandmom used to shake the burnt ashes through the grate of her old cook stove in the mountains. The ashes would settle and cool before they were shoveled into a metal bucket and emptied outside behind the cabin to eventually blend with all that had been and all that would be.

But Jack wanted more. He wanted both of them to confess their love for one another. He tried to open up the discussion, but found it too difficult. He supposed it was a desire for eternal connection. Was that what religion was? Sort of a final testament and covenant? He had believed for years that you cannot know the Father if you don't have a father… He felt a wound to the soul to see Grandpop standing at the door with him waiting for his cab, unable to speak his mind, feeling all the loneliness of final separation.

When the cab arrived, Jack did something that he had failed to do when he went off to Nam. He reached out and shook Grandpop's hand, then pulled him close. They hugged and kissed one another for the very first time ever. He was 87. Jack was 30.

"I love you, Grandpop," he whispered. There was no response. Jack remembered how fragile and bony Grandpop felt when he hugged him. As Grandpop drew back, he held out his scrawny fist and put a wadded $20 bill into Jack's hand.

"Good-bye, Jack."

Jack turned away, and climbed into the cab. He remembered how he cried during the cab ride to the airport. He was so damned angry and sad, too, because the only father-man in his life was dying and he was sent away with a twenty-dollar bill. It brought back dying buddies in Nam. Some were embarrassed to have a friend witness their death. Others hated to read your eyes and know from them that death was coming.

As the taxi passed through a black section of Charleston, he opened the cab window and threw out the $20 bill. He could not bear to keep it another moment. He surmised Bryan was experiencing the same kind of pain from not knowing a father-man. It was pain from realizing deep down that he would never, ever have the missing ingredients.

Harvey sat before him, no longer touching his coffee, waiting for Jack to talk.

"Sorry," said Jack, glancing up at Harvey. "Somehow, thinking about Bryan reminded me of my Grandpop. Funny how the mind plays tricks."

Harvey's face was solemn. "True. You cannot control what your brain think," he said, pointing to his head. "Only God can do that."

Jack lifted himself out of the chair and looked glumly into the darkness of the boulevard. He knew that Bryan was lost and that he could not help him any more than he could keep his Grandpop from dying or Bernice from leaving. He reached into his pocket, drew out his wallet and began pulling out bills.

Harvey stood up and pushed Jack's hand with the money away. "You are my guest tonight, Jack. Keep your money."

He dropped a dollar on the table for Mary.

"I am sorry that Bryan does not understand your kindness," Harvey said, patting Jack's shoulder. "Perhaps later he'll know we both tried to help him."

"Yeah. You're a fine man, Harvey. And a wonderful baker."

"Thank you. Not to worry. It will turn out all right. You must be patient. Remember what I tell you. From this night on, everything in your life will be different."

They shook hands. A strange thing for him to say. Somehow, he knew Harvey's prophecy would be true. From this night on, everything would be different. Except, in Jack's mind, it was a bad omen, not a good one.

Chapter 11

Late Thursday Evening, May 16.

Leaving Harvey's, he drove slowly down Seaview Boulevard, watching the sidewalks for any sign of Bryan. He already knew where he would be: at the Civic Center. They were setting up props tonight. Two weeks from now, the senior play was to be held there to accommodate the large crowds. They had always drawn outsiders, people from as far away as West Palm Beach. Tourists also attended the three-night production. It was the best G-rated live show around.

The drama teacher, Mr. Enright, was a former director of off-Broadway productions, semi-retired, living in Seagate. Those who knew said that if you were trained by Enright and he thought you were talented, he could get you into the finest acting schools. That meant you were almost assured of a career on Broadway. Jack marveled that Em was willing to take that risk. Truth was, ninety-five percent of all the work was done by five percent of all the actors. Same with set design, props, directing. It was a tough business. But so was photography. And he had made it sufficiently to keep house and home together...until now.

Stalker

The white limestone Civic Center loomed ahead. He parked and walked along the esplanade of date palms, tasting salt air on his lips. The dark was almost shiny and liquid tonight, a white aggie marble of moon glowing brightly in star-filled heavens. Silently, scudding puffs of cloud ran across the sky, pulling more of themselves along from the Southeast. Oh, to be on the water tonight, racing with the moon. He rounded the bend and before him, sitting on the shadowed steps, was a dark hulk. The form changed shape as it arose and moved off toward the azalea garden. It carried something about the size of a shirt box.

"Wait, Bryan! We can still talk."

The dark form did not answer, but disappeared into the blackness along the canal where water oaks and palms shook themselves in the tepid ocean breeze. A bike's kickstand snapped. The silhouette of Bryan and bicycle reappeared as he crossed the canal bridge.

Jack did not enter the theater because Em did not like for her Mom or her Dad to do so. She was with friends doing her thing. He respected that. He returned to the car and headed for home.

Half way down Pine Avenue, there was Bryan on his bicycle, knapsack on back, pedaling hard. Jack opened the window on the passenger side. Bryan slowed, recognized who it was, and cut sharply into an alley.

"Bryan! Don't be afraid of me!" His dark silhouette made another turn to the right and was gone.

When he got home, he found Bernice watching television, wine in one hand and a cigarette in the other. She was still dressed in business clothes.

"Hi," she said, seeming to be in good humor. "How'd it go? Did you and lover-boy have a cozy chat?"

Classic Bernice, he thought.

"He didn't show," he replied, keeping his temper in check. "He was down at the Civic Center. When he saw me, he took off on his bike. He's probably back at the Center waiting for Em to come out."

"Um! Too bad."

She drew on her cigarette, flicked the ash partially into the ashtray, and resumed watching her sit-com. Ashes surrounded the tray on the table. Canned laughter exploded at the end of a dumb one-liner. She reached for the remote and punched the volume up another decibel. Case closed. No further questions.

Jack entered the kitchen for a glass of wine and a bowl of pretzels. He was heading toward the studio when Bernice stopped him with her voice.

"I don't suppose you would remember, but Suzanne is expecting us to provide her with a division of property by Wednesday. What do you want to do about it?"

What's there to do about it, he thought? It was her divorce. He returned to the living room doorway and leaned against the frame. "We've already settled on the big assets: house, cabin, cars, sailboat. What's left?"

She assumed her Joan Crawford look, full of wide-eyed fury and disgust. "What's left? For God's sake, Jack, are you blind or something? Look around you. We've got to decide who gets all this junk."

He held his tongue. Such a bitch! She could not even be civil for the few weeks before they split. "Hold on a second," he said. In the studio, he opened the cabinet where all his mailing materials were stored, and took out three rolls of yellow bulk mail stickers. Returning to the living room, he placed them on the table next to Bernice.

"Use these. Stick one on every damned thing you want, except leave Em's stuff alone. Make a list for Suzanne. When your packers come, they can simply pack whatever has a sticker. How's that?"

"Well," she said with amused haughtiness. "What a brilliant idea!"

He did not answer. Bernice examined the rolls and gave him a friendly smile. "Bulk mailers. Where'd you get these?"

"Post office, obviously. I've got more if you should run out."

Bernice was glowing, effusive. "You mean you're not going to hassle me about any of this stuff? Mementos? Pictures? The paperweights? The print collection?"

"Take what you want, Bernice."

"That's very sweet, Jack. I do appreciate it... What about the studio, though? All the cameras, lights, action! All that stuff. Can I put stickers on the equipment?"

Her pretend smile had changed to pure acid. He took a deep breath to steady his voice. She hadn't been in the studio in over two years.

"Stay away from my equipment. It's what I need to earn a living. No court in the country would allow you to take away my means of supporting Em. Touch any of it and you've got a big problem."

She put her cigarette in her mouth and raised her hand. "Not to worry! I won't touch your God-damned precious equipment." She coughed and removed the cigarette. "Hell, I won't even go in there."

"Fine."

He could not let it go, however. He set the bait. "You know, Bernice, you make twice the money I do. All those rich clients. What the hell would you do with my camera equipment?"

She mashed the butt in the glass ashtray. "I don't know," she said breezily, her head nodding from side to side in a haughty swagger. "Donate it to the Boys Club? They're always asking for computer and photography equipment."

"Fine," he said, setting the hook. "When you donate your $6,000 computer and $800 laser printer, I'll match it with my darkroom and cameras. How's that?"

"Damn, Jack! Can't you take a joke? Jesus! I know you can't survive without all those gizmos you hide back there. You know I was only kidding."

"I've never understood your kidding, Bernice. I never see the humor." He turned and walked down the hall while calling over his shoulder. "Let me know when Em comes home, will you?"

"Don't go away mad. The sticker idea is great!"

She seemed unfazed, getting him riled. He could not wait for her to get the hell out. He slammed the door to his citadel. War on all sides. It did not pay to be a nice guy, either to your daughter's stalker or to your bitchy wife. The volume on the television suddenly jumped several decibels. More of Bernice's jokes, he supposed.

He sat down in the swivel chair and tried calling Adelia Cutler. The phone rang for a long time. No answer.

Using a felt tip marker, he crossed off the photo assignments from today and checked the list for tomorrow: a building dedication, a planning commission hearing, publicity shots of Sea Siren, a tall ship that had arrived at the municipal pier today. It was a light schedule. Maybe Bryan would think more about his offer and give him a call.

He was studying a book of California photographs by Max Yavno when he heard Em come home. Her voice was loud above the canned laughter on the television. She was saying something excitedly to Bernice. The sound of the television died. He put the book down and hurried out.

Bernice's face was distraught. "Wait 'til you hear this, Jack."

Em turned. "Dad! Bryan was waiting in the parking lot behind David's car when we came out of rehearsal. He was really nasty. I think he was on something."

"Why?"

"His voice was slurry. He tried to pick a fight with David. He called him a queer and a fag and all. And he blocked us from getting in Chuck's car."

"So what happened?"

"David didn't want any part of him, you know what I mean? He's not a fighter. Chuck stepped in front of David and would've swung at Bryan, but David and I grabbed him. Thank God Bryan didn't retaliate. He woulda killed Chuck, you know? It was like... Bryan was waiting for Chuck to hit him first, you know? So he could say Chuck started it."

"Hm. Chuck and David together couldn't win against Bryan," he said, recalling Harvey's description of the Barnes fight. "So what happened?"

"David and I pulled Chuck back toward the Civic Center. Bryan just leaned against Chuck's car, calling him more names."

"Bryan didn't follow," Bernice asked.

"No."

"So what happened next?" he asked. "After you and Dave pulled Chuck away."

"We went in and told the Russells and Mr. Enright what happened."

"Who are the Russells, hon," asked Bernice.

"Jim and Mary Jane. He's a carpenter and a really big guy. He and his wife are volunteers in charge of set construction. Anyway, everybody, including Mr. Enright, came out with us. Naturally, Bryan was gone."

"Glad nothing else happened," Jack responded.

"Chuck says Bryan's got a bad reputation for fighting."

"For sure. You tell Chuck and David not to mess with Bryan. Walk away and report what happened to authorities."

Em looked apprehensive, seeming to recognize he knew plenty about Bryan. "What happened between you and Bryan tonight, Dad?"

"Unfortunately, nothing. He didn't show. Harvey clued me in. Bryan nearly killed a bully out in front of the bagel shack one time. He showed no mercy."

"Really?" asked Bernice, looking like he was exaggerating.

"Really. Ask Harvey."

Bernice studied him, then took a drag on her cigarette before grinding the butt in the tray.

"What's all this about," asked Em, starting to giggle and pointing.

"What's all what..." said Bernice, following Em's eye across the room. "Oh, that..."

The entire room looked like it had been hit by a pox. Yellow stickers adorned every item: pictures on the walls, lamps, chandelier, furniture, paperweights, prints, and every book in the bookcase.

"Your father gave me mailing stickers to identify what I want to take when I leave," Bernice said with a sheepish expression. "Clever, don't you think?"

The amused look evaporated from Em's pretty face. "I guess so." She turned to Jack. "Well, Dad, what do we do now?"

He shrugged and glanced at Bernice. "I think we've been patient enough. I'll try calling his mother again tomorrow. If I don't reach her, I might just drive over and pay her a visit."

"Cool. Why do you think Bryan didn't show at Harvey's?"

"He'd been there, Harvey said. Probably watched me arrive. I think he was too afraid I was trying to trap him somehow. Anyway, I won't waste any more time like that."

"So then what did you do," Em asked, while wiping make-up off with a tissue.

"I visited with Harvey 'til eight-forty or so, drove to the theater, saw Bryan sitting on the steps, and tried to talk with him."

"He ran off?"

"Yeah. On my way home, I saw him on his bike and tried to talk with him again. He turned in an alley and I guess he doubled back to the Civic Center and waited for you in the parking lot."

"Did anyone call the police," asked Bernice.

"I don't know," Em replied. "Mr. Enright may have."

"Be sure," he said, "to write down the times and places in your Bryan log."

"I will. He really scared me. I'm afraid he's going to hurt Chuck or Dave, you know? They wouldn't stand a chance. And I feel like I'm responsible." She wiped a tear from her cheek.

"Jack, you've got to do something," Bernice said, using her best Bette Davis voice.

He ignored her. "Have you ever noticed Bryan carrying a box with him? He had one tonight."

"That's his portable computer," said Em. "He plays chess games on it. He's a whiz."

"Can't you do something, Jack," asked Bernice. "This boy's a nuisance."

"I'm doing all I know to do."

"Well, you two," Em said with a false yawn, "I'm going to bed now. Good night."

"Night, love," said Jack.

"Good night, Emily."

She gave Bernice and Jack a hug, got a Coke from the kitchen, and went to her room. "Don't forget you have to drop me off at Julie's tomorrow morning, Dad," Em called from her doorway.

"I won't."

"What's she going there for," asked Bernice.

"A costume fitting. Julie's mother is making her a gown for the play. She's got permission to be late to school."

"I see." She drew on her cigarette. "What are you going to do about this boy," Bernice asked in a lower, Lauren Bacall voice. "He's getting on my nerves."

"As I said, I'll try to reach his mother. I'm also going over to Ocean State and talk with the counselors there. Maybe I can get some help from them."

"Good luck! I think we ought to get a lawyer on this myself. Send his mother a legal letter. That will get their attention."

"Yeah, well, good night, Bernice."

"Night. By the way, I need more stickers. What a great idea."

"I'll get some."

How quickly women changed their minds. One moment, he was dirt; the next, he was the benevolent prince who was giving away the family treasures with a mere pasting of a sticker. One moment she thought Bryan was just a boy going through puppy love, the next he's a nut-case.

He grabbed a flashlight and slipped out the side door, tiptoeing around the corner of Em's playhouse. Without using the flashlight, he waited for his eyes to adjust to the darkness and moved along the fence, into the moonlight. Across the street, leaning against a lamppost in full light was Bryan, gazing toward Em's bedroom. Jack moved, low to the ground, breaking into a run across the front yard. Bryan bolted down the street toward Eisenhower Park and into the trees.

"Stop, Bryan. We've got to talk," Jack called in low tones, fearing he was waking neighbors. He paused at the edge of the trees, heart pounding and breathing heavily and listened. Nothing.

If I am honest, he said to himself, I'm afraid that I'll actually catch up with him and be forced to deal with him on his terms. He wiped sweat from his face with the front of his T-shirt. He turned on the flashlight and moved the beam across the line of trees. No sign of him. He switched the light off and walked back to the house, relieved that Bryan had had the sense to run rather than turn on him.

Yes, Em, he said to himself, I'm more cowardly than Bryan–unless he corners you or Bernice or me or your friends. Then, I don't know what I'd do.

His body shivered as he felt the rush of adrenalin. An Ocean City police car turned the corner at the end of the street. It had missed Bryan by two minutes. Bill was keeping his word about extra monitoring.

As he crossed the lawn, a dry breeze warmed the back of his neck. The smell of burning wood and grass was palpable. There was a fire somewhere. The air was coming from the south, southeast. He would shut the windows and doors. With the windows closed and the air conditioner running, they wouldn't know whether Bryan came back and sat beneath the plum tree behind the evergreens under Em's window. He decided to set his alarm for two o'clock and check. He switched on the security lights, front, back, and sides, even though the neighbors would protest that the lights kept them awake.

A siege mentality was taking hold. Without thinking about it, his mind and body were already preparing themselves against what Bryan might be planning. He was not going to sit and wait. Tomorrow, he would take the offensive and make Bryan wish he'd never, ever laid eyes on Em. He paused at the sliding glass door. Big talk. All big talk. He did not have the foggiest notion of a plan… only a growing anger.

He quietly entered Em's room and closed her windows and locked them. He did the same in every room of the house. He passed through the living room where Bernice sat, cigarette in hand, watching television.

"What's burning," she asked.

Before he could answer, a news alert interrupted the television program and announced an emergency: brush and grass fires were getting out of hand in several places across Florida. He paused to listen before he switched on the air conditioning and set the thermostat.

"Think we're in danger, Jack?"

"The closest fire is north of Baytown. Unless the wind shifts, we should be fine."

He went to his bedroom, undressed, and tried to sleep. The television was blaring. He imagined the level of wine in the jug in the refrigerator receding slowly, like a miniature tide, emptying into a glass and into Bernice, one sip after another, working up to one last drink as Johnny Carson said goodnight and waved his hand. Bernice would likely smoke a final cigarette, which would prompt her to open another jug, already cooling next to the nearly empty one. And the new cigarette and fresh glass of wine from the new jug would likely prompt Bernice to turn the channel to a late night movie and before she realized it, the second jug would be half empty and the ash tray full and would need emptying before she opened a new pack of cigarettes.

He sometimes watched her when she sat in her chair fantasizing during the late night movies. She became mesmerized, almost in an out-of-body state. Her face reflected the heroine she was watching. She silently voiced the lines she had memorized, becoming the star character in the movie, changing expressions with every situation. Her favorites were Lauren Bacall, Joan Crawford, Bette Davis and Greer Garson.

She mimicked Greer Garson to a tee. Every nuance. She must have seen her movies dozens of times to accomplish the feat. Even so, when she applied her movie roles to real life with Em and him, she looked and acted silly. He could not imagine living in the same house with her any longer. It would be the greatest blessing when she moved out.

He lay thinking about all the prompts in Bernice's life and how they must affect her sleeping, waking, dreaming, and working. One prompt led to another, like the stimulus-response system Pavlov made famous with dogs. Except her system was built on time frames, pulsed by segments of television and commercials which dominated what Bernice did from eight until two every night of her life except when she went out with friends and her special friend she never talked about.

Come to think of it, her professional life was one big sequence of commercials, campaigns, and promotions fertilized by money from companies wanting television exposure. Yes, Bernice watched television with an eye toward sensing what the public liked and disliked. Only, she could not take it anymore without lots of wine and cigarettes.

Even she must cringe at the shill laughter and dumb one-liners. Yet, she made her money from being able to anticipate what people would like six months from now on television. She was a master of the superficial, an expert in forming the half-truth and putting it to music. She was the inventor of the crass commercial, the jingle you couldn't forget. How in hell could she have changed so, he wondered? He supposed she hadn't really. He used to admire her ability to promote as being creative. He mistook her clever manipulation of people as being an admirable intuitive skill. Her shallowness had always been there. He just hadn't notice it. And when he did, he was appalled.

The television noise snapped off. No late, late movie tonight. The silence was deafening. Echoes of the voices, laughter, commercials, and music lingered in his mind, playing a trick so that somewhere inside his head, he still believed the television was playing. He swore he heard voices and laughter. It was two thirty.

He waited until he heard the door to Bernice's bedroom close and water running in her bathroom. He got up, slipped on a pair of shorts and moccasins, and crept out the sliding glass door. The grass was drier tonight, probably because of the fires. Clouds filled the sky so the hazy moon darted behind one cloud after another, appearing to ride jauntily across the smoky sky while casting eerie shadows upon the light-covered neighborhood.

He moved past the playhouse and into the spotlight's glow at the corner of the house. No sign of Bryan. He walked past the garage and along the other side of the house beyond the crepe myrtle bushes. He stood listening. Nothing. He entered the sliding glass door and locked it.

He had a strong sense that Bryan was nearby. He had acquired it in Vietnam, when the enemy was within spitting distance, deadly quiet, waiting, watching. A sixth sense.

In Nam, men would use that sixth sense to turn and fire at point blank range into jungle, sensing something there. It was usually nothing. Sometimes, though, it would be Viet Cong who, caught off guard, would cry out in misery as they fell out of hiding places onto the ground. The faces of the two boys glared at him. So young...

Although he sensed that Bryan was close by, he did not have the strong feeling, yet, of knowing instinctively where. He was content in knowing all the windows were locked and the doors bolted, the sliding glass doors double-braced. As he returned to bed, he knew he would eventually be able to find Bryan at will.

He dozed and came wide awake from a nightmare. A unit of infantrymen had surrounded the house and lay in wait. Then Bryan appeared across the street beneath the lamp in his dark clothing. His face was expressionless. He puffed on a joint and leaned against a lamppost, shifting one foot across the other. Platoon Sgt. Robbins appeared and ordered his men to form a line in the yard. They came out of bushes, from around both sides of the house, wearing full combat gear, their boots making an eerie, swishing sound on the wet grass.

On hand signal from Robbins, all dropped to one knee and raised their M-16's toward Bryan. The Sergeant dropped his hand, and the air crackled with shell bursts. Bryan's body jumped and danced with tiny explosions as he fell to the curb in a twisted heap. The firing continued. The hump of flesh and black cloth jumped and popped, growing smaller, bloodier. The barrage continued until the body had evaporated, leaving only a pool of blood spilling over the curb beneath the soft lamplight.

He tried to fall back to sleep and discovered upon waking that the dream was continuing. The lieutenant was commanding his men to fall in and follow. Jack's face, neck and back were wet. He tried to shake the dream off, got up, and washed himself at the lavatory without turning on a light. He toweled off, seeing in his mind's eye Bryan's body taking hits, getting smaller and smaller, disappearing as the men were ordered to stop firing. The squad moved off without a word, crossing Archie McAllister's yard. He found it incredible that, after waking, he could return to the dream and recall it in minute detail. He put the towel on the rack and returned to bed, realizing that he had enjoyed seeing Bryan struck down and, as they used to say when he was a kid, liquidated.

He considered how he should arm himself. He had long ago given up firearms. Yet, he knew Bryan was much stronger than he. With Bryan's rage in full gear, it would be like fighting a man high on cocaine. He wouldn't stand a chance. Mace? Perhaps Chief Winters could give him a can of mace. Misused, it could do as much damage to him as it would do to Bryan. Mace wouldn't do. A club? He'd have one swing, probably, before Bryan took it away from him.

All sorts of weapons danced in his head. He dozed only to come awake again in a sweat. Was it a noise? Should he get up and go outside?

He arose and checked the doors and windows. Bernice and Em were quiet. Their doors were closed. Four o'clock. Images of shooting Bryan swam in his head. Back in bed, he tried to sleep, but he could not.

Chapter 12

Friday Morning, May 17.

The St. Pete Times was reporting major fires across Florida from Tallahassee south to the Everglades. Towns and cities were losing power. Some fires were out of control. Jack checked the morning news on television. He waited while Em got dressed. They grabbed a quick breakfast at Em's favorite cafe.

As he pulled to the curb in front of Julie Becker's house, he caught a glimpse of Bryan half a block away, sitting on a bench at a bus stop. His portable computer was open on his lap. Bryan seemed oblivious to their approach.

Em did not seem to notice him. Jack let her out and watched her go in the door. He turned back. Bryan and his bike were gone. Was it his imagination? Was it a Nam-type illusion?

He drove down to the corner and parked. He crossed the street to the bench, checked out the streets in all directions, then entered the corner grocery market. Bryan was nowhere to be seen. How did he know Em would come here rather than go to school this morning? It was as if she were carrying a signaling device on her. He returned to the Becker's house and knocked on the door. Julie opened it.

"Sorry to bother you, Julie, but can I speak to Emily for a second?"

"Sure. Come in, Mr. Kaufman. She's in the dining room."

Em, already in her costume–a lovely powder blue lace and satin gown—stood on a green plastic milk crate next to the table. Mrs. Becker with pins in her mouth was on her knees pinning the hem. She looked up and waved.

"Hi, Dad. What's up?"

"Is someone taking you girls to school this morning?"

"We thought we'd walk," Em replied. "Why? Is our phantom friend out there?"

"Yeah. If you won't be too long, I can take you. I'll wait in the car."

Mrs. Becker removed the pins from her mouth. "Not to bother, Jack. I need to drop off some hats at the Drama Department. I'll be glad to take them."

"You sure?"

"Of course."

"All right. See you later." He paused and turned back. "By the way, Em. When did you guys set up this appointment for this morning?"

"How do you mean?"

"Did you and Julie talk about it yesterday at school?"

The girls looked at one another, then gazed at him with wide eyes like he was speaking a foreign language.

"I called Emily," Mrs. Becker explained, getting to her feet. She glanced up at Em. "When was it, honey? Two days ago?"

"Yeah. You called me around five, I think." Em looked at her father. "Why?"

"Oh," he shrugged, "I dunno. I can't figure out how our friend knows what you are up to all the time."

Em put her hands on her hips. "Me, too. It's like he's got spies out"

"You're talking about Bryan Cutler, that gross guy who's always hanging out at play rehearsals," asked Julie.

"That's him," Em said with a sigh. "My one and only hound dog."

They giggled, except Em's laugh was forced.

"It really isn't funny," said Em. "I'm afraid he's losing it."

"Like, how?" Julie asked.

"Scary. Saying bad things to Chuck and David. Trying to pick a fight. I think he's on something."

"Not cool," Julie replied.

Jack wanted to get back to the street to look for Bryan. "See you later."

Julie opened the door for him. He walked to the street and looked in both directions. No sign. He was puzzled. I'm not covering all the angles, he thought.

After doing his assignments, he drove to Ocean State College. He couldn't help thinking there had to be some professionals who could reach Bryan before it was too late. Unfortunately, he found the college counselors less than interested in talking with him. He got nothing except carefully worded, textbook responses that felt to Jack like psychobabble.

"You must understand," said James Rice, a counselor, "that we can do nothing for a student unless he or she seeks our help. From what you tell me, Mr. Cutler hasn't committed any crime and is apparently doing very well here at college."

The other counselor, Nathan Sands, sat across from Jack and nodded agreement. "We're here purely for the sake of being available if and when a student or prospective student seeks our advice. We cannot initiate any type of counseling, group or individual therapeutic activity, unless requested to do so either by the student or a faculty member or an authorized referral source. And in the case of a juvenile, we would also need approval from the parent or guardian."

"Yes," added Rice. "Even a faculty member has no authority except to recommend. He or she cannot require a student to participate in counseling sessions the student does not wish to attend."

It sounded like they were reading their lines from the faculty handbook of policies and standards. "I thought you were hired to identify students with problems and to help them solve them," Jack said with growing sarcasm.

The counselors shook their heads.

"Well," Jack said, gripping the steel arms of the chair tightly, "I had hoped you and I could work together on this. I've offered to meet with Bryan, but right now he's frightened of me. And I am becoming frightened of him. The kid needs help. Surely, there's somebody who can help him."

"Sorry," said Rice.

Jack laughed hollowly. "Hell, I am frightened for my daughter. I'm frightened for all the young women he may be trailing. I want to do something. I thought the college where this fellow is enrolled would help. What about all the young women on this campus? How do you know he isn't stalking several of them as we speak? His letters mention trying to get dates with women in his classes. It's part of your responsibility to warn these women that this guy may be stalking them."

"Do you know any names," asked Rice.

"Only one... Helen, I believe."

"No last name," Sands inquired.

"No."

Both nodded gravely.

"It's not easy," said Sands. "That's what we're telling you, Mr. Kaufman. It's like any other matter involving law and people's rights. You can't act until something happens which either compels a person to seek help or else the person is forced by authorities to get treatment. Either way, unless the person is willing and cooperative, the treatment won't work. The person must want to overcome his problems."

Jack got up and shook hands. "Thank you gentlemen. This has been interesting."

"Sorry, we can't help you," Sands replied.

He returned to the car feeling exasperated. What could he do that was positive? Hell, he would pay a visit to Mrs. Cutler and put her on notice. He drove down East Bay to Seagate, looking for Harlan Street. It was on the left. He turned into the narrow street, which was filled with potholes. The brick building at 122 was four stories and dilapidated: open windows, shoddy gray curtains, broken blinds flapping. He parked and entered the building. Adelia Cutler's mailbox showed Apartment 202.

He climbed the worn carpeted stairs, entering a semi-dark interior hallway that was pungent with a variety of odors ranging from urine to mildew. The second floor was bare wood and creaked under foot. A ceiling light bulb gave off a vacuous yellow light, casting a dull glow on grayish green walls. Standing before a darker green door of chipped paint with the number 202 stenciled in black, he rang the doorbell. No answer. He knocked, sending dull echoes down the hallway. Nothing. "Hello!" he called loudly. "Mrs. Cutler, may I speak with you? Hello!" Dead silence.

He walked to the end of the hallway and peered through the dirty window into a dismal sand lot filled with trash and broken furniture. Chained to a palm tree was Bryan's bicycle. So, he was home. He went back and knocked harder.

"Bryan! It's Jack Kaufman. I want to talk with you and your mother. Is your mother home?"

No response. A door squeaked open down the hall. A young woman carrying a small baby eyed him suspiciously. She slammed the door and gave him a wide berth as she passed by. He nodded and smiled. Her face was taut, expressionless. She was wearing a bright miniskirt and low-cut blouse, showing great cleft and puffed breasts. She looked like she might be an exotic dancer. She said nothing. She knocked at another door down the hall. It opened without a word. She went in. The door slammed. He returned to the car.

He drove home. Archie McAllister was mowing his front lawn. Archie limped along in a loping gait behind the mower. He had lost his lower left leg on Pork Chop Hill in Korea. He was a good guy to drink beer with and to share war stories. Jack had come to depend on Archie for his carpentry and plumbing skills. Never charged a dime beyond materials. He decided Arch needed to be aware of the Bryan situation. He crossed the lawn. Archie shut off the mower and wiped a hand across his brow. "Glad you came along," said Archie. "I needed some excuse to quit for the day. Time me and you had a beer or two."

"I don't mean to stop a working man from his job," Jack quipped. "I'll take a rain check on the beer..."

"Ain't these fires something? If the wind keeps up, we might be in trouble."

"They say not, but you never can tell. Wind has a way of quartering."

"That's so." Archie took off his Atlanta Braves hat and smoothed thin strands of wet gray hair. "What can I do you for?"

"You mighta noticed a tall, heavy-set kid hanging around, Archie. His name's Bryan Cutler. Dresses in dark clothes. Always has five o'clock shadow."

Archie replaced his cap. "Yeah. I've seen him different times. Seen him come out your front walk a couple days ago. Why? Is he a problem?"

"Yeah. He's stalking Emily."

"God-a-mighty! Ya don't wanta mess with one of those mothers. My sister–the one I mentioned worked in the Winn Dixie–Louise?"

"Yeah."

"She was stalked for weeks, 'cept nobody knew who it was. The bastard tried to climb into her bedroom one night. She woke just as he was halfway in. She screamed like bloody hell and drove him off."

"Damn..."

"She got so scared she hired a body guard to stay at her place and take her back and forth to work. She'd get obscene phone calls. Obscene mail. You know, the whole nine yards. She was afraid to go out... and she was afraid to stay home. She was a nervous wreck."

"Did they ever find the guy?"

"Oh, yeah. The damn bodyguard didn't keep him away. He came back different times. Eventually, Louise spotted him putting an envelope in her mailbox. Recognized him, by God."

"Yeah?"

"One of the box boys. A kid just out of high school. A misfit. Louise worked the cash register right next to him without knowing. They'd practically rub hips, they were so close. She never knew 'til the day he put that letter in her mailbox... Louise was never the same after that. Even therapy didn't do much good. Always scared 'til she died."

"I'm sorry."

"How's Emily taking it?"

Jack looked down at the grass before nodding affirmatively.

"Pretty good so far. She has a nightmare now and then. Fortunately, she's getting great support from all her friends. Anyway, if you see Bryan hanging around, I'd appreciate you calling 911."

"Know what I'd do, if I were in your shoes, Jack?"

"No."

"I've got a friend down in Miami who owns a whole bunch of apartments. Any time a tenant gets behind on rent or takes off without paying, he calls up a couple of very big, tough guys out of Hialeah. One visit is all it takes. They talk direct, no bullshit, you know? They ask for the back rent. Any static and they scuff the guy up some. He pays. I can get you their number, if you want it. That's what I'd do. Hire them to pay a courtesy call on this SOB. I think one visit would do the trick..."

"Hell, Arch, with my luck the two guys would screw up and I would be thrown in jail for attempted contract murder."

"Believe me, Jack," Archie said, tapping Jack's arm firmly, "this SOB understands only one language and that is brutality. I'd a done it for Louise if I'd a known. Police are no damn good in this situation. And a stalker won't stop until he gets what he wants or is killed trying. That's what Louise's lawyer told us. Ya got a problem, Jack. Get to him before he gets to Emily."

Jack scuffed his shoe through the cut grass, watching the blades scatter. He did not see hiring some goons to hurt Bryan. For one thing, they'd underestimate Bryan's strength. For another, he would outsmart them. "Well, I've got to check my messages, Archie. Thanks for the advice."

"I'll be on the lookout," he said, starting the mower. "I'll keep my Smith & Wesson .38 handy, too, just in case he comes on my property. You better believe he won't do it a second time."

Jack ignored Archie's bravado, crossed the lawn and entered the front door. The coolness of the air conditioning was unpleasant. Perhaps it was the recycled smoke from Bernice's cigarettes and the brush fires. He entered the studio and checked messages. One. Call Bill Winters ASAP. He called and asked for Bill. Florese put him through.

"Chief Winters."

"Bill? This is Jack."

"Got some info on Cutler, ole buddy. It isn't good."

"How so?"

"Your boy's got a record with Seagate police."

He could hardly breathe.

"Oh?"

"Seems about a year ago, the kid was driving his mother's car and struck a kid about his own age."

"Ran over him?"

"Correct. He was arrested and charged with manslaughter, marijuana possession, reckless driving, along with a whole bunch of lesser charges. Got off with an involuntary manslaughter conviction, a $1,000 fine, and a year's probation. Took away his driver's license for a year."

"Holy hell!"

"Of course, this is off the record—strictly between the two of us."

"Right."

"He's had previous arrests for loitering and aggravated assault."

"I don't understand, Bill. With all those arrests, why isn't he in jail?"

"Hey! He's a juvenile. He's twenty. Now, if he were to kill you in cold blood, he'd be tried as an adult. But as of now, he's a ward of the juvenile court system."

Jack felt sweat running down the sides of his ribs, pooling at the waistband of his trousers. "What can I do?"

"First thing I'd do is see that my weapons are in good working order. You do own a pistol or two, don't you?"

He took a deep breath. Something in him kept seeing Bryan as just a kid. Crazy, maybe, but he was still a kid. Hell, he had seen so many like him in Nam. One minute, they were fearless; the next, they were scared rabbits. "No. I sold my guns after Nam."

"Yeah, well, don't say I didn't warn you. I know you think with Nam behind you, you can take out this guy by some other means. Believe me, Jack, you can't. I'm telling you as a buddy, not as chief of Ocean City PD. Get gun permits for Bernice and Emily. They need self-protection. You and I know my people can't protect you every minute. We usually arrive too late to do any good."

Jack's heart was beating faster. He could not see Emily using a gun. And Bernice with a gun would be downright dangerous to them all. "I can't see us doing that."

"Think about it, Jack. You're trying to protect lives, here. Get two guns and learn how to use them pronto. Go down to Tony's Gun Shop. Tell him I sent you. He'll give you a good discount on handguns, ammo, all you need. Then, come down to our range.

I can provide an instructor to teach all of you gun safety and self defense procedures. Be glad to do it."

"Thanks, Bill. I'll think it over. What else?"

"You've got to get proactive with this jerk. Contact his parole officer and report what he's been up to. Take her those letters. The sooner you get in touch with her, the sooner she can figure a way to get Cutler off the street. She can take him back into court. If he's found in violation, they'll probably put his ass in jail. You want the officer's number?"

He grabbed a note pad and pen. "Yeah."

"She's Probation Officer Sally Brand. Her office is in the Seagate police department. Her number is 322-4735, extension 526. Got it?"

"Yup."

"Would you like to borrow an automatic for the next few days?"

"Not yet. I'll let you know."

"Don't play around with this bastard. I'm telling you from experience. You and your family are very vulnerable if this guy should really get pissed."

He did not want to hear it. Then he remembered something important to tell him. "Oh, before I forget it. Bryan seems to know every move Emily makes. He's there waiting for her. This morning, I drove her to a friend's house, Julie Becker's. Sitting on a bench up the street was guess who?"

Bill chuckled. "Unbelievable, isn't it?"

"Yeah. I asked how the appointment was set up for Em to go over there and found Mrs. Becker called Emily day before last. Nobody else knew, except Julie. You figure that one out."

"Easy. The bastard's got a device with him. He's monitoring your phone calls."

"You really think so?"

"I know so. Hell, there are monitoring devices available so he can listen to conversations from half a block away. He knows every word you say. Has he been in your house?"

"Once."

"Then he probably placed a bug so he can monitor from a mile or so away. Check the whole house: in lamps, under tables, inside drawers. Check the bathrooms closely and also the smoke detectors."

"You really think he's planted a bug?"

"Could be more than one. The kid's smart. You can buy the equipment most anywhere. That's part of your problem, Jack. You see this guy as an average twenty-year-old kid. He isn't. He's ten steps ahead of you. He's hearing everything you say. Warn the family not to divulge any information while in the house or on the phone that could be of use to him. Meanwhile, I'll put another car in the area. I've already alerted Seagate police to watch this dude. Okay?"

"Thanks, Bill."

"Are you calling from home?"

"Yeah."

"Ha! Are you aware that Cutler is taking all this in? Can you hear me, Bryan Cutler? This is Chief of Ocean City Police, Bill Winters. You mess with these people any more, and I will get your ass and put it so far away you'll never bother any body except moles and groundhogs. Got that?"

"He can't use this against you by recording it?"

"Nah! He's scum. I'd love for him to come in my direction. Hear that, Cutler? You're a sneaking, son-of-a-bitching coward. You're nothing but green, slimy, filthy scum! Anyway, now he knows I recommended you talk with his probation officer. He'll be watching to see whether you follow through. It'll be interesting to see how he handles it."

"For sure..." He was thinking how he and Bill had just escalated Bryan's emotional state by about a thousand points on the Richter Scale with this conversation.

"I'd talk with Sally as soon as possible and get the hell out of the line of fire. Let this probation lady take the heat. Know what I mean?"

"Right."

His head was swimming. Listening devices! Aggravated assault! Manslaughter! Guns! "Talk to you later."

"Bye."

Jack clicked off the phone. All my big talk and bright ideas, he thought... I am being outflanked by a juvenile, a very bright mentally ill thug. Well, I might as well put him on notice that I intend to follow through. There are no options. He dialed the number for Officer Sally Brand, punching in the extension.

"Officer Brand speaking. How may I help you?"

Her voice was firm yet feminine with a soft, lilting quality. "This is Jack Kaufman, Miss Brand. Chief Winters from Ocean City suggested I get in touch. I'm calling regarding a young man who may be one of your probationers."

"Yes?"

"Bryan Cutler. Is he on probation with you?"

There was a pause. "Tell me why you need to know."

"I have some very troubling information, including several letters he's written to my daughter. I believe he's stalking her. Could I come over this afternoon and discuss this with you?"

"Oh, I've got three court appearances this afternoon. What about Monday?"

"It's quite urgent."

"Hm... How 'bout right now? Where are you?"

"Practically next door, north side of Ocean City. I can be there in fifteen minutes."

"Okay. I'll be expecting you. Do you know how to get here?"

"I know where the police station is."

"Good. When you come in the headquarters, walk straight down the hall to the very end and turn left. My office is the first one on the right side."

"See you."

Chapter 13

Friday Noon, May 17.

Jack sat in Sally Brand's little office, watching her as she read Bryan's letters to Em. She was thirty-five or so, freckled with orange-red hair, a large mouth, lively green eyes. She looked sexy in her khaki uniform. Nice breasts. She grimaced as she looked up.

"Good news and bad news..." she said, rising. "I'd like to make copies of these."

"Go ahead." He stood up too.

"I'll be right back." She rushed out of the room and he sat down again. Bryan Cutler's file was lying on her desk. He was tempted to open it. Before he could decide, Sally rushed back in, handed him the originals, and sat down in a swivel chair behind her desk.

"You said you had good news and bad news."

"Oh! Sorry." Her cream colored hands shifted Bryan's file around, opened it, and inserted the copied letters. Deft fingers with unpainted nails attached the letters to the top edge of the folder with a paper clip. Her open mouth showed pretty teeth.

"These letters will give me what I need to recommend an extension of Bryan's probation. Another week and it would be up and he'd be free as a bird. You've bought me extra time to work with him."

"Is that the good news or the bad news?"

Her expression was more wince than smile. "I wish I did have better news. Keeping him on probation means he has to come in and report regularly. Any small infraction such as hanging out across the street from your daughter's window all night can get another extension... maybe. It isn't exactly breaking the law unless Ocean City police catch him at it and arrest him for loitering. Really, I can't expect the court to do much unless he breaks a law."

"I understand he was busted for smoking pot and was found guilty of manslaughter. What if he were into pot again?"

She began rocking back and forth in her chair. "You're not supposed to know that, you know..."

"I know." He attempted to smile, but felt hollow inside. He looked away. "It's something I heard through the grapevine. So... Can you answer my question? Could smoking pot put him in jail?"

She stopped rocking and looked toward the window. "That might get him arrested and put in jail for a day or two, but it wouldn't solve your problem. You see, Bryan is a juvenile. He's not quite twenty-one. So the juvenile court bends over backwards to keep him out of jail or youth detention. Now, if we caught him high and in possession, that might bring the house down. He could go to jail for a while. He'll be twenty-one in a few weeks and could be tried as an adult then."

"What about his mother? I tried to call her several times. I haven't been able to reach her."

"Both of them are difficult to reach by phone."

"Is he into electronics?"

"What can I say? Bryan's into computers, electronics–all the latest equipment. He lives and breathes it. Got his own lab set up in his bedroom, he tells me."

"So it wouldn't be hard for him to tinker with a phone or conceal a listening device?"

"A piece of cake. He could probably build a microphone when he was ten. He's a very smart guy. Why?"

"I think our house is bugged."

She nodded without committal. "Hm."

"You aren't in contact with his mother, then?"

"I really can't speak to that."

"When's her next appointment?"

She checked a calendar book. "That's confidential... It isn't for a while though. It won't help you."

He felt like he had reached a dead-end with this lady. Moreover, he had compromised Bill Winters by mentioning Bryan's confidential record. He could see the sandbags building in her mind across the desk. He decided to make one more attempt to talk off the record.

"Look, Officer Brand, I'm feeling very frustrated. Everybody I talk with says they can't help me. Either I'm violating Bryan's personal rights or they can't help me until he's committed a crime. I've got a lovely daughter who is about to graduate from high school. She's the star in the senior play. She's graduating with honors. I don't want her final weeks of high school ruined by this guy. I need to find someone who can help me deal with him."

She started rocking again, studying him from behind a closed fist. He tried again. "I guess there's no more pretending where I got my information about Bryan's police record. I'm not trying to hide anything. I want to be as candid with you as I possibly can. I will say off the record that Chief Bill Winters told me about Bryan's arrest sheet and what happened with the manslaughter verdict. Please.... I don't want to get Bill in trouble over this."

She tapped her nose lightly with her fist. "I understand."

He was not certain she did. He spoke in a softer tone. "Are there any additional facts I ought to know… or can't you tell me?"

She pointed to the closed folder. "You know that's a confidential file. I can't discuss it with you. I've already told you more about Bryan than I am supposed to. And you've reciprocated by telling me your friend Chief Winters has given you information from a sealed record. You've given me evidence of a criminal act. Bill Winters was totally out of bounds in sharing that information with you. What do you expect me to do?"

Her face was flushed and she held her arms out, palms flat, in frustration with him. A wave of embarrassment brought heat to his cheeks. He knew he had compromised Winters. He was now afraid she was going to report it to her supervisor and get everybody in hot water. Winters could lose his job or worse.

"I'm very sorry for my indiscretion, Miss Brand. I hope you won't tell anybody what Chief Winters shared. I am only trying to protect my daughter."

Her eyes watched him closely. "I know... I won't unless I'm called upon to testify."

"Thank you. I understand."

She gave him a look of admonishment. She dropped her fist to Bryan's folder, opened the file, ran a finger down the sheet, flipped it back, and continued, repeating the process through eight pages. She closed the folder and looked contemplatively at him. "I really can't divulge any information contained in this file without written permission of Mrs. Cutler and the courts. What Chief Winters told you is off the record and cannot be discussed. Can you see that?"

"I see."

Another stonewall. She studied him with her soft green eyes. She glanced at the doorway.

"Would you mind closing the door," she asked in a low tone.

He closed it and sat, leaning in expectantly with both his elbows on his knees. She fixed her eyes on him.

"I understand where you're coming from, Mr. Kaufman. I wish I could tell you more, but I can't."

"There's nothing more you can do?"

She pursed her lips and winced, tilting her head slightly to one side. She glanced at the door and back. "I didn't say that..."

"What can I do? I'll do most anything at this point."

She fingered Bryan's file. "I can't advise you as a parole officer. On the other hand, if I were in your situation, I would consider filing an Order to Show Cause with the court. Has Chief Winters suggested that?"

"No. What does it do?"

"It requests the court to grant you a Temporary Restraining Order. The TRO would restrain Bryan from coming within a certain distance of your daughter, making phone calls, writing her letters, that sort of thing. It would keep him from harassing her in any way."

"Would it work?"

She shrugged. "It could. Off the record, I doubt it. What it would do is provide you with a legal means of keeping him at bay. Any violation and he would be hauled into court. That's serious. And by then, he would be tried as an adult rather than a juvenile."

"Great! How do I file one? Through my attorney?"

"Yes. Or you can save money doing it through a paralegal."

"Good. I know one. Suzanne Wilkes."

"Oh, you know Suzanne? She's very competent and one sweet lady."

"I'll touch base with her this afternoon."

"Perfect. If you make the request, I can write a letter of support. Coming from the Probation Department, it ought to add weight. When will you file it?"

"As soon as Suzanne prepares it."

"You know, of course, this action must be initiated by your daughter. She'll have to state the reasons for the order and swear to the facts."

"I see. She's got to go with me to Suzanne's?"

"Yes. Suzanne will ask her several questions. The answers must be in your daughter's own words, not yours."

"Good! She can answer for herself very well."

"And she'll have to be prepared to testify in court. Do you see a problem with that?"

"No. I'd like for Em to answer that one for herself, though. It's her choice."

Brand's expression relaxed as though he had given her the answer she wanted. "Of course. Let me know."

"Getting back to a time frame, it might take a couple days then?"

"I'll have my letter ready."

"Officer Brand, you're the first person outside of Bill Winters who's been helpful and supportive."

"Glad to help. I wish I could tell you more, but I can't. Off the record, it's my opinion that a Show Cause and TRO might be just what Bryan needs at this point. We've tried about everything else we know to do."

He rose to shake her hand. "I so appreciate your helping us."

"Glad to do it. Just don't mention who suggested the TRO, okay?"

"Oh, right."

She gave him a wan smile and leaned against the desk. "Would it be okay with you if I had a talk with Emily," she asked, still holding his hand. "I'd like to hear her side. She might give me information that would help me deal with Bryan more effectively."

"Sure. Any time. Want her to call you?"

"Um... No. I'd like to contact her directly. Any problem with me meeting her alone?"

"Fine by me. She has nothing to hide."

"Good. Call me whenever you need to. In case I'm not here when you come by with the Show Cause papers, I'll leave the letter in a manila envelope at the front desk."

He left Sally feeling like she had given him sound advice. As he pulled out of the parking lot, he looked both ways on Seagate Boulevard. No sign of Bryan. He drove home and parked inside the garage. He entered the studio and began to list tasks. He must immediately search inside and outside the house for bugs and devices. Get the telephones checked. Map plans with Bernice and Em. Check security: windows, doors, locks. He realized he was now spending most of his time on this Bryan business and not enough on making money.

How stupid it was, he thought. Bryan had the freedom to move about as he pleased while the Kaufmans were locking themselves inside a house and fearing for Em anytime she went out. All the police, social workers, probation officers, counselors, courts, and lawyers could not keep Bryan from getting to Em, if that's what he wanted to do.

He considered Archie's suggestion. Hiring two goons to rough Bryan up sounded more and more like a viable alternative. Except... with his luck, something would go wrong. Seagate police would investigate. He would be arrested on charges of hiring these guys to hurt Bryan. And Bryan? Hell, he'd say–his lawyer would say—Jack Kaufman had hired two thugs to kill Bryan Cutler for no reason at all. And guess what? Good old Jack would be the one going to jail for attempted murder. No. There had to be a better strategy than using thugs.

He spent the afternoon going from one room of the house to another, examining lamps, drawers, undersides of tables, chests, beds. Disappointed by not finding anything, he went out the front door and began searching bushes, window frames, shutters, sills, trees and flowers around the house.

Throughout the afternoon, Bill's and Archie's warnings kept interrupting his concentration. "you're protecting lives here... Get two guns and learn how to use them... Police are no damned good in this situation... Get to him before he gets to Emily... Don't say I didn't warn you... We usually arrive too late to do any good... This SOB understands only one language, and that is brutality..."

He went into his studio and studied the black and white photograph of the rifle squad. Tears filled his eyes. How was it he could feel such rage at their deaths, wanting to run through the jungle shooting every goddamned Vietnamese in sight, and yet experiencing utter remorse and guilt over killing two teenaged Cong who moments before had been shooting at him? Yes, that was what he couldn't understand. That was the crux of it. None of it made any sense. He looked closely at the familiar faces. It was duty no matter what. No matter what you understood, believed, or thought. Duty. Duty always came first. Yes. They were resolute.

Their faces told him he had a job to do, no matter how he felt about killing. He picked up his car keys without thinking anymore about consequences and slammed the front door.

Chapter 14

Friday Afternoon, May 17.

Instead of taking Bill Winter's advice and going to Tony's Gun Shop, Jack decided to buy a gun at The Arsenal, which was across the county line. It was unlikely that anyone he knew would be there. And he certainly did not want to draw attention to his purchasing a gun.

He drove past Luko's Fish Packing Plant and over the river bridge. The Arsenal was just outside Baytown, a few miles across the wetlands. The sky was white with smoke from one of the larger fires raging twenty miles north. His nerves were on edge as he swung into the parking lot. When he entered the shop, it was like a time warp: the scents of gun metal, oil, leather holsters, gun powder, were just like in Nam. A middle-aged man wearing a blue pinstriped apron came out from behind a counter. Peaking out from the side of the apron was a nickel plated automatic in a holster. The man seemed to be sizing Jack up before saying anything.

"Can I hep ya?"

"I'd like to buy an automatic handgun."

"Any particular brand or caliber?"

"Yeah. A Colt .45 is preferable."

"Yes, sir. 1911. A good weapon. You must be a veteran. Vietnam?"

"Yeah."

"Thought so. New, reconditioned or pre-owned?"

Jack scratched his jaw. The idea of a gun with a history somehow did not appeal to him. If he were going to kill somebody, he wanted to do it cleanly with a new weapon. There had to be a certain ceremonial tone to it.

"New."

The clerk pointed to a display case, took out a key, and unlocked it. He drew out a Colt from among several brands and handed it to Jack.

The weapon felt at once heavy and all too familiar to him. Hell, he had qualified with one every year for the past nineteen years. It felt satisfying in his hand. He pointed it toward the ceiling and removed the clip, pulled back the breech mechanism, checked the chamber, and clicked it shut. He ran his hand along the barrel and felt the tension of the trigger pull. The trigger clicked. How many times had he fired one of these? The newness made it different from all the others, though. There was no wear or velvety smoothness; all the mechanisms were tight and rigid. It would take some getting used to.

"Can I try it out?"

"If yer a buy'n, you can. It'll just cost you the price of the gun and a box of ammo."

"Okay."

"Prefer hollows or hardballs?"

"Hardballs."

The clerk reached behind him and placed a box of live rounds on the counter. "You seem to know what yer do'n, so just go through that door to the range and Lou will hep ya."

Jack entered the semi-dark range, which consisted of two bays with backlit targets twenty-five yards away. The scent of spent gunpowder filled his nostrils. Lou was sitting on a stool, cleaning what looked like a Glock automatic.

"Muffs are over there," Lou said, pointing to four sets hung on wall pegs. "Help yourself."

Jack set the weapon and ammo box on a loading table and put on the ear protectors. There was a tremor in his hands as he opened the box and loaded the clip with seven brass and copper rounds. He had done it a thousand times, but this was different, he thought. He stepped up to the firing line and cocked the gun. He raised it above the target with a straightened arm. He slowly lowered the Colt and squeezed off a round as the sights centered on the bull's-eye. The kick was solid and good. He lifted and dropped the automatic down again and squeezed off another round, then repeated the procedure again, and still again. Perspiration dripped from his armpits even though the range was air conditioned and actually chilly. He emptied the clip. Lou pushed a button and the target was retrieved.

"Damned fine shooting. Perfect bull's-eyes," Lou said, removing the paper target and handing it to Jack.

"Thanks"

"Is that it or would you like another target?"

"That's it. I just needed to check it out."

Jack returned to the shop and placed his American Express card on the counter. The clerk put the Colt in its box and placed it and the box of cartridges in a brown bag.

"Care for a belt and holster? We've got some fine shoulder holsters."

"No, thanks."

The clerk processed the credit card and Jack signed the slip.

"Appreciate the business. Come back soon," said the clerk with a wry smile.

"Sure."

Jack felt exhilarated and drained at the same time. He hurried back home, trying not to think anymore about what he had done. Upon arrival, he closed the door to his studio and placed the Colt and cartridge box on the light table. He stared at the weapon and ammo for several minutes. You do not buy a gun and bullets without intending to use them, he whispered. And what if the situation were all wrong? What if I had a gun in my hand and was chasing Bryan? What would prevent me from firing at his back? Or how would I feel if I killed Bryan at close range when Cutler was unarmed. It would all depend on split-second judgment. I've been known to be wrong…

There was no question in Jack's mind that he would shoot to kill. That was how he had been trained. You did not intentionally "wing" the enemy; you aimed at the vital organs. He had learned well. And for nineteen years in the military, he was an expert marksman in small arms. He drew his right hand to his nose. The scent of gunpowder was pungent. He loved the smell of it despite all the images it incited. He loved the smooth feel of the steel and wood grips of the automatic. It was strange how a gun held such intoxicating power while it could cause such immeasurable harm.

He sat down, attempting to untangle the jumble of emotions. And the more he sat looking at the gun, the more he became convinced it was wrong of him to buy it. There had to be some better way to protect Em and Bernie without resorting to a Colt .45. He resisted the temptation to drive back to Baytown and get his money back. Instead, he opened the small safe beneath his desk and put the weapon and cartridges there and locked them up. Only as a last resort would he take them out. And after all this was over, he resolved to sell them back to the man at The Arsenal. He did not need a gun and live ammo in his house.

He called Suzanne Wilkes and arranged an appointment for Monday morning. Maybe the courts would issue a TRO and keep Cutler at bay. He hoped so.

Chapter 15

Saturday-Sunday, May 18-19.

The Kaufman family awoke Saturday morning to no power. The house was beginning to warm from a lack of air conditioning. According to the *Times*, fires had destroyed high tension power lines up and down the Florida coast. Over 4.5 million people were without power. Major highways were cut off from heavy smoke and raging infernos. Play practice was cancelled. Everyone was warned to stay inside rather than endure the smoke-filled air. Easier said than done with temperatures in the high eighties. Jack and Em drove to the icehouse and filled two coolers with crushed ice and bought a twenty-five pound cake for the refrigerator. There was no predicting when the power would be back on. At least they could save the food until it was eaten.

By Sunday afternoon, Flagler County reported over 2,000 people were homeless: burned out of their houses. Wild fires were sweeping across Florida in so many places that Governor Bob Graham was considering calling out the National Guard. Hordes of shoppers stripped the shelves of grocery stores. Generators were selling at a premium. The Kaufmans were too late to obtain extra food and a generator, but Jack had a couple dozen MREs (Meals Ready to Eat) stacked in their black plastic bags among his USAF Reserve equipment. These were in addition to a variety of canned soups, beans, pasta, and other stores they kept in the pantry just for such emergencies.

The Kaufmans stayed cool, enjoying air conditioning in Archie's RV parked behind his house. Archie, Em, and Jack played games of Hearts while Bernice stayed glued to the television and kept them informed about the latest fire news.

By Sunday evening, the winds decreased. The worst fires were north of Daytona. There was a sixty-percent chance of rain in the forecast for Monday. And by ten o'clock, power was restored to Seagate and Ocean City. The Kaufmans were able to return to their house the following morning.

Chapter 16

Monday Morning, May 20.

As Em and Jack approached the front door, Jack's eye caught the pink colored envelope with pasted butterfly stickers lying on the front step. A new tactic: delivering letters in the early morning. He handed it to Em and they climbed in the car. Em read the letter aloud.

Dear Emily:

I can't take it. You people are killing me slowly. I think of death a lot, thanks to you, Bitch. I could kill you and your friends but I won't. No way. Why should I waste my energy on killing damned fags and whores like David and Chuck and you? You are a whore, aren't you, Bitch? I know you'd like to do it with me... Except you fear I'm too big to fit. Is that the problem, Bitch? Don't worry, you'd like it so much you'd want more...

Every time I think of you, I want to kill myself. Could you do it for me, Emily? Put me out of my misery? We could meet in E. park. I have a razor blade. It wouldn't take long. Could you at least do that much for me? Pleeeeeese?????

I can't stand your coldness any longer. Come to me. Help me end it all. Kill me so I don't have to suffer.

All My Love,
Bryan.

"He's really lost it, Dad." Em handed him the note as tears trickled down her face.

He read the words slowly. It was clear that Bryan wasn't on drugs when he wrote this one, which was even more chilling. He wanted to call Bryan and encourage him to slit his wrists and end it–before he hurt somebody else.

"You'd think this letter by itself would be enough to put him away. Add it to your log and we'll give it to Suzanne with the others."

"Okay." Em continued to weep as she opened the pocket notebook and entered the latest episode using a fat imitation Mont Blanc fountain pen.

Jack had complete faith that Suzanne Wilkes could provide the paperwork that would put Bryan in a mental hospital or jail where he belonged. A wispy, sixty-something spinster, Suzanne had the reputation of having trained most of the attorneys in Ocean County. Her father and grandfather were attorneys and later judges. Some say she never married because she considered men a distraction from her passion for law. Her offices were on the first floor of a rambling Victorian house situated on East Beach across from the breakwater.

When they arrived, Claudia, her receptionist, took them into an airy parlor that had been converted into Suzanne's office. One was struck immediately by the view of the channel and harbor through the large bay window in front of which Suzanne sat, surrounded by computer equipment.

"Hi, there, Jack," she called in a soft, whiny voice. She got up and came around the table to grasp Em's hand. From years of sitting before keyboards, her narrow shoulders had taken on a permanent stoop. "Aren't these fires something awful?"

"Yeah, they are, Suzanne."

"My, my, child. How you've grown since I last saw you."

Em leaned down toward her and smiled. "I think I was twelve or thirteen. You came over to school and spoke to our class."

"Yes..." Suzanne patted Em's hand and looked at Jack. "I see your dad much more, you know... He's been a great help to our association of paralegals over the years with his picture taking for our newsletter."

"Yeah," said Em glancing at him, "he's quite a guy."

"You both have a seat." Suzanne beckoned them to chairs on one side of the gray computer console. Suzanne slipped between desk and credenza and sat in her swivel chair. She touched the keyboard and turned back to Em.

"Your father has explained the circumstances, Emily. In order to complete the request for the Show Cause, I will be asking you questions. I want you to answer each question using your own words without trying to be formal. I want you to tell me in the natural language you use in everyday conversation. Will you do that for me?"

"Sure." Em straightened her back and smoothed her hair.

"Explain the circumstances of how you met this young man, Bryan Cutler..."

Em answered the several questions posed as Suzanne entered the responses into her computer. Em was totally composed, sitting up straight, hands relaxed on the chair arms.

"Now, Emily, has Bryan physically harmed you?"

"No."

"Has he caused you emotional stress?"

Em looked at Jack for help. He shrugged.

"He's caused the whole family emotional stress," she replied.

"I'm sure. Tell me briefly the nature of this emotional stress as a result of Bryan's conduct. Give details as to why you want to file against him."

Em took a deep breath. Tears welled. "I'm afraid of him... and what he might do to me."

"Good. Continue."

"I get upset when he leaves obscene notes on our door."

"Yes."

"I am afraid when I know he's watching my house at night or following me."

"Do you fear for your safety?"

"Yes."

"Has he threatened physical harm?"

"In the parking lot at the Civic Center. He tried to pick a fight with my friends, you know what I mean?"

"Did he actually strike anyone?"

"No. He called David and Chuck names. Like fag and queer..."

"Very good."

Suzanne's fingers fluttered over the keyboard. She stopped, checked the screen, and added more information. She turned back to Em.

"Emily, can you tell me why you need a Temporary Restraining Order before the court can hear your case?"

"To keep him away, you know what I mean? We don't know what he'll do next. We're all afraid of what he'll do to us. His last letter, which we got this morning, has all kinds of swear words. He says, 'I could kill you and your friends but I won't... I want to kill myself... I have a razor. The letter says he wants me to kill him... he wants to end his life. It's crazy, you know?"

"Yes...." Suzanne lifted her hands off the keyboard and began examining the stack of letters and Em's log. "My word," she muttered, stopping to read. "I can see why you want a TRO." She set the stack of letters to one side and thumbed through the log notes Em had entered in the little notebook. "Your notes are quite thorough. Did you think of this yourself?"

"No. Dad asked me to do it."

Jack winked at Suzanne. "Actually, Chief Winters suggested we keep a log."

"I didn't know that," said Em, a surprised look in her eyes. "Why didn't you tell me?"

"I wanted to play it low key, thinking Bryan would eventually quit–like your mother said."

Suzanne shuffled through the log and put a crystal paperweight on a page and began to enter information into the computer. She shifted to reading Bryan's letters again and arranged certain pages for reference, like an explorer might set out maps and itineraries to study.

"I'm going to prepare a narrative based on all the incidents. It won't take but a few minutes."

Her fingers began to fly like bony talons over the keyboard, reminding Jack of Wanda Landavska playing a Bach concerto on a harpsichord. Em grinned at him. Both were in awe of Suzanne's prowess. Now and then, she stopped and checked the monitor, scrolling backwards and forwards, adding words or deleting them. She added three more paragraphs, checking Em's log, and drew back. "I believe that'll do it. You'll have to go over what I've put here, Emily."

"Okay."

Suzanne struck a key with her index finger. The computer began whirring and soon printed pages spilled into the tray. She looked them over, and handed them one-by-one to Emily.

"Read them carefully. Any words you want changed, just tell me." Suzanne turned her head toward the open doorway. "Elaine?"

Elaine appeared in the doorway. "Yes, ma'am?"

"Please make copies of these letters and Emily's log showing Bryan Cutler's activities. Be sure the letters are assembled in date sequence. I've been shuffling them a bit."

"All right."

Suzanne handed Elaine the stack and the notebook log.

Em read the pages and gave them to Jack. The first two were the Order to Show Cause (Harassment) and Temporary Restraining Order. The remaining pages were a narrative description of details almost word-for-word of what Em had said.

"I don't see any changes... Do you, Dad?"

"No. Suzanne's letter-perfect," he said with a smirk. "How fast do you type?"

Suzanne grinned and brushed the keyboard. "Oh, when I'm in the groove I do about one-twenty to one-thirty."

"Cool!" said Em.

Suzanne took the pages, checked their order, and placed them before Em. She retrieved a pen from the computer desk and gave it to her. "I want you to initial in the places indicated at the bottom of each page and sign your name at the bottom of each form, Emily."

She did so.

Elaine returned with the letters, neatly arranged by date in two stacks, envelopes attached. She handed Em her notebook.

"Elaine, would you make ten copies?"

"Sure."

Jack stood up. "What's the next step?"

"You don't have to raise a finger, Jack. That's my job." She rose from her chair. "My process server will take your court request over to Seagate Police Station, attach Sally's letter to it, and deliver it within the hour to Ocean County Courthouse. Bryan will be served by the court as soon as possible."

"Super." They moved into the outer office.

"You poor dears." She patted Em on the shoulder. "This on top of the pending divorce."

"Yeah. It's tough," Jack replied. "Hope this court order will keep the kid away."

"Are you all able to get any sleep?"

"I think Bernice is. What about you, Em?"

"Pretty much. Sometimes I hear something and wake up." She giggled. "It's usually an older man I know out wandering around at two in the morning... Right Dad?"

He chuckled. "I get up a couple times a night and check the bushes."

"That's terrible, Jack. It must be simply awful to live constantly under threat."

"It isn't fun."

"For sure," added Em.

"I received the signed separation forms. I take it you aren't haggling over who gets what?"

Jack heaved a sigh. "Enough hassle for one lifetime. She can take it all except for my studio."

"Has she said where she's relocating?"

He shrugged and looked at Em, who was shuffling, looking at her feet.

"Mom's moving onto her boyfriend's boat at Fort Lauderdale until the final papers are sent."

Jack pulled back. Em hadn't shared... How much more was going on that she hadn't told him? He regained his composure and tried smoothing it over. "Bernice doesn't share directly."

Suzanne looked from Em to Jack and back to Em. She was asking too many questions. He wanted to leave.

"At least you're parting amicably," Suzanne added.

"Guess you could say that..." Jack said, knowing Em was trying not to smirk.

"Too bad most couples don't dissolve their marriages like you and Bernice. Saves money, emotions, and is really better for the children. Don't you think so, Emily?"

"I suppose," she replied, biting her lip. "Dad's made it easier for me... I can say that. Still no fun, you know what I mean?"

"Some of the cooperation," Jack said, "is due to your handling the paperwork, Suzanne. You knew where all the mine fields would be."

She smiled, hands on her hips. "That's what you pay me for. Which reminds me... Did Bernice tell you I need final property division papers filed by Wednesday?"

"Yeah. She's taking care of that end."

"You should see our house," Em said, giggling. "Dad gave Mom a bunch of those bulk mail stickers to put on stuff she wants. The place is covered with them."

"You don't mean it..."

Even though Suzanne was a dependable buddy, Jack was getting antsy with all her questions.

"What do I owe you for Em's filing?"

She waved both hands at him.

"Not a penny. My privilege. After all the work you did for our association convention."

"You sure?"

"This one's for Emily–on the house. After what you-all have been going through, you don't need to be shelling out money for a Show Cause."

"Thanks, Suzanne. See you later."

They waved and went down the steps. Suzanne watched from the porch as they got in the car. He put the car in motion and glanced at Em. "So what's this about Bernice moving onto her boyfriend's boat?"

Em tilted her head. "I guess you weren't supposed to know. She's moving into this guy's boat at the Ft. Lauderdale Marina. He'll stay in his condo 'til the separation papers are received."

"Have you met him?"

"No. Mom wanted me to. There hasn't been any time."

"True."

"You should ask Mom about him. She'd probably tell you."

"Yeah. It's not fair to you. Sorry. I don't mean to put you in the middle..."

"That's okay. Just don't tell her I said anything."

"I won't," he said, feeling like a kid instead of an adult.

Em's eyes filled. "I hate secrets, you know? Why is it parents think they have to keep these deep, dark, stupid secrets?"

"I dunno. I guess we don't want to face truth. What do you think?"

"Probably. But you know something? It's worse when the person finds out. I mean... who wants to be made a fool of?"

He forced a smile, feeling the full impact of her words. "It's no fun." He pulled up in front of the high school. Em's eyes were clear again.

"See ya later, Dad."

She gathered up the pile of books and the fat play script and climbed out of the car. He watched as she entered the front doors, then made a U-turn and pulled up near the Bagel Shack.

Chapter 17

Monday Noon, May 20.

Teen-age boys were sitting on the two planters between which a line of kids was waiting. He loaded two cameras and took several photos, starting with some long shots in which he got the shop, the crowd, the boulevard, and the school. Then he came in closer, shooting mid-range at different angles, including some shots from across the street. He tried not to be so obvious that he attracted too much attention; otherwise, the kids would be making faces at the camera. He came in for close-ups, first from an oblique angle, getting the boulevard, a corner of the school, and to the left to capture a crowd of seniors and juniors. They suddenly caught on, and the photo session was over–outside, anyway. He stowed the cameras and entered the shop.

Harvey was serving up trays of enormous sandwiches, chips and soft drinks. Jack entered the kitchen and crouched down behind the partition next to the bagel kettles. He pulled out both cameras and adjusted them for the interior light conditions. He began shooting over the counter, capturing the long line and crowded tables without a flash. Using the 28mm lens, he switched on the

Stalker

flash, and got two shots of Harvey handing a tray of food to Jim Sheraton, one of Em's friends.

There was no use taking any more shots. All the kids were now primed and waiting to make gestures, raising fingers, making faces. He put the two cameras back in the bag as several kids groaned and complained that he hadn't taken their picture.

"You should have a nice sandwich after this work, Jack," said Harvey over his shoulder. "What can I get you?"

"Nothing, thanks. I need to rush home and tend to some business."

Harvey looked at him closely. With his baldhead, sturdy body and large eyes, he reminded Jack again of Pablo Picasso. Harvey wiped his hands down the white apron like a woman might run her hands over her breasts unconsciously. "Your eyes tell me it is about serious business, eh?"

"Yeah."

"Can you come by later, maybe around seven, so you can let me worry for you?"

He chuckled. "I'll try."

Jack moved through the throng of kids, glancing around to see whether Em had decided to catch lunch here. He did not see her, but spotted Chuck and David outside, near the back of the line. Chuck greeted him. "Hi, Mr. Kaufman. Looking for Emily?"

"I just dropped her off at school."

"She sick this morning," asked David.

"No. We had to fill out some papers. We're filing a complaint against Bryan with the court."

"Oh, cool," said Chuck.

"I want you both to know Bryan Cutler is somebody you need to stand clear of. He's dangerous. When he gets served with papers later today, there's no telling what he'll do."

David snickered and looked down at his shoes. "We know all about it, don't we Chuck?" They grinned at each other. "That jerk called me a fag. Chuck wanted to take him on after he insulted me, you know?"

"Emily told me. It's good you didn't. He shouldn't be messed with. He's not worth it."

Chuck didn't seem convinced. He tilted his head and grinned.

"Would you two fellows make sure Emily isn't ever left alone?"

"Sure," said Chuck. "Everybody in the Drama Department is on notice, including the parent volunteers."

"Good. If you see Bryan milling around campus, contact a teacher or security immediately. Okay?"

"Will do," said David.

Jack got in the car and headed home. When he arrived, he checked messages and continued the search for bugs. What was he missing? After spending half an hour looking inside, he went out back and checked each shrub and tree in the yard for signs of wires, microphones and transmitters. Nothing. He turned the corner past Em's old playhouse. He paused in front of the door. How long had it been since she used it? Five years? He had wanted to tear it down or else donate it to a daycare center.

He opened the latch and poked his head in. Cobwebs. He brushed them away and entered the single downstairs room with the little latticed Plexiglas windows on three sides. The place was a mess. Some papier-mâché fruits and vegetables Em and he had made when she was in sixth grade lay on a shelf. They were mildewed and dust-covered. Empty hulks of insects hung trapped in spider webs in the corners.

He ran his hand over the lattice moldings, examining the glued joints. Did a good job, he thought, making Em's house look like one you might see on *Little House on the Prairie.* Em wore long, gingham dresses then, just like Laura Ingles'. He stepped inside, shoulders bent, and flicked a spider's web aside. The ladder up to the trap door invited him upstairs. He pushed the hinged trap door open from below and climbed two steps.

As he emerged at eye level to the second floor, his nose responded to a slightly sweet scent. He looked around, sensing danger. The window overlooking Em's back bedroom window was slightly open. What was the smell? The top floor was empty except for a few of Em's orange and yellow plastic dishes and cups stacked neatly in the corner below the opened window.

He climbed all the way up and shifted his body onto the plywood floor so that he could put the trap door down. A plastic dish next to the stacked cups was half filled with grains of tobacco and ashes. His hand shook as he picked up the dish and smelled the contents. Fairly fresh. Son-of-a-bitch! He's been using the playhouse to spy. He checked the angle of the window and realized that Bryan could probably see Em's bed in the space of light between window and blind. He's been watching Em getting undressed. God almighty!

He pushed the latticed window open and looked down. In the window box was a candy bar wrapper. Tiny sugar ants were furiously running about, collecting minuscule flakes of chocolate. The wrapper had obviously been there a very short time. Damn! How long had Bryan been using the playhouse? His hands continued to shake as he closed the window. He wanted to grab the son-of-a-bitch with his bare hands and choke him to death.

He climbed down the ladder, letting the trap door slam over his head. As he turned, he walked through a spider web. He pushed the door open and brushed the strands of web from his forehead and hair. He strode across the back yard and into the garage in search of hammer and nails. He would nail the damned door shut until he had time to tear the whole thing down.

He pulled open the tool drawer of his workbench. He took out the claw hammer and looked around. Sixteen penny nails were what he needed. See if the bastard can open that door after he got through… His hand stopped short of the box containing the sixteen-penny nails. He wiped beads of sweat from his forehead and laid the hammer down on the bench. Was that the best strategy, he asked himself? What would it accomplish? Would it keep him out of the playhouse so he would be compelled to seek another place where he could play voyeur? Is that what he wanted? No. He wanted to keep Bryan thinking they didn't know he was using the playhouse.

He remembered the upstairs window was only cracked slightly and that he had closed it. He retraced his steps, not quite understanding why he was choosing this plan. He climbed the ladder and looked around to be sure the dish with the ashes and the candy wrapper were in their original places. He positioned the window exactly as it was when he first saw it. He carefully checked the stacks of dusty saucers and cups for other signs of use. Nothing. He put them back where they were. Sally's face with all those orange-red freckles suddenly came to mind. He had to let her know.

He rushed back to the house, adrenalin pumping, and phoned Sally Brand.

"Officer Brand. How may I help you?"

"This is Jack Kaufman, Miss Brand…"

"Hi. No bad news, I hope."

"Bryan's been using the upstairs of Emily's playhouse to spy on her. I found fresh tobacco ashes and a candy wrapper up there. He can see her when she's undressing or getting into bed."

"Yuk! Coming on your property is not a good sign. I need proof. Have you called Bill Winters?"

"Not yet."

"Ask the chief to send an officer over and get some fingerprints. All I need is a match. The ashes and wrapper can also be used as evidence. Tell the investigating officer to call me when he's through."

"Fine."

"You don't sound fine," she said in a soft voice.

"Guess I don't. I'm shaking with rage. I've got to get this guy off our backs."

"I know. But you've gotta stay cool, though, and let us professionals do our thing. Call Bill and let his guys get busy."

"I will. By the way… You ought to be receiving a copy of the court papers from Suzanne's server this afternoon."

"Good. I can use them as an excuse to get Bryan and his mom in here for a little chat."

"We got another letter today, too. It's filled with obscenities and threats of suicide. He's pleading with Em to kill him."

"God! Sending it over?"

"It's included in the court papers."

"Perfect!"

"Thanks." He hung up. His hand was unsteady. The phone rang.

"Hello."

"Mr. Kaufman?"

An involuntary shudder whisked through his abdomen.

"Yeah, Bryan..."

Should he confront him about the tobacco and ashes or what? He tried to control his breathing and calm myself.

"Can we talk?"

Bryan's voice was nervous, too, higher, shriller.

"When?"

"Now. I can meet you some place. How 'bout Eisenhower Park near the swings?"

No. He did not want to meet him without other people around. "What about Harvey's? I can be there in ten minutes."

"Okay. Harvey's is good. It may take me a few minutes longer. I'm on my bike."

"All right. By the way, how come you changed your mind?"

"I'll explain when I see ya. I need yer advice on somethin'."

Another involuntary shudder wrenched his torso. His shoulders started to shake. "I'm leaving right now."

"Can't wait ta meetcha," Bryan replied.

He hung up and considered. Should he take his pocket-sized tape recorder? Get their conversation on tape for Sally? He grabbed his car keys and dismissed the thought of doing anything that might spook Bryan. Maybe he was ready to square things. He stopped midway through the front door. What if I need to defend myself, he thought. He walked to his studio, opened the safe, and took out the box of cartridges and automatic. His fingers shook as he loaded the clip with seven hardballs. He snapped the magazine into the handle and retracted the loader, slipping a live round into the chamber. The problem now was how to hide the gun. He pulled a raincoat from the hall closet and placed the Colt .45 in the right side pocket and carried the coat to the car.

He backed the BMW out of the driveway, and turned left on Palm. The shivering in his body persisted. It was Nam-type nerves, the same as he used to get just before going on a night mission. They were not butterflies. More like bats bouncing back and forth against his stomach walls. They would disappear for a while during the actual mission... until all hell broke loose. Then his stomach would be calm until the worst was over. And after that, they came back, big time.

He had to calm down. What could Bryan possibly want to talk about other than to admit he was being dumb and wanted help? Too late for the buddy-buddy thing, pal. They had some serious issues to talk about, like ashes and candy wrappers and spying and hanging out on his property. Yes, Bryan, you've got some explaining to do, he thought. He just hoped he could keep his cool like Sally said. He glanced at the bulge in the raincoat. Yes, he had to stay cool.

He turned the corner and drove the few blocks on Seaview Boulevard to Harvey's and parked in front. He entered, carrying his raincoat over his right forearm. The lunch crowd had already eaten and left. Some businessmen were holding forth in the corner booth over coffee and sandwiches. Mary waved from behind the counter.

"Hi, Mary. Harvey in the back?"

She shifted her hips and touched the back of her hair.

"He's gone to Rotary. Should be back soon. Come for lunch?"

"Not really."

He studied the five men in dark suits and white shirts. They were nearly finished with their sandwiches. They would be leaving soon.

"Who's helping you in the kitchen?"

Mary gave him a mock scowl.

"Nobody. John's taken the afternoon off. Just me is all for now."

"Guess I'll have some coffee."

He chose a table where he could watch the boulevard. Bryan should be arriving any minute. He put the raincoat on the chair next to him with the right pocket opening closest to his right hand. Mary put the coffee and spoon before him.

"How 'bout a pastry, Mr. Kaufman? We've got fresh cherry cheesecake."

"No, thanks anyway."

He sipped the hot coffee, feeling it warming his entrails. He grew calmer, anticipating that by the time Bryan arrived, he would be in full control. He glanced at the raincoat and realized it would be so easy to reach down and retrieve the weapon and flash it in Cutler's face. The image sent shivers down his spine.

He took another sip, aware the men in the corner booth were leaving. They joked with each other about the check. A ruddy-faced guy Jack recognized vaguely as a former member of the planning commission finally agreed to buy lunch and threw several bills on the table. They left.

He took a menu from the clip on the back of the napkin holder and read the lunch specials. One day he'd have to try Harvey's sauerkraut with bratwurst, rye bread on the side. Mary came by and refilled his cup. He took another sip and checked his watch. Damn! He had been here twenty minutes and Bryan... Son-of-a-bitch! He jumped up. "Where's your pay phone, Mary?"

"There's one outside on the corner. Go ahead and use Harvey's in the office. He won't mind."

"Got a phone book?"

"Behind the desk."

He rushed inside the office and picked up the book. No, dummy, he said to himself. Just dial 911. He tossed the book aside. His finger nervously punched 911.

"This is the police department. Please state your name and the nature of the emergency."

"There's a young man who is stalking my daughter. And I believe he's on my property as we speak. My home address is 442 East Pitcairn."

"Your name?"

"Jack Kaufman. I take pictures for the police department sometimes."

"Can you describe this person?"

"Yes. Six feet, two hundred pounds, a twenty-year old white male. Always dresses in black pants and shirt."

"His name?"

"Look, time is of the essence, ma'am. Your chief, Bill Winters, knows all about him. If somebody isn't sent over immediately, he'll be gone."

"I'm sorry, sir, but I need basic information. Please give me his name."

"Bryan Cutler."

"And where are you calling from?"

"From Harvey's Bagel Shack. This guy has tricked me into leaving my house. I need to hang up so I can get home."

"I'll send an officer to your residence, sir."

"Thanks."

Jack picked up the raincoat and rushed out without paying for the coffee. Mary said something as the screen door slammed. What a dumb, stupid guy I am, he whispered, as he climbed into the BMW and pulled it into traffic. The phone. The damned phone. Out of habit, he had used the phone and spilled the beans to Sally about the ashes and candy wrapper. Bryan must have been nearby, listening. All Bryan needed was a listening device and a pay phone to call and entice him away from the house. Bastard!

He turned the corner at Palm and made a right onto Pitcairn. Two cruisers, lights flashing, were at the curb in front of his house. He swung in the driveway and jumped out. An officer came around the corner of the house and ducked under the overhanging limbs of the plum tree. Another came up behind Jack, evidently coming from around the other end of the house.

"Jack Kaufman," he said to the officer striding across the lawn.

"Sergeant Nelson. Do you live here?"

"Yes, sir."

"Aren't you the city photographer? I've seen you around City Hall a lot."

"Yeah." He was tired of everybody asking. It was easier to lie than to say he was on contract with the city as a free lancer. They never understood. He had to go into long explanations about free-lancing. Most still didn't get it.

Nelson motioned over his shoulder. "Checked all around outside. Nobody on the premises. No signs of forced entry into your house."

"Did you check the playhouse? Upstairs?"

The other officer closed the distance.

"This is Corporal Schneck." They shook hands.

"Yes, sir," said Nelson, "He's not in there either."

Jack explained how Bryan had suckered him into driving to Harvey's and gave them the background information. Schneck whistled. "Sounds like a smart cookie. Next time he calls and says he wants to meet you, call us first."

Jack's face warmed. "Yeah, and I won't use the phone in the house to call, either," he responded. "Let's see whether he's been here and removed the evidence."

They went to the playhouse and Jack climbed the ladder. The dish that had held the tobacco and ashes was gone. The window was shut. He crawled across the plywood floor and opened the window. The wrapper had disappeared. A small cluster of tiny ants swarmed in random activity around the area.

"Yup, he's been here. He's cleaned up. No ashes or candy wrapper. Son-of-a-bitch!"

Nelson's head appeared in the opening. "Why don't you come down, Mr. Kaufman? Let me and Jim see if we can get some prints."

He climbed down and stood in the backyard watching as Corporal Schneck opened a black suitcase of equipment on the grass. They dusted the door, trap door, window, and a few dishes. When they finished, Nelson came over, wearing an expression that was a mix of amusement and dismay.

"Got plenty of prints. They all appear to be from the same person."

He caught his meaning. "You think they're mine?"

"Quite likely. Can we take your prints for comparison?"

"Sure."

Schneck opened an inkpad and placed a print card on the top of the suitcase. Jack squatted down next to him. "I see you all the time with yer camera. Whatcha do with all them pictures?"

"Give them to Sommers in Public Information."

"I was just wonder'n." Schneck guided Jack's fingers, rolling each one on the pad, then on the card, creating a perfect set of prints. He compared them with the lifted prints.

"Whatcha see, Schnecky?" asked Nelson.

Schneck handed Jack a tissue and looked up. "Same."

Jack stood up and wiped the ink off his fingers. He felt totally stupid. "You sure you don't have at least one print from Bryan?"

Schneck and Nelson glanced at one another.

"We'll check 'em all back at the lab, sir," said Nelson. "But I don't believe so. You're dealing with a savvy kid. He probably wears latex or cotton when he's stalking. He won't make many mistakes like he done with the ashes and candy wrapper. Just too bad you didn't think to call us first from a pay phone."

"Yeah."

Jack's head was reeling at the thought that the evidence would have put Bryan in jail. So stupid!

He followed the officers around the house to the front yard. Old man Wallace was standing across the street, watching. The officers got into their cruisers and left. Wallace started to cross the street, but Jack ignored him and went into the house. He had had enough humiliation without anyone else telling him what he should have done.

Chapter 18

Monday Afternoon, May 20.

Despite his resolve not to use the home phone, he called Officer Brand. She answered.

"Have time for me to come over? I need to tell you what happened since our last conversation."

"You sound awful... I'm sorry. That's rude of me. What I mean is, are you okay, Mr. Kaufman?"

"Yeah. Humiliated and mad as hell is all."

"Tell you what. I've got to deliver some papers to Ocean County Courthouse. Could you meet me in the lobby in fifteen minutes?"

"Sure."

"See you."

It was starting to rain. He slipped on a short windbreaker. He left the house and drove slowly toward the courthouse, his long raincoat and Colt .45 still on the seat next to him. Every time he spotted a heavyset man in dark clothing, he thought it was Bryan. His heart quickened like he had seen a ghost. Bryan was everywhere, yet nowhere. It was like he was sparring with somebody in a ring with one eye closed and the other one swelling. He had lost his focus. He could not make out what was real and what was unreal. He was staggering like a punch-drunk fighter, while his opponent danced around him, poking him whenever he chose. He touched the hard bulge in his raincoat pocket. His impulse was to shoot the bastard on sight. After parking, he folded the raincoat and slid it beneath the passenger seat.

When he walked through the swinging doors of the courthouse, Sally Brand tilted her head in that unique way she had and gave him an, 'I'm sorry it's this way' smile. Her liquid green eyes and pretty mouth cheered him up without her needing to say anything. She reached out her freckled hand. He grasped it and held it a moment.

"Hi. Sharp looking windbreaker you're wearing, Mr. Kaufman," she said lightly.

He looked down at it self-consciously. It was a gift from a boat racing team out of Hialeah. He had taken their pictures when they won the Miami to Jacksonville regatta.

"A gift from some buddies."

"Nice. Why don't we go downstairs to the cafeteria? I'll buy you coffee."

"I'll buy you coffee," he insisted. "And by the way, I prefer Jack to Mr. Kaufman.

She turned. "In that case, call me Sally."

He followed. Her red hair had golden glints in it when she passed beneath the ceiling lights. He'd never seen hair like hers. They walked down the stairs instead of taking the elevator. The cafeteria was practically deserted. He poured their coffee and paid the cashier. She carried the cups to a table away from the few customers. They sat down.

Sally leaned in, seeming to make herself smaller and more intense as she placed her elbows on the table, her hands beneath her freckled face.

"So... what happened?"

"He overheard me telling you about the cigarette ashes and candy wrapper. As soon as we hung up, he called and invited me to meet him at Harvey's. Said he wanted to talk."

"Oh, jeez!" Sally put one hand to her forehead.

"Yeah. I know. I waited for him twenty minutes before I realized I'd been done in. I called the police and got officers there, but he'd already left..."

"With the evidence."

"Yeah."

"Oh, god... Maybe you've given him a wake-up call, though. I don't see this as being totally negative."

"I do. Had I immediately called Bill Winters and stayed the hell home... Pardon my language..."

"That's okay. I understand."

"...I could have gotten you the prints you needed."

Sally reached over and patted his arm. Her eyes were compassionate. "You're too hard on yourself. You're doing the best you can... It's just that... Wait a minute..."

She pulled her hand back and tapped forefinger to chin. Her green eyes squinted. She seemed to be studying the counter of the cafeteria where all the drink dispensers were. "What time was it when Bryan called you?"

"One? A few minutes after we talked. Why?"

She ignored his question. "Today is Tuesday, right?"

"Yeah."

"Trig class. Bryan's got Trigonometry at one on Tuesdays and Thursdays."

She pulled her portable phone from her belt and punched in a number.

"Latasha? Get me the number of that counselor at Ocean State. You know, the one I talked with last week…"

"That's him. Thanks!"

Sally entered new numbers.

"This is Officer Sally Brand. We spoke last week about Bryan Cutler. I'm his Probation Officer."

"Is Bryan playing hooky today? I'm thinking he's supposed to be in Trig class right now. Can you verify that for me?"

"I'll hold, if you don't mind. I'd also like to know his current status, whether he's missing classes regularly, whatever you can get from the registrar."

"Yes. Please do."

She cupped her hand over the receiver and whispered. "This guy isn't too cooperative with the probation department. I have to prod him to get any information out of him. When I leave messages for him, he never calls back."

Jack nodded agreement, remembering how Rice and Sands stonewalled him. After a few minutes, a voice came back on the line.

"Oh, shoot… You're sure of that?"

"Did he give any reason?"

"Appreciate the information, Mr. Rice."

She switched off the phone and replaced it in a leather holder at her hip.

"Bryan dropped all his classes Friday… No reason given."

Sally drummed her fingers. "It figures. Now he's unemployed and just quit college. All his energies are focused on Emily."

A hardness formed in Jack's chest. "Is he breaking probation by dropping out of school?"

Sally pulled her lips tightly together in an "o" shape. "Noooo.... Nobody thought to include that as a condition. He's always been such a good student. It was the one thing he had going for him."

"All for an obsession."

"Uh-huh. He's going to come totally undone when he's served notice of the Show Cause and TRO request. It means you've gotta be on alert twenty-four hours a day. Can you handle it?"

"Whatever it takes," he said, not feeling any bravado.

"How long does Emily have before she finishes school?"

"Three weeks."

"What are her plans afterward?"

"She leaves immediately for Spain. Part of an exchange program."

"Super! Between Ocean City and Seagate police departments, I think we can keep Bryan away until she goes to Europe."

"I hope so," he said quietly.

Sally shifted closer. "Off the record," she whispered, "I know Bill Winters is taking this case personally."

"Yeah?"

"Yeah," she said, imitating him with a little smile. "I can see why."

"Why?"

"You're one of the good guys. He doesn't want anyone to hurt you... or Emily. And I don't either."

Her sudden intimacy was almost more than he could bear. She had a personal interest. She was lovely, sitting there in her khaki uniform, giving off a clean, fresh scent. She was like a spring flower that is full of good health, high hopes, and positive thoughts. They sat and gazed at one another a few seconds before the reverie was broken by her beeper. Her eyelids flicked as she reached for her phone.

"Officer Brand."

"Oh, hi, Phil," she said flatly, looking at Jack strangely.

He looked away, feeling too awkward to get up and leave without saying good-bye. His watch said two-thirty-five. He needed to be getting back. He had to make prints for the mayor. Em was getting home at five today. He stared at his coffee cup and took a sip.

"Let's talk about it after duty hours, Phil. But no, I won't."

"No. Phil. We'll talk later. Good-bye."

She switched off the phone. "Sorry," she said, looking distracted.

"Don't apologize."

"I don't like mixing business and personal life."

"Me neither. Except sometimes," he said with a wry smile, "we don't have any choice, do we?"

"Too true."

Chapter 19

Monday, Late Afternoon, May 20.

Jack paced the floor as five o'clock approached. He went to the front door and watched the street for Chuck's car. There was something white on the walk. He unlocked the door and pushed the screen door open. It was another letter from Bryan. Two in one day. He ran out to the street and looked in both directions. The street was empty except for Prescott's kid and another boy clicking down the sidewalk on skateboards.

He was tempted to open the letter as he walked toward the house. The envelope had <u>Emily</u> scrawled in harsh, ugly strokes with a ball point like one would carve letters with a knife on the side of a tree. Before he closed the front door, the familiar sound of music and laughter swept down the street. Chuck's green bomber screeched to a halt at the curb beneath the palm tree. Four boys and three girls were somehow piled in it. Em climbed off David's lap and slammed the door as everybody waved and raucously greeted Jack. Then, the car zoomed off in a cloud of exhaust fumes.

"So, Dad," Em said, apprehensively, glancing at the envelope in his hand. "Looks like the dark phantom struck again!"

Stalker

"Yeah. Twice by letter and once by phone. We've got to have a pow-wow."

"That bad, huh?"

"Worse. I called your mother's office. She's coming home early."

"Not cool. What's Bryan up to?"

"Let's open this and see what he says first."

"Okay."

Em used a long fingernail to break the seal and pulled out four pages. "Wow! This guy's insane. Look at this stuff, Dad."

She handed him the first page. There were five lines scrawled in inch high letters, like a series of ugly screams let loose one mark at a time across the page. The style of printing was that of a first grader. The point of the pen had in some places punctured the paper.

EMILY: YOU FUCKING BITCH!!!
I HATE YOU FOR WHAT YOU ARE DOING
TO ME. WHY??? WHAT HAVE I DONE TO
YOU??? I ONLY HAVE LOVE FOR YOU...
DON'T YOU KNOW THAT???

"God, Dad..." Em whispered, handing him the second page. "Same stuff as this morning."

YOU WHORE!!! YOU WON'T GO OUT WITH A REAL MAN!!! YOU LIKE FAGS AND LESBIANS LIKE YOUR QUEER DAVID!!! AND THAT LITTLE DYKE JULIE.

WHY CAN'T YOU LOVE ME? ALL I WANT TO DO IS BE WITH YOU A FEW HOURS???

Em handed him the remaining two pages.

IS THAT TOO MUCH TO ASK, BITCH??? I DREAM OF TOUCHING THOSE LOVLY TITS. STROKE YOU. YO WOULD LIKE THT, WULDN'T YOU, BTCH?

FOR GIVME, EMLY. IM A LITTL HIGH RIGT NO.

YOU KNOW I JUST WANT TO LOV YOU. YOU KNO THAT, DON'T YOU???

Jack read the final page.

TEL YOUR DAD TO STOP CAUSNG PROBLEMS. I DONE NOTHN WRONG TO HIM. HE TRIED TO GET ME ARRESTED TODAY. IT DIDN'T WRK, DID IT, JACK????? HA, HA... STAY OFF MY CASE, MR KAUFMAN OR U'LL BE SORRY TOO.

I MEAN NO HARM, EMLY. YOU KNO IN YER HEART I DON'T. OH, PLEASE, EMLY, YOU ARE ALL I'VE GOT NOW. NOTHING ELSE MATTERS. I DON'T CARE ABOUT ANYTHING ANYMORE EXCEPT U. SEE ME JUS FOR A MINETTO NIGHT AFTR PLA RHRSAL. I'M GOING CRAZY WITH UT YU. PLEASE EMLY BE MI FRIND.

LOVE,
B.

"Damn him! Let's go inside and wait for your mother."

They entered the kitchen. Em filled a glass with ice and opened a can of Coke and poured the glass full.

"Want some, Dad?" Her hand was shaking.

"No, thanks."

She held the glass with both hands and watched him glumly.

"Bryan's bugged our phones..." he whispered. "Maybe the whole house."

"That's shit!"

It was the first time he had ever heard Em use a bad word in conversation. She put the glass down and wiped her arm across her lips. Her clouded face was fighting tears. She swallowed and took another swig of Coke.

"Anything you want kept secret can't be discussed here," he said in low, hushed tones.

The door burst open. Bernice was wide-eyed.

"What's happened, Jack?" She was breathing hard as though from running. "You never call my office. Thank God you're okay, Emily."

She went to Emily and embraced her before turning to Jack for explanation. He handed her Bryan's letter.

"Jesus!" she exclaimed as she finished the last page. "This boy is loony! You mean to tell me, John Lincoln Kaufman, that he can't be locked up in an asylum for sending this? He's absolutely bonkers!"

He took the letter from her hand and replaced it in the envelope.

"Maybe we should hop in the car and take a ride," he said, adding bewilderment to Bernice's already horror stricken face.

"A ride? What for? Where are we going?"

"I'll tell you in the car."

He opened the door to the garage. They trooped into the garage and Jack pressed the garage door opener. They climbed into the BMW and headed toward Ocean Drive. He turned onto

Seaview. Jack explained to Bernice and Em all that had happened today.

"Good heavens, Jack," said Bernice, breathing hard. "Don't you think we ought to call Floyd Baker and see what he can do?"

"We've already got a Temporary Restraining Order in the works. That's the most Floyd could do."

"What about Jim Smith? He's been a prosecutor. He could lean on those legal bureaucrats in the courthouse."

"An attorney can't do any more than Chief Winters, Suzanne or Officer Brand."

"But why didn't you do what this Brand woman told you? Called the police immediately? He could have been arrested by now."

He winced at the stab. Bernice never let up when she had the upper hand.

"When Bryan called me, I got caught up in the idea of meeting him face to face. I thought right then it was more important to see Bryan than to call Bill. I did exactly what Bryan wanted. It was dumb. I made a mistake."

"Well, Jack, we've got to do something. Now!"

"We're doing all we can..."

Bernice interjected. "I think we ought to have a gun in the house myself. We can't wait until Bryan really goes off his nut and attacks her some night. Good Lord, Emily is a sitting duck!"

She was talking like Em was not there. She had a way of making the weight inside his chest feel doubly heavy. He glanced at Em in the rear view mirror. She was biting her knuckle and gazing out the window.

"And you say he's been watching her from upstairs in her playhouse?"

"That's right."

"My God! Let's go back and tear the damn thing down!"

"I'm thinking it's best that we don't disturb it. He might come back and use it again. I can rig a trip wire to a camera and flash and get his picture when he opens the playhouse door."

"Oh, Good Lord, Jack. Have you lost your mind? The boy'll grab your camera and dash it to pieces!" She forced a laugh. "Sometimes I think you're as crazy as this boy is."

He glanced at her. She was avoiding eye contact. He knew the idea sounded foolish, but it could work. He tried to explain. "I'd have the camera hidden where he can't get to it. And when the trip wire is pulled, I would have one of those screeching auto alarms to go off, scaring him so he wouldn't have time to do anything except turn and run."

"And what if your Rube Goldberg creation doesn't work? What then?"

"He might discover the trip wire or not. If he does, he won't use the playhouse again. If he doesn't, he might come back. I'll have another crack at him."

"I think you're going to a lot of trouble for nothing," grumbled Bernice under her breath.

"It's worth a try, Mom."

"Another part of my plan is that Em and I switch bedrooms. With the fires gone, I'll open the back window at night. I should be able to hear Bryan moving around."

"What about hiring a body guard? Put him in Emily's room at night instead of risking your neck? Have him escort her whenever she goes out."

Em leaned forward so her chin rested on the back of his seat. "I'd really feel dumb, Mom. What would everybody think?"

Bernice turned. "Better dumb than dead."

Jack swung the car around at the cul-de-sac at the end of Seaview and started for home. "I considered asking Chief Winters for a couple cans of Mace. But I decided against the idea. I don't think Bryan would risk a direct attack in daylight. And I wouldn't try using it at night."

"So far, you've been one hundred percent wrong about him."

How quickly she forgot that it was she who wanted him to play Daddy to the guy. He was tempted to mention Archie's suggestion about hiring two goons to deal with Bryan. Then, he thought better of it, knowing Bernice would want to do it immediately.

"Any discussion inside the house ought to be about trivial stuff," said Jack.

"Isn't it always?"

"Come on, Mom. Let up."

"When we want to talk about Bryan or about where we'll be or when we're leaving or returning, let's write notes. Okay?"

"Good idea, Dad," chimed Em.

Bernice lit a cigarette and blew a puff of smoke at the dashboard. The smoke was swept up by the air conditioner and blown back in their faces. She knew he did not allow smoking in his car, but said nothing. Em let her window down. He did the same.

"Whenever you have a spare minute, I suggest you look around for bugging devices. I'm taking the phones out to have them checked tomorrow," Jack said.

"Do you really think this boy's gone to all that trouble, Jack? He's only been in our house twice: when he picked Emily up for the date and when he left her off after. It seems to me he's probably using an electronic listening gismo from outside. They say you can pick up voices with them half a mile away. There wouldn't be any need to bug the house."

"He came in the house after the date?"

"For a second," said Em. "Maybe he used the bathroom. I don't remember that well."

Bernice looked at Jack incredulously. "And you believe the boy was already putting bugs in our house? On the first date? Come on!"

"We don't know Bryan hasn't been inside the house since then, when we were away. He could have come in through an unlocked window. He hears every word we say on the phones. He certainly knows when he can leave letters on our front door. Had I not put the car in the garage today, you can be certain he wouldn't have left that letter. He's very clever and very sick."

"All the more reason you should get some legal help and some bodyguards on this. We're at his mercy. You're going to be sorry for your dilly-dally approach."

"I've just told you what Chief Winters and Officer Brand advised. We're asking the court to grant our petition. I'm taking advice based upon law and practicality. Sally Brand says Bill is taking our case personally. He's doubling surveillance of the neighborhood."

"Besides, Mom, it's when I'm out of the house that Bryan is most obnoxious. All my friends and the cast are going to be with me from now on."

"Your friends are puny. All together, they wouldn't be a match for this boy."

"I don't see me being followed around by some bouncer-type bodyguards, Mom. I'd be a laughing-stock."

"As I said before, better a laughing-stock than raped or murdered."

"Mom...." cried Em plaintively. "I think we're doing the best we can. The whole police forces of Ocean City and Seagate are on Bryan's case. He's bound to do something really dumb, and they'll get him."

"Wishful thinking, my dear," Bernice whispered. "But then, what do I know?"

Jack said nothing. He was sick of hearing Bernice's strident voice. Her snide jabs had numbed his ears. He found himself watching every foot of the way for signs of Bryan. This section of town would be out of his normal range, yet you never know. Above, an echelon of pelicans swooped low in front of them, coasting, their wings tilting, balancing. Then, as one, they flapped their wings, climbed in a graceful arc above the street, and dove toward the sandy beach. How he wished Em could fly. Fly off to some island out of harm's way for a few days. The downside of that idea was she would miss all those special senior activities that only come once. Flight was not an option.

His eye automatically fastened on a person sitting on a bench at a bus stop. Behind the bench was a bicycle. He knew it was Bryan even before his features came into focus.

"There's Bryan."

Emily drew her arms under her chin on the back of the seat. "He doesn't see us yet," she said. "He's doing his thing with the computer. Probably playing chess."

He turned right at the next intersection.

"What're you doing, Jack," cried Bernice.

"Going around the block so I can pull up on his side."

"But why? What will you do?"

"I want to tell him what I think. It'll do me more good than him, but I want to have my say."

"Oh, God, Jack," cried Bernice. "What if he's got a gun or a knife? I don't want you doing this. Let's go home. Please, Jack!"

"Yeah, Dad. Mom's right. You don't know what he'll do. He could throw a rock through our window or something."

He made a left and then another, coming out at the traffic light across from the bench. It was empty. No Bryan. No bike. "Gone," he said under his breath.

"Thank heavens," sighed Bernice. "Let's go home. I don't think I can take much more of this."

Jack turned onto Ocean and drove slowly, looking down side streets. The car was silent. He swung in the driveway and parked in front of the garage. They trooped silently into the house. Strange to say, he did not look around, as though his instincts told him automatically that Bryan was not close by. How could he be? He was probably still near where they had spotted him. The image of him sitting on the bench with his computer was annoying. It was the identical image of him the other day at Julie's. He was sitting at a bus stop, playing games on his computer... unless his listening devices were somehow connected to it.

Bernice poured herself a glass of wine. Em got a glass of milk and put crackers into a bowl.

"Want some wine, Jack?"

"No, thanks."

Bernice carried her wine to the living room and flicked on the television. Em sat on the arm of Bernice's chair, watching her mother change the channels. Jack retreated into his studio and returned with a bunch of small, yellow note pads. Bernice immediately used her pad as a coaster on the table next to her chair. Em took hers to her room. He followed her.

He jotted down a message: CHANGE ROOMS WITH ME TONIGHT?

Em shrugged and wrote: OKAY. YOU REALLY THINK HE WOULD BREAK INTO MY BEDROOM?

He responded: YES.

She picked up her script, using it as a tray for her glass of milk and bowl of crackers, and headed to his bedroom.

Jack entered the bathroom and was stopped by the array of yellow stickers. Sometime between when he got up this morning and when Bernice went to work, the rest of the house had contracted the yellow sticker pox. Nickel sized stickers were on everything, including the soap dish and most of the towels stacked on the shelf over the toilet. Bernice was taking everything in sight. He did not see her loading all this stuff onto her lover's Good Ship Lollipop. He suspected she would donate it all to Goodwill or to The Salvation Marine just for spite.

She showed an extraordinary ability to attach stickers where you wouldn't think they could stick. One was stuck on a plastic food container in the refrigerator. Another was on a Teflon fry pan. Perhaps she uses glue. He expected stickers to appear on his bathrobe and underwear any minute now.

He went to the studio and fed Cutler's letters into the copier. He printed out three sets. He composed a little letter.

Dear Mrs. Cutler:

Enclosed are copies of letters Bryan sent to my daughter. He is stalking her, spending nights outside our house. He is following her everywhere. I have filed a Cease and Desist Order at Ocean County Courthouse. I am also in touch with Bryan's probation officer, Sally

> Brand. The Ocean City and Seagate Police Departments have been alerted to Bryan's behavior.
>
> Please know this is a very serious matter. I do not want harm to come to my daughter or to Bryan. You've got to make him stop this stalking. Bryan's future is at stake.
>
> I'd like to talk directly with you. Call me at any time at 742-8688. Or, I'd be glad to meet you at Officer Brand's office.
>
> Sincerely,
> Jack Kaufman

He made three copies of the letter. He placed two copies of the letter and Bryan's letters in two envelopes and addressed them to Adelia Cutler. He put regular stamps on one, thinking he would send the other Certified Mail. The regular one would arrive tomorrow; the certified would take longer. He wouldn't provide any outside return address on the regular one, knowing Bryan would open it. He probably opened all the mail anyway. At least he would have a shot at reaching his mother. The third set he placed in a manila envelope for Sally.

He slipped into a pair of shorts and tank top and went for a jog. Running down the beach, he realized that he was two miles from home. He walked, then sat down on a bench and watched the moon beginning to rise. It was a perfect sailing night.

By the time he returned, Em and Bernice were gone. Em left a note saying she would be home at nine-fifteen. Bernice left nothing as usual. He decided to forego a visit to Harvey's tonight. He needed to clean up the lab.

Em and Bernice returned around nine-twenty. No sightings of Bryan. Em took homework to Jack's bedroom along with a box of crackers. Bernice turned on the TV to an old *I Love Lucy* show.

Jack grabbed his old softball bat from behind the door and pushed the swivel chair down the hall and into Em's room without turning on the light. He leaned the bat against her bookcase and positioned the swivel chair so as to have a clear view of the front and side windows. He closed the blinds.

He entered the main bathroom just like Em would do, brushed his teeth, and then entered her room and turned on the light, waited a few seconds, and turned off the light. He opened the blinds and sat down next to the bat.

He leaned back, adjusting his hearing to night sounds. It was difficult at first because Bernice had the damned television on so loud. He wanted to tell her to turn it down except that she always had the volume up. He did not want anything to be different from the way the house would normally be. He tried to relax his body while keeping his eyes and ears super vigilant. His body, however, was not cooperating. The muscles along his ribs and stomach kept contracting wildly like they did on photo assignments in Nam.

Around one, the television went silent. Amen. Bernice was going to bed early tonight. Crickets sang noisily in the ivy along the side fence. A screech owl's low, whirring song was answered by another farther away. Suddenly, a light thrashing sound, getting louder, along the fence near the playhouse made the hair on his neck stand up. His heart thumped loudly. He nervously grasped the baseball bay and slowly pulled it across his knees. He shifted his weight onto his feet and prepared to stand up and take a home-run cut.

The thrashing grew louder. He got to his feet and raised the bat. A dog barked. Something small and dark flew upward, a blur, until it settled atop the fence. Jack fell back in the chair, heart still pounding. A cat. It was McAllister's cat, Rambo. Rambo sat on the top rail of the fence, seeming to peer in at him, wondering, he supposed, why in hell Jack was sitting in the dark brandishing a softball bat.

Rambo raised himself up on all fours, stretched languidly, and walked along the top of the fence to the corner. He jumped down, making more noise before crossing the lawn and disappearing across the street. Jack was so worked up that beads of sweat were running down the sides of his face. His shirt was wet. Tomorrow night, he would wear a sweatband. He also decided to set up a camera on a tripod so he might get a dated photo of Bryan, if he were standing across the street or attempting to enter a window.

He knew Bernice was right. It is stupid to think about setting up cameras to take photos of Cutler. If the guy was to enter the playhouse or come through a bedroom window, Bryan was committing a crime whether he had a picture of it or not. No, that was not the reason for a camera. He realized that he associated his cameras with life and death situations; his cameras must be with him and ready to use—just like in Nam—if and when Bryan made a forcible entry. Somehow, his cameras were his protection, his shield against thinking about the consequences of violent action. And, ironically, they were at the same time the recorders of the violence so that he must witness time and again the carnage they revealed in the quiet of his darkroom. Yes, his demons forced him to record and develop and replay the tragedies over and over until every detail was etched in his brain. That was the hell he had created for himself and he could not stop it. What crazy thoughts, he muttered beneath his breath. It was all so stupid.

Around four, he had a cup of coffee and ate some crackers. His antennae told him Bryan would not be coming. He relaxed a bit. He watched first light appear above the gable of McAllister's house. A flock of gulls, having spent the night on the soccer field in Eisenhower Park, circled in the coming light and headed toward the beach. He got up to lower the blinds and glanced outside. Just beyond the pool of light from the street lamp, a dark figure sat in the shadows between old man Wallace's house and the Jacksons: Bryan.

Jack crept down the dark hall into his studio, loaded a camera and snapped on a telephoto lens. He slipped out the front door, breaking into a run across the yard, but Bryan saw him and disappeared between the houses before he could get close. Jack's heart was thumping loudly.

So much for stalking the stalker. His whole body was wet with perspiration. He crossed the yard, feeling the dew cooling his bare feet. He went inside, undressed and showered. He felt utterly wiped out. Why hadn't he called the cops when he spotted Bryan? Why hadn't he clicked off a couple shots of Bryan from inside the bedroom? It had been dumb to chase him. Somehow, he had to get control over his emotions or else he could get himself or Em killed, he thought.

Chapter 20

Tuesday Morning, May 21.

According to *The St. Pete Times*, fires still raged north of Daytona Beach. The sunrise was bright and clear at Ocean City. Jack jogged past Eisenhower Park, scanning the pine trees at the edge of the soccer field. He didn't expect to see Cutler. No, he was probably home in bed asleep, now that he had spoiled another night's sleep for Jack.

After dropping Em off at school, Jack drove to City Hall and took some publicity shots of the mayor and council members. He stopped by the police department afterward, carrying all the house phones to Winters' office in a grocery bag, while in the other hand, he lugged his attaché case.

Florese greeted him with a bright, toothy smile when he came through the door.

"Good morning, Mr. Kaufman!"

"How're you doing, Florese?"

"Great." Her smile evaporated into concern. "Your family okay? You look like you've been up all night."

"We're fine... Do I look that bad?"

"Uh-huh," she said, rising. "I'll tell the Chief you're here."

She disappeared for a second, then popped her head around the corner. "Come on back."

Bill's office was like that of most politically successful police chiefs. The walls were covered with photographs of grip-and-grins, parchment proclamations, and engraved awards mounted on walnut, along with assorted memorabilia. Several of the black-and-whites were photos Jack had taken. Winters' desk, however, was cleared for business. To his left was a wall of video screens and two computer consoles. Red and green lights blinked. One silent monitor showed cops going through a search exercise in an urban setting. Jack recognized it as part of Ocean County's new law enforcement training complex.

"Come on in, tiger," said Winters, raising a hand. They did a high five. "Sit down, sit down."

Jack sat down and glanced at the action on the screen.

"That's live," Winters exclaimed. "My guys are getting tested today. They've been working with Academy instructors a week now. Getting proficient in how to clear a high-rise apartment building... The coming thing, you know?"

Jack nodded. Winters pressed both elbows on the desk. He looked sharp in his navy blue uniform with gold service stripes at the cuffs. His smooth, shaved face was almost pink and the orange tinted pilot's glasses made him look younger than his fifty years.

"The creep been around?"

"At daybreak, he was sitting across the street between two neighbors' houses. I ran out and tried to get a picture, but he jumped up and ran back to the alley. I clicked off some frames. All I got was his back disappearing in shadow."

"Damn it, Jack. Why didn't you call 911? We coulda had two cruisers and our foot patrol there in seconds!"

Jack looked down at his hands, asking himself again why he hadn't. "I figured he'd be gone before your guys could get there."

"Come on, fella. You gotta let us do the dirty work. You're lucky he ran."

"I guess so," he admitted weakly.

"Watcha got in the bag?"

"Phones. I thought one of your men might check them for bugs. I wouldn't know what to look for."

"Oh, sure. You did the right thing. They're hard to find. Florese?"

"Yes, sir?"

"Take these across to Corporal Lake. Have him drop what he's doing and check 'em out in the next ten minutes."

"All right." Florese took the bag away.

"Got more letters to show me?"

"Yeah. I have a copy of Suzanne's papers she sent over to the courthouse, too." He opened the black leather attaché case and handed Winters a copy of Bryan's latest letters along with the papers. Winters laid the letters out across his desk by date. "He wouldn't make 'A's in penmanship," Winters quipped. He read them and whistled through his teeth.

"He's your typical stalker... vacillating between love and hate, wanting to hug and to strangle... You notice how he pleads, then threatens?" Winters pointed to several scrawled paragraphs.

"And notice the progression. This letter here is reasonably lucid... This other show's he's high and on the edge of self-destruction. He's a time bomb waiting to explode..."

169

There was a knock on the doorframe. A young, pale-faced policeman appeared. Winters looked up. "Come in, John. That was sure fast."

Lake carried the bag of phones to Winters' desk and set them down. "The phones are clean, sir."

"John Lake... Jack Kaufman."

They shook hands.

"I was hoping they weren't," Winters said. "Appreciate the turnaround."

"No problem, sir." Lake left the room.

"I'd like to tap your phone. You got any problem with that?"

"None. The sooner, the better." Jack closed the case and got up. He could not think of anything more to talk about. He felt tired and out of sorts.

"I can provide you with a voice scrambler, too. Make it so this jerk can't monitor your conversations in the house."

"That's swell. How much will it cost?"

"Not a dime. I'll send Schnecky by either later today or some time tomorrow. He'll call first."

"Good. Does it take long to install?"

"Nah! Won't take more'n a couple minutes."

Winters came round his desk and slapped his large hand on Jack's shoulder and gripped it hard. "Come on, buddy... Stay outta this creep's way and let me do my job."

Jack forced a grin and hit him lightly on the chest with the back of his hand.

"I do appreciate all the special arrangements, Bill. Really, you've gone above and beyond..."

"Hey! You'd do the same in my shoes... which reminds me. When are you going to take some time off to work on your boat? Hell, we need to do some fishing, man."

"Soon."

"Soon's not good enough. Set a date. Give me a call."

"I will."

He entered the parking lot just as the first clap of thunder announced a shower. He was reminded that his raincoat with the loaded Colt .45 was still under the car seat.

Chapter 21

Tuesday Afternoon, May 21.

Jack returned to the house after a photo assignment and found a letter attached to the screen door. It was addressed to him. Three pages filled with obscenities and threats. Cutler claimed Jack had caused him great harm, and was responsible for his mother being sick. Bryan was thinking of hiring a lawyer and suing Jack. Bernice and Em arrived. He shared the contents of the letter with them, after which Em went to her room to get ready for play practice. Bernice poured herself a glass of wine. Everyone, thought Jack, was damned sick of Bryan's rages and obscenities. He carried Bryan's letter to his studio and reread it. One paragraph in particular kept his attention.

YOU ARE KEEPING ME FROM EXERCISING MY RIGHTS GUARANTEED IN THE CONSTITUTION, JACK. I AM TALKING TO A LAWYER. HE AGREES YOU ARE A BASTARD FOR INTERFERING WITH MY FREEDOMS. YOU KEEP ATTACKING ME AND SEE WHAT HAPPENS, ASSHOLE!

Jack picked up the phone and dialed the Cutler number. No answer. The doorbell rang. He replaced the receiver.

"I'll get it," shouted Bernice. The door opened. He heard a male voice.

"Corporal Schneck wants to talk with you, Jack."

Schneck peeked around the corner in the hallway. He was holding a black box with a cord.

"Sorry I didn't call first... Chief asked me to set this up," he explained. "It's a scrambler. It picks up voice vibrations and changes them so's a person using a bug or listening device can't hear your conversations inside the home."

"Terrific!" Jack replied. "Where should we put it?"

Schneck looked around. He nodded his chin toward a double outlet at the end of the hallway near the living room. "How 'bout there?"

"Fine."

He went over and plugged it in, then adjusted dials. "Would you say something, Mr. Kaufman."

Jack tried to think of something clever, but couldn't. "The weather outside is mild with a chance of late evening thunder showers," he said in his natural speaking voice. "The low front, which is expected to remain over South Florida–particularly over the Kaufman household–throughout the day tomorrow–is expected to..."

"I think that's got it, Mr. Kaufman," said Schneck, apparently not impressed either with Jack's knowledge or delivery of personalized weather information.

"Good."

Schneck stood up and tugged with both hands to hitch up his sagging pants and gun belt.

"Now you people can have normal conversations again. You might wanna put the machine on a table there so nobody trips over it."

"Great."

"That was very sweet of you to bring it over," said Bernice, watching from the living room. "Tell Chief Winters we deeply appreciate it."

"No problem, ma'am," he said, going out the door.

Jack opened the hall closet and pulled out a wooden TV tray. Bernice lifted the machine off the floor and Jack placed the tray beneath it.

"So much for the pads of paper... They make good coasters, though," Bernice said in good humor.

"Yea," cried Em as she strode down the hall toward the kitchen. "I can sing again without fear of being recorded... or do dumb weather reports just like Dad..."

She skipped into the kitchen and rustled in the pantry while humming a tune from a Broadway show. Jack presumed she was into her second box of crackers. She was a regular cracker nut, which he supposed was better than being what her mother was: a nutcracker.

He returned to the studio and examined the proofs from Harvey's. Good, clear thumbnails. He had caught the flavor of the place. Even got Harvey smiling and handing a tray with a mounded sandwich and chips to a customer. He looked closely at the shot of Harvey, then placed the loupe over the thumbnail and looked again. There was something written across Harvey's left forearm. He drew the loupe back, enlarging the image. It was numbers. Of course! A tattooed number Jews got in concentration camps. So that was why he felt close to Harvey, Jack mused. They both had demons from war.

175

Em interrupted his reverie.

"Whatta-ya-think, Dad?"

He looked up. Em was wearing a yellow sticker on the end of her nose and others on her clothing. They laughed together as she pulled them off and put them in the wastebasket.

"Cool."

"I was tempted to wear them to rehearsal. I told all the guys what Mom's done. They all want to come over and see. Can I have a sticker party for the cast?"

"Sure. Why not?"

They laughed, and Jack gave her a hug and watched her go back to her room. Good old Em. Only a teenager would find something funny in all of this. The television kicked up several decibels. An announcer was talking about a major oil spill in the Gulf of Mexico. He went into the living room to listen to the report.

Bernice looked up, deftly dropped the volume with the remote control, and took a sip of wine. So much for the audio portion of the oil spill news.

"I've been meaning to ask you," she began in her sultry Bacall tone, "about your retirement."

He knew she would hit on that sooner or later. They had agreed that Jack would keep it three months ago. He figured she would change her mind.

He took a deep breath. "Yeah?"

"How does that work again? I know you told me, but I've forgotten."

On top of everything else happening today, she had to bring this up. He took a second deep breath and tried to explain for the umpteenth time while watching the TV screen. They were trying to rescue wild ducks that were coated in grease.

"I hafta have twenty good years before I qualify for retirement. Right now, there is no guarantee I'll make it. I've got to stay in the good graces of the general and maintain perfect health. Once I make twenty good years, I can receive retirement payments when I reach sixty."

"And how long before you qualify?"

"One more year. I'll have twenty good years, hopefully, just before my forty-second birthday."

Bernice shifted in her chair and lit another cigarette. A fireman knelt on the blackened sand next to an otter covered in a thick black glaze of oil. The otter was gasping for breath. Jack braced for what he knew was coming.

"I think I ought to get half, Jack. After all, Reserve duty has taken you away from me two days a month plus summer duty for sixteen years–plus your time spent away in Vietnam. Two years, was it?"

"No. It was eighteen months. Look, Bernice... We've been through this...You've got all kinds of 401s, IRAs and savings. You make twice or three times the money I do. My Reserve retirement and Social Security are all I'll have."

"And why is that, Jack," she asked smugly. Her eyes had taken on the satisfied look of a cat that has just pounced on a mouse. The announcer on television was pointing to a dead fish on the oily sand.

"Because I'm not obsessed with making money like you are, Bernice. I don't work day and night so I can drive a Mercedes. But let's be clear about my contributions to this family. For one thing, I've put money into Em's account for college just as you have. For another, I've been paying the household bills all these years. I've never asked you to contribute, except when we were business partners." The irony of his statement nearly brought a smile to his face.

"Why is it you want to take everything I have, Bernice? It's a few hundred a month when I'll need it most: age sixty. Do you hate me so much that you want to see me in poverty?"

Bernice grimaced and held her finger up to her lips while looking toward Em's room.

"Shush, Jack," she whispered. "Don't talk so loud or else Emily might hear."

"Maybe she needs to hear," he hissed. "Maybe she needs to see her mother for what she really is…"

"Oh, go to hell, Jack! There's no talking to you any more. You can bet your life I'm out of here the day Emily leaves for Spain. I can't wait…"

"Neither can I. And for what it's worth, Bernice, you can go straight to hell, too. I've taken all the crap from you I can stand. You have been a nasty, sour bitch too long. You've been ugly to me for the last time. From now on, you will either be civil with me or else you will shut your damned mouth. Do you hear me?"

Bernice sat there, frozen in place.

"I want you to answer me."

"I heard you," she whispered, eyes filling. "I'm sorry." Her mouth began a slight quaking as his words took effect. Damned if he hadn't gotten to her for once.

He turned without another word and went into the studio. He pulled Bryan's letter out of the envelope and set about making copies for Bill and Sally. Damn the woman! She deliberately sets up these situations so that when he becomes angry, she can feel justified in wanting to divorce him. Well, he thought, she better not try it again…

It was like in the military, when the old man didn't like your style anymore. He put out the word that you had to go. And so all the underlings–the colonels and the majors–began setting you up in impossible situations where they could write bad reports, create the necessary paper trail. When they'd got enough, the old man calls you in and gives you a choice reassignment, like, to Guam. Take it or get out. Your choice. He had seen it happen. It was the military equivalent of what Gottlieb was pulling; getting rid of good guys to make room for cronies.

There was a knock.

"Come in."

Em appeared in bathrobe, a towel wrapped turban-like around her hair. She gently closed the door behind her.

"Whatcha do'n?" She sat on the stool next to the copy machine.

"Oh, making copies of this letter for Bill Winters and Bryan's probation officer."

"Did you say her name is Sally?"

"Yeah. Sally Brand. Why? Do you know her?"

"I think I've seen her around campus a few times. Does she have great red hair, lots of freckles, and a tan uniform?"

"That's Sally."

"She's really cool looking, don't you think?"

He looked at Em and gathered the copies and began stapling the pages. "She's a pretty lady. Told me she wants to talk to you about Bryan one of these days."

"Really?"

"Uh-huh. Would you mind handing me that stack of proof sheets over there on the counter?"

"Sure." Em picked them up, stared at the top one and began sorting through them, recognizing faces.

"Harvey's. Yea! There's Chuck. Dave. And here's one of Jerry. Half the senior class is standing in line! You got a great picture of Harvey. How come you took all these, Dad?" She handed them to him.

"A favor to Harvey. I'm going to deliver them tonight. He's using some cuts in a flyer about his shop."

"Neat... By the way, I heard you and Mom arguing. What's that all about?"

He fumbled with a manila envelope. Em took one corner and helped him stuff the proof sheets inside. "Thanks. You should probably ask her."

Em smirked in a droll way. "You know I'll hear her side. I wanted to hear yours."

He didn't like to play these sorts of games with Em. But he decided to make an exception. He figured that in this instance she needed to hear his side. He took an extra loupe and grease pencil and put them in the envelope with the proofs. "She wants half my retirement from the military... which I won't get 'til I'm sixty."

"Yeah? That's not right, Dad. Her boyfriend's a rich guy. She doesn't need your money."

Jack turned and looked her in the eye. So he's rich, yet? He was stunned. Bernice? Bernice has a sugar daddy? He tried to suppress the image of her cozying up to some baldheaded dude twice her age.

"How do you know?"

"Mom told me. He's a boat dealer in Ft. Lauderdale. He's loaded."

"Really? Incredible!"

Em leaned against the counter, playing with a round photo-sizing calculator. "I'm not supposed to tell you. I just thought you ought to know, you know what I mean?"

"Thanks for telling me. Just out of curiosity, how old is he?"

"Don't know," said Em with a growing leer. "I know what you are thinking. Probably some old guy, huh? God, Dad, you are so funny sometimes." She laughed.

He felt embarrassed. "Doesn't matter," he said, knowing damned well it did.

"I can find out."

"As I said earlier, I don't like you being in the middle."

She shrugged and threw the sizing calculator down on the counter. "Can't change the script, Dad. That's my role in our little soap opera: Emily, the big kid in the middle of the little mess? Or is it the little kid in the middle of the big mess? Just ask the Duchess or the white rabbit. Anyway, no matter how you look at it, I'm Alice..."

"Right... You're Alice and I'm the Dodo."

She gave a little laugh and hugged him.

"Well, I gotta get ready for play practice. See ya, Dad."

"Chuck picking you up?"

"My twin bodyguards, Big Chuck and Little Dave."

"What time?"

"Around seven. We can be a few minutes late tonight. Chuck says it'll keep the black phantom guessing, know what I mean?"

"Anything you guys can do to change your routines is good. Tell Chuck I like his creativity."

"I will. Oh, one more thing." She looked intently at him. "Why would Mom give you such a hard time? Is she getting back for stuff I don't know about? Were you mean to her?"

"No. Never." Jack flattened the metal fastener on the manila envelope and set the package down. "I think she's more angry with herself than with me right now. I don't know why. Maybe she's got to hate me long enough for the divorce to go through. Who knows?"

"Ya know something? I really don't believe she's going to take all this stuff she's got those stickers on. Where would she put it all on a boat? She'd need a battleship or an aircraft carrier."

They laughed.

"See ya later."

She left. The phone rang. He picked up the receiver.

"Hello?"

"Hi, Jack. This is Sally. Is this a good time to talk?"

Jack glanced toward the open door. He did not want to talk to Sally with Bernice nearby.

"Not really. I got a letter addressed to me today. Suppose I call you later. Will you be at your office?"

"Call me at home after seven. 482-2150."

"I will."

Chapter 22

Tuesday Evening, May 21.

After Em left for play practice and Bernice had gone he knew not where, he locked the house and headed over to Harvey's. He parked and used the pay phone at the corner.

"Hello?"

"Sally? It's Jack."

"Hi! I wanted to apologize again for the other day."

"For what?"

"Well, you didn't need to hear my problems with all you've got on your plate."

"Sally, these past several days have taught me that you have to deal with situations when they come up. You can't put them off. Anyway, no need to apologize."

"I appreciate your understanding."

"No problem."

"I got a letter from Suzanne today. Did you receive the original?"

"Not yet."

"It's about the Order to Show Cause forms she filed."

"Yeah?"

"She says the court wouldn't grant a Temporary Restraining Order. The judge refused to sign the request without a four-hour notice to the defendant. She's been trying to reach Bryan by phone. So have I. No answer."

"So what does it mean?"

"To obtain the TRO, Suzanne's got to serve Bryan. Otherwise, the judge won't grant it."

"How come he can't be served?"

"They can't find him. He's staying away from his Mom's apartment. And she's nowhere to be found either."

"So what happens if he isn't served? Is there a time limit?"

"The court will set the case without the TRO."

"Will we have long to wait before it comes up?"

"Could be days or could be weeks. One way or another, Bryan will have to answer the court."

"But meanwhile, he can come and go at our place whenever he chooses?"

"I know you're disappointed, Jack. I talked to Bill about it. I think he will put some pressure on to move the case up."

"It can't be too soon."

"Is the scrambler working?"

"I guess so. He sent an officer over to install it. So far as I know, it's working fine."

"Well, I'd still be careful on the phone."

"Yeah. Bill told me he's tapping our phones."

"What's the latest?"

"Got another letter this morning."

"Oh?"

"It's to me. He switches back and forth between obscenities and pleading his love for Em. He says if I don't get off his case, I'll be sorry. Is that a threat in the legal sense?"

"Um… Not really. Had he said, 'I'm going to hurt you,' that would qualify as a clear threat of harm. Can you drop a copy to me tomorrow?"

"Sure. Each one gets crazier."

"I need to touch base with his mother. I want her to understand."

"You try Seagate Center? Harvey Gold told me she cleans offices at night."

"No more. I checked. She left four months ago."

"Nobody knows where she went?"

"Nada."

"That's bad… Did I tell you I dropped by the apartment on Harlan Street?"

"No, you didn't. A swell place, huh?"

"Yeah. Nobody answered the door. Bryan's bike was parked in the back, so I think he was home."

"Maybe she's moved out. Had all she could take. If that's the case, she's violated Bryan's probation conditions. She's 'sposed to report any change of address for her or her son."

"It gets curiouser all the time. Anyway, good night, Sally."

He hung up the phone and walked across the pavement to Harvey's. It was like 1942: bad news on every front. He opened the screen door and entered the Bagel Shack. The same couple was there, occupying the same table, looking into each other's eyes with that stricken, expectant glow of sexual longing.

A busboy he hadn't seen before was wiping tables and filling salt and pepper shakers. Mary and another young woman were in back preparing the vats for making bagels. Harvey appeared in the office doorway, wearing a clean white shirt and dark pants. Funny how he didn't look the same without his usual spattered apron. He barked a greeting.

"Welcome, my friend!"

"Thank you."

They shook hands and sat at a table.

"I was not so sure you'd come by tonight," Harvey said, scratching his cheek with a pink hand.

"I just talked with Sally Brand, Bryan's probation officer. She says they can't find Bryan to serve papers and the judge refuses to grant a Temporary Restraining Order. She said it could be days or weeks before they set a court date. Meanwhile, he is free to wander any place he chooses."

"Not good news. Sorry, Jack. I know Sally is doing everything she can to help you. She's a lovely woman."

"Yeah. She's bending over backwards." Jack handed him a fat manila envelope.

"What is this?"

"Proof sheets of the lunch crowd. I put a grease pencil and a loupe in the envelope, too. Look them over and circle the ones you want. I'll make five by seven prints for you."

Harvey opened the package and poured the contents onto the table. He began scanning the thumbnails. He picked up the loupe and examined it. He put it to his eye like a spyglass and aimed at the proof sheet. He put it down. "I'm supposed to know how this works? I see nothing."

"Put it over the thumbnail print. No. Let it rest on the print. Then look through the glass without moving it."

"Ah! Yes." He moved the glass to the next frame and peered at it. "You take excellent pictures, Jack. How much do I owe you?"

"Nothing. My pleasure."

He slid the proof pages and loupe back in the envelope. "Thank you, my friend. I see in your eyes much trouble. Tell me about it."

Jack explained all that had happened. Harvey sat glued to his chair, leaning in with both elbows, listening to every word. "How is your wife taking this?"

He explained the pending divorce. Harvey leaned back and reached for the saltshaker.

"Oy Vey! A house of difficulties. I feel so sorry for your daughter."

"Me, too. She cries and she's frightened. Has a nightmare now and then. Still, she can joke about it with her friends."

"You must be a Jew for her to see humor in such experience."

He chuckled. "Not that I know. Still... Kaufman. That is a good Jewish name, isn't it?"

"Oh, yes." Harvey scratched his baldhead. "Getting back to Emily... To have such a daughter must be God's greatest blessing."

Jack grinned self-consciously. Emily had done him proud, that was for sure. He shifted away from the subject out of consideration for Harvey. "What about you? Have family?"

Harvey looked wistfully. "No family for me."

"Really? No wife or kids? I thought family was the center of Jewish life."

"Yes. You are right. But not for me," he said, scratching the corner of his mouth and looking toward the kitchen.

Jack had touched a nerve, but did not have the sense to stop asking questions. "Divorced or widowed?"

"No. I cannot have that joy of wedded husband and father of children."

"But why? Injuries?"

A grim smile broke across his pink face, crinkling around his wide, staring eyes. "I suppose. Yes. In a matter of speaking, it is a permanent injury. But not the physical type of which I think you're thinking." He twirled the saltshaker on the table, watching it rather than Jack.

"You would make a great husband and father."

"No. There you are wrong. I would be worst father and husband."

"I can't believe it."

"Believe it. It is for this reason." He unbuttoned his left shirt cuff and pulled the sleeve up, exposing blue numbers tattooed on the inside of his lower arm.

"Nazi prison camp?"

"Birkenau, a death camp. I witness my two sisters, my mother, my father, my uncle and my grandmother on my mother's side–everyone I ever loved–exterminated. They went into one line and I into another."

"Damn! How old were you?"

"Twenty-five. I was strong and big. They put me in a soap factory. They put my family first in gas chamber and then in oven. They were the lucky ones. I was not so fortunate."

"But you survived."

He pointed with some force to his nose. "I still to this day can smell the fumes of those ovens."

Harvey pushed the saltshaker into the middle of the table. "Survival is not living. You know something, Jack? We are all made differently. Many survivors come out of death camps able to start a new life. They go to school and learn a trade. They create a new family, new dreams. Not so with me. I try to do the right thing. I learn how to bake, thinking some day I, too, will marry and have a new life.

"Unfortunately… I am forever damned by the experience of concentration camp. I come out with nightmares so bad I wake up screaming in the middle of the night. The rage inside me cannot escape. At times I awake and find I have torn my blankets and sometimes I sweat so the entire mattress is wet. How could I ever be a good husband and father when I am like this? Eh? You tell me!"

"I'm sorry. I had no idea." He looked at Harvey, appalled by his revelations, knowing they were kindred spirits. Yet, Harvey seemed so gentle.

"Ach! Not to be sorry. It is like Bryan Cutler that nobody can do anything about, you know?"

"Have you been to therapy?"

"Ha! Therapy Schmerapy. I try therapy many years. Psychiatrists, psychotherapists, psychologists, counselors… to rabbis I've been. For many, it helps. For me, nothing helps… except my bagels. I go in there…" He pointed toward the kitchen. "And I mix the dough using my own hands and a paddle. That is my therapy. See how strong my arms become?"

He made a muscle. His arms were quite powerful. He looked at Jack, squinting and wiping his hand across his forehead. "At four o'clock in the morning when the demons come, I brush them away with my hand and get up. I tell myself it is time to make bagels. To the demons I say, 'You cannot haunt me while I work.' And it is true. Making bagels keeps them away."

He threw up his hands. "Hey! For what am I telling you this? I meet you two times and say things I tell no one for years! How is that, do you think?"

"Maybe you sense I have my own demons... I spent a couple years in Vietnam watching people being blown to hell. Maybe it has to do with Bryan. We both tried to help him."

"Perhaps. I did not know you were a soldier. I will not ask the usual question everyone always asks."

"What is that?"

"When they hear you are in war, they always ask, 'Were you wounded?' Hell yes! You damned well were wounded! Everyone who witnesses war is wounded. Yes, Jack. You and I share wounds of the soul, do we not?"

"Yeah. That's true."

"No. Who can you talk with about such things? Nobody."

"You're right. Nobody understands unless they've been there."

"I am sorry you suffer too."

"I guess I was lucky, though. I was a photojournalist. I only had to shoot pictures and develop proofs of dead and dying civilians and GIs and Vietcong. Photographs of mayhem. Tracers. Napalm. Explosions."

"And you call your job lucky?"

"Compared with others," he said, trying to conclude this topic. "I'm curious, Harvey... What did you see in Bryan that made you want to help him?"

"Oy!" Harvey chuckled. "I see me as an angry young man when Bryan stands before me, asking for a job... I try to use my technique with him. I tell him not to use the electric mixer each morning. 'Work out the demons from your life,' I tell him. I make him use the paddle to stir the dough."

Harvey gave a half smile and gazed absently around. "Bryan does not understand why I want him to use his powerful energy and strength to good purpose. He thinks I am punishing him. And we cannot talk about it as you and I are doing."

Harvey looked down at the table. When he looked up again, his eyes had turned watery. He tapped a finger and looked across, a hint of wildness in his eyes. "It goes further back …to the fight. In Bryan, I saw me… when he got into that fight with the Barnes boy. He was doing what I yearned to do to those guards—especially at Dachau. I took pleasure in the release of his anger. I know it is bad to admit, but I felt thrilling sensations as Bryan knocked down this bully and tried to kill him… I am sure you can't imagine this. But I did nothing myself to stop him…."

"Yeah?" Jack's mind was swirling with conflicting emotions, "I've had some fantasies myself recently. Except it was Bryan I wanted to strangle…"

"When he comes asking me for work, I think to myself, 'Harvey, this is you seeking help. Would you turn down such a needy person as yourself when you were a troubled boy? Help him, Harvey. You might save him from becoming a Harvey Gold…' I say to myself. It was a mistake. There is no helping those who are possessed by demons. We are damned to a life of torment. Do you not believe so, Jack?"

He was bowled over by Harvey's candor.

"Yeah, I agree. In Nam we called it 'nutting up' whenever we went off the deep end. I still have nightmares too… about two young Viet Cong I may have killed…"

There. He had finally admitted it to somebody else. He was all too familiar with his demons. Ever since the war, they had been there, scaring hell out of him. They scared Bernice, too. She could never figure out why he lashed out at her. Surprise attacks came often in their early years of marriage. Maybe that was what she was paying him back for now...

Jack picked up the saltshaker from the middle of the table and slid it back and forth between thumb and forefinger. He thought of all the Nam vets who, like Harvey, were possessed so badly that they could not live in society. At least Harvey could hold himself together during the day. Many of the Nam guys couldn't. They were up in the mountains of Montana or Alaska or in the California desert, living out their days as raging hermits continuously nutting up, incorrigible human animals, warning everyone not to come near them.

"I don't know what to believe, Harvey. I know all of us have demons of one sort or another."

"Some can hide them and some cannot," Harvey whispered ruefully.

"You hide yours well."

"Ha! God controls me by day; the Devil by night. For Bryan, there is no respite. He is untouched by God. The Devil has his way with Bryan Cutler day and night. Do you not think so?"

He considered Harvey's words. Years ago, if anyone had told him Bernice would be divorcing him, he would have said they were crazy. And had it happened back then, he might have raged, too. He might have threatened her life. He might have taken his military knife and slit her throat from ear to ear and afterward not remembered a damned thing. It was not too much different then from how Bryan probably felt now. He was lonely, lost and crying out in pain.

It had taken years for Jack to gain some equilibrium and control over his emotions, years of biting his tongue as well as his fingernails. Turning the other cheek. Walking away. Taking time out to sit by the edge of the water. Sailing alone in heavy seas. But nothing could erase the images of death…

He thought he owed most of his sanity to Em. Raising her, loving her, seeing her grow into a lovely person, had been his best cure. She was his reason for surviving.

He still could not quite get it through his head that anyone would hurt Emily. At the same time, he was thinking about how he might kill Bryan. He realized that Harvey was gazing at him, waiting for a reply.

"I know now you are right about Bryan," Jack admitted. "He's beyond our help."

"I think so."

"I'm awfully sorry for what you've been through, Harvey. You do a helluva good job hiding it. I can understand how you and Bryan came together like two magnets."

"Ya. Two magnets." Harvey placed his fists knuckles-to-knuckles on the table. "There was great attraction. And when we part," he said, twisting one fist opposite the other, "it is like one magnet is turned around so they never can touch again. Isn't that so?"

Bernice's face appeared in Jack's mind.

"Yeah. That's so."

Chapter 23

Late Evening, Tuesday, May 21.

As Jack went about making preparations in Em's room, Harvey's story about the concentration camp and his pent-up rage remained in his mind. It was as though he was the ancient mariner who grabbed you with his eye and compelled you to listen. Why him? Jack knew why. They both saw the presence of demons in each other's eyes. The moment he walked into Harvey's shop the first time, he felt a dark affinity, an electric charge between them. There was instant connection, like the magnets he talked about. And tonight, Jack had confessed his deepest secret to Harvey: his fear that he had killed two young boys in Vietnam.

He arranged small pillows beneath Em's blanket in her shape. He retrieved a wig Bernice no longer used and arranged the hair on the pillow. You just don't know, he mumbled to himself. Who'd expect that a man who appeared so ordinary by day could be a raving maniac at night, screaming and ripping his sheets and blankets.

He pulled a comfortable chair into the corner where he had a clear view of both windows. He set up a small tripod and mounted

195

a camera and his largest flash. He considered: the screens on the windows would reflect flash. He should have asked Bill Winters for one of their infrared camcorders. Get all the action. No flash, no reflection. He propped the softball bat against Em's curio cabinet. On top of the dresser was Jack's raincoat where the butt of his new Colt .45 was visible. He covered it.

He supposed he had stirred Harvey up when he went to see him about Bryan that first day. Must have touched him deeply. Raised his memories and dashed hopes. He had never met a stranger like that where he felt such instant rapport, a kinship between a victim and–could he say it–another victim? He had never wanted to admit that he, too, was already a victim–the victim of what he had experienced. There were pictures that never left his mind, so etched on his brain that nobody, not even the best therapist in the world, could scrape them away.

Harvey sees me as directly in Bryan's path, he thought. It was what in the military they used to call in the line of fire. In order to get to Em, Bryan would have to deal with him. Harvey saw him doing that.

He chuckled. What the hell do you think you're doing, setting up this ruse? You are baiting Bryan, aren't you, Jack? A tremor whisked through him. Yeah, dopey, that's what you're doing. You want him. You intend to get him.

He made a thermos of coffee and set it on the bed table. What was it Harvey said? He and Bryan were too alike to help one another. They both had fatal flaws? In Harvey's case, it wasn't that he hadn't come to earth with all the ingredients. He'd had critical ingredients burned out of him at Treblinka and Dachau. Who's to say Bryan didn't have his burned out, too? Did his father beat him when he was a little boy? Perhaps it was his mother who was abusive. What difference did it make how he got this way? He was the way he was. He was dangerous. Feeling sorry for him won't change him.

He checked the time. Nine o'clock. Play practice would be over soon. He suddenly thought of Sally. Light brown freckles and cream. It was so bizarre how inextricably sexual energy was bound up with emotional experiences involving fear, anger or sadness. He recalled the night after Bernice and he had attended his grandfather's funeral. They hadn't had such lively sex in years. It was like coming home from Nam. He kept wanting more until they both collapsed, exhausted, and slept like babies.

That was how sex was in Nam, too. You returned from night missions with so many pent-up emotions and looked around for the nearest, softest woman for release. You wanted to get lost in her flesh. You wanted to be held in strong arms and legs that would make you forget... for even a little while. Sometimes, he thought, sex after missions was the only way he knew that he was still alive.

The front door opened and banged closed.

"Are you here, Jack?" Her majesty had arrived with her loud, strident voice.

"In Em's room."

She stepped into the room. "Good grief! What on earth are you doing?"

"Hoping to get a decent shot of Bryan."

"I still think you should call Floyd. Or better, why don't you get one of those private investigative agencies to help. They've got surveillance cameras, recorders, the whole nine yards."

"You don't think Bryan would notice all the activity?"

"Suit yourself." She leaned against the doorframe. "You know? One of the reasons we're getting a divorce is that you're so damned stubborn."

Stalker

She was down the hall before he could retort, leaving a trail of cigarette smoke behind her. He grinned sadly. He thought she was divorcing him because she was in love with another man. Maybe it was battle fatigue, but she could not push his buttons any longer. His mind was focused on Bryan and the prospect of being free at last... Yes, free at last... Martin Luther King's voice echoed the words over and over in his mind. He turned off the light and went into the studio, carrying the camera and tripod with him.

He mounted the 28mm lens and loaded the camera with film. He lit the two floods in front of the easel and placed a copy of today's *St. Pete Times* on it. His eye caught on the headline: "Septuplets delivered; 6 survive". He shot two frames for good measure, making sure the flag and dateline were in focus. His method of dating film was the best. It held up in court every time.

He carried the loaded camera and tripod into Em's room and positioned it so the view took in both windows. All was ready. He switched off the light and returned to the studio. The television suddenly snapped on with an explosion of forced laughter. He closed the door and slumped down on the sofa. He would still like to rig the trip wire on the playhouse door and install an auto alarm and camera. Perhaps later, after he saw how this plan worked.

He left the studio and passed by the living room toward the kitchen. Bernice looked up, aimed the remote and lowered the volume.

"I apologize for what I said, Jack. Will you forgive me?"

"No problem, Bernice. Hell, what's to forgive? When you're a bitch, you're a bitch and nothing I say can change it. Bitchiness is a permanent state, like having blue or brown eyes, that neither God nor man can fix."

"You see it like that," she asked, using her soft Greer Garson voice. She looked off toward the bookcase where yellow stickers adorned all the books and furniture. "I was apologizing. Can't you forgive me once and for all? This hasn't been an easy time for me."

"Okay, then I forgive you. I forgive you whatever."

"We're all uptight. Can't we at least be civil? We've gotta work together through settlement."

Yes. Settlement. She takes nothing except the entire household. He felt the lather of a good fight coming on.

"Yeah. I understand. We're all uptight. Still, you attack me personally. You've come and gone as you pleased. I've stayed the hell out of your way. What more could you want, Bernice? And despite all my bending over backwards to keep some semblance of calm in this house, you snipe away at me like you hate my guts. You are an ungrateful bitch and I'll be the happiest guy in the world when you go out that front door."

Bernice's hand froze on the wine glass suspended before her lips. She blinked at him and put the wine down next to the ashtray. She glanced at the cigarette in the ashtray, but made no effort to pick it up. Instead, she fell apart.

"I know I've been difficult," she said in her very best Bette Davis voice. She clutched her hands to her face and began to bawl. She reached for the napkin under the glass and used it to sponge up the mascara running down her cheeks. She looked up like a little girl caught in a lie. "I'm sorry, Jack. I know I'm bad. Please forgive me... You don't deserve this. You're the good person. I'm the one who's bad. Please. I won't say another mean thing to you. I promise."

He took a large swig of the Chardonnay, watching Bernice. It was interesting how, when a person cut you off, you saw her as ugly. That is how he had seen Bernice these past two years, ugly.

Now, in the half-light of the table lamp, Bernice's tear-streaked face suddenly looked attractive and vulnerable. Her eyes had an uncertainty about them and those lips he used to kiss were quivering. It was like she was trying to be reborn in a split second. He loathed her yet he also felt pity for her. Or was it another one of her acts: Myrna Loy in a 1943 sob story where war bride Myrna falls in love with the milkman.

She watched him with a plaintive expression, her fingers touching her ring finger, as though to check whether there were any. Finding none, they slipped up and down the ring finger in a nervous rhythm, reminding him of other strokes. Bernice looked down at her hands, stopped the movement, and raised her head. Tears formed again and trickled down.

"It is sad how we each went our own way after we split the business," she said, an attempted smile forming. It was vintage Ingrid Bergman. "I got so caught up in the swirl of the game I forgot what was important. It cost me a husband and a daughter."

He handed Ingrid his napkin and responded with a Cary Grant line. "Em still loves you, Bernice. I hope you know that."

"Yeah, well…" She reached for her cigarette and flicked ash across the ashtray with a dramatic flair. "From the time she was a baby, she always preferred you."

Ingrid was gone from her face, leaving only a sad Bernice. It was her great excuse for not giving her daughter proper attention. They had done this scene a hundred times over the years. He would say his part, like Van Johnson, trying to be convincing. "Not so. She loves you. You see that, don't you?"

Tears continued to trickle down Bernice's face. Jack went into the kitchen and retrieved a box of tissues. He handed one to her.

"Thanks."

"It's not too late for you and Em, Bernie," he said, realizing he was using the loving nickname for the first time in years. "She needs you now more than ever. Take time off. Be with her before she leaves for Spain."

Bernice sniffed and sat up straight. "Excuse me."

She went into the bathroom. Jack sat down and took another swig of Chardonnay. Bernice returned, tugging at her skirt to smooth it. She had regained her composure. Except for red eyes, you'd never know she'd broken up just five minutes ago.

"I don't know what came over me..." She sat down and lit another cigarette like Joan Crawford might. "You're right, Jack. I've been working seven days a week. I've become a workaholic. I've gone without vacations for three years. I've worked nights until all hours. It's a wonder you both put up with me this long."

"Yeah, well... As you say, PR and advertising are your passions. Mine's photography. Em's is acting. Nothing wrong with passions. It's just that there was never any balance. We didn't have any real family life, you know?"

"Yes... And I'm sorry for that. I hope some day you'll forgive me."

The sound of music from a car radio came blaring through the closed door. Shouts, laughter, a car door slamming. Em was home safely. He gave a sigh of relief. Bernice went into the kitchen and refilled her glass.

Em came through the door, carrying her script and overnight case. Her stage make-up was exaggerated, her eyes encased in heavy black lines and blue shading.

"How'd it go?"

"Great. Dad. No dark phantom tonight. Everybody was watching for him."

Stalker

"Good," said Bernice, coming into the living room carrying her wine. "Perhaps he's getting the message."

"Yeah," Em replied, giving her mother a quick look. "You okay, Mom?"

"Yes, hon. Your father and I have been having a little chat."

Em turned back to him. "The gang went to Harvey's for coffee after. Harvey said you were over there tonight. He's such a neat man."

"Yeah. I took those proofs to him."

"He told me he was keeping an eye out for Bryan. I guess you guys talked about it."

"Bryan used to work for Harvey."

"I remember him there. Well, I'm going to bed. Goodnight, guys."

"You're in my room again. I'm going to be in your room."

She went down the hall. "Hey, this is too cool!"

She came back down the hall with a large smile. "I'm a dummy in there!" She guffawed. "The wig does it. Where'd it come from? Yours, Mom?"

"Yes, it's mine, darling."

"Can I have it after?"

"What on earth would you do with it," asked Bernice.

"I think it would look great on Chuck. We could make a fantastic entrance at the prom with him wearing it. Wouldn't that be a smash?"

Bernice and Jack looked at each other and smiled, the first honest-to-God smiles they had exchanged in a long time.

"How do you come up with these ideas," he asked.

"Same way you come up with stupid dummies," she replied, laughing again.

He went into the kitchen and got a bag of pretzels and some crackers and carried them to Em's room. Time for Operation Dummy, although he was not sure who the bigger dummy was. He waited until Em turned off the shower and went into his bedroom. Then, he switched off the light, pulled the blinds up, and opened the curtains. It was totally dark, overcast. He could not be seen in the farthest corner of the room. The security lights, however, did cast a pale glow so a person would be visible when approaching either window. He checked the lens for reflection. None.

The television switched off early–around eleven. It was very unlike Bernice. He heard her knock on his bedroom door and say something to Em. Their whispers filtered down the hall. Apparently, Bernice was doing a motherly thing for a change: having a heart-to-heart talk with her daughter. He closed Em's door, cutting off their conversation.

Around one, Bernice closed the door to her room and soon the house was quiet. His head fell to one side, jerking him awake. Too much wine. He was not used to it. How long he had been asleep, he did not know. It was four o'clock. No Bryan Cutler. At first light, he checked the street. All was clear.

Chapter 24

Wednesday Afternoon, May 22.

When he returned home from shooting the groundbreaking for a new mall, Jack discovered a thick envelop on the driveway. The flower stickers adorning the top and right side of the envelope seemed to epitomize the irony of it all. Em's name and address were barely legible scrawls.

He checked the mail: a letter to Em from Suzanne, the paralegal. He threw the letter on his desk and set about developing the film he had shot. He was just coming out of the photo lab when Em peeked around the door.

"Hi, Dad! Guess what?"

He braced, reading bad news on her solemn face.

"When Chuck went out to get in his car this morning, there was a dead rat full of maggots on the front seat."

"Damn."

"Yeah. He wanted to take the rat over to Bryan's and leave it in front of his door, but Jerry and Dave convinced him not to."

"Good thinking. Did he report it to the police?"

"Yeah. He talked with Chief Winters."

"Good." He nodded toward the desk. "Another missile from him and something from Suzanne. I believe it's what Sally received having to do with the court not being able to grant the TRO until Bryan is served notice."

Em opened Suzanne's envelope.

"Yup. You're right. She says they'll try to serve him today."

"Super."

"Well, let's see what phantom boy has to say..." She opened the letter and pulled out several sheets of notepaper showing GEORGE'S TOWING SERVICE at the top. She laughed. "How cool! George's Towing Service stationery. I think I'll get some like it. Maybe, Ethel's Full Service Garage. Wouldn't that be cool?"

"Very." He watched her face change serious as she read. She handed him a sheet.

EMILY

YOU ARE KILLING ME... I HAV NO RESON TO LIVE WITHOUT YOU. CAN'T U SEE THAT, BITCH????

I NEVER DID ANYTHN TO U. ALL OF U ARE KILLING ME. YOU, YOUR DAD, CHIEF WINTERS, MISS BRAND. I KNOW YOU ARE ALL AGAINST ME AND WANT TO SEE ME DIE.

I ONLY HAVE LOVE FOR YOU. YOU AND JEAN... SHE'S A WOMAN I WORK WITH... WE WORK ACROSS FROM EACH OTHER. SHE'S GOT GREAT TITS LIKE YOU. YEAH, EMILY, I GOT A NU JOB. BETTER MAKING SOME MONEY THAN SCHOOL. IF YOU MUST KNOW, I QUIT. I KNOW YOU ARE DISAPPOINTED IN ME FOR THAT. I AM TOO IN SOME WAYS. IT DOESN'T MATTER ANY MORE, YOU KNOW? SCHOOL'S ABOUT FUTURE AND I DON'T HAVE ONE.

I WANT TO ASK JEAN OUT. I'M AFRAID TO. SHE'D REJECT ME LIKE U. I'M NOTHIN!!! DO U KNO HOW IT IS TO BE NOTHIN, BITCH?

PLEASE, JUST ONCE GO OUT WITH ME. PLEASE. THAT'S ALL I ASK BEFORE I DIE. ONE NIGHT WITH U. IS THAT TOO MUCH TO ASK?

YER DAD AND HIS FRIENDS SALLY AND BILL THINK THEY'RE REALLY BIG SHITS. THEY DO ALL THIS STUFF JUST TO MAKE ME FEEL BAD. AS THO I DON'T FEEL BAD ALREADY. DO YOU KNOW HOW A PERSON FEELS WHEN PEOPLE GANG UP ON THEM? ALL OF YOU HATE ME.

TOO BAD I CAN'T CALL YOU ANY MORE. I MISS HEARING YOUR VOICE.

YOU TELL THEM TO STOP HARRASSING ME AND MY MOM, EMILY. YOU TELL THEM I HAVEN'T DONE NOTHIN WRONG. HAVE I? HAVE I TOUCHED YOU???? IT'S ALL IN YOUR MIND. I'M NOTHIN BUT SCUM IN YOUR EYES. RIGHT, BITCH?

CAN'T YOU SEE I WON'T HURT YOU? YER SO SPECIAL. I COULD NEVER HURT U.

IF U WOULD ONLY TALK TO ME. MAYBE YOU COULD TELL JEAN HOW MUCH I LIKE HER. SEE IF SHE'D GO OUT WITH ME... COULD YOU DO THAT? I KNOW YOU WON'T. CAUSE YOU HATE ME SO.

I GOT TO GO NOW. IT IS TIME FOR WORK AND I AM LATE... AS USUAL.

LOVE, PLEASE ANSWER THIS LETTER. LET ME KNOW YOU CARE JUST A LITTLE BIT. IS THAT TOO MUCH TO ASK?

I LOVE YOU.

BRYAN

"How could he know Chief Winters had our phone tapped?" Jack mumbled under his breath.

"Our phone's tapped?"

"Yeah. Winters did it as an extra precaution... Bryan doesn't mention my letter to his mother."

"When did you send it?"

"Yesterday."

"It probably didn't get there yet. Ya know something?" Em pursed her lips and looked at Jack speculatively through half-closed eyes and drooping hair.

"No, what?"

"Do you think Bryan's working himself up to committing suicide?"

He sat down in the swivel chair and swung back and forth. "Could be. Sally says that he's given up."

"At least there are two women in the picture. This woman he works with, Jean. God, I'd love to get the two of them together. Get him off my back. 'Cept, I wouldn't wish that on anybody."

He looked across at Em, realizing she was not his adolescent kid any more. Somehow, he could not fathom that she would soon be on her own, away from him for most of the remainder of their lives. The realization made him doubly aware of how precious these moments were.

"Want to drive down to the boat?"

"Sure. Why?"

"Thought I'd check her out."

"I need to be back here by six. First dress rehearsal tonight."

His watch said ten-of-five. There was plenty of time.

"We won't stay long. Chief Winters has been pestering me to take him out fishing. I need to see how much work I've got to do before she's seaworthy."

"Cool. You need a break. I'd like to go sailing too, before I go to Spain. You wanna?"

"We can do it."

"Could we take the gang?"

"Not more than ten."

"Oh, I mean Julie, Robin, Jerry, David, Goliath."

"Who's Goliath?"

"Chuck... Jerry calls him Goliath ever since Chuck wanted to take on Phantom Boy."

He locked the door and they headed into rush hour traffic on Seaview Boulevard. He never ceased to marvel at Em's ways of absorbing worrisome events and turning them into humorous situations. She and her pals must talk through all the episodes until one or another sees the lighter side.

He had seen them do it. He recalled watching them one night sitting around the kitchen table drinking coffee and listening to Chuck's latest problems with the bomber. They listened quite respectfully as he admitted he didn't have enough money to buy the used transmission he needed. The old one was apparently slipping badly. They began joking about which junk yard they would steal one out of, then went into an absurd discussion about who would stand look-out for the junk yard dog and how many it would take to carry the transmission out of the place. By then, everyone was howling with laughter, including Chuck. In the end, they pooled their money and made a list of all the friends they could tap for the difference. This set them off into another fantasy in which they decided to hold fund-raisers with kissing booths. More gales of laughter. They were imperturbable.

He looked over at Em. She was unusually quiet. Perhaps she was working up to something funny.

"You talk to Mom last night?" She was dead serious.

"Why?"

"She came in after I went to bed. She'd been crying."

"Oh?"

"She said she was sorry for all the times she wasn't there for me, you know what I mean?"

"That's good."

"We hugged and cried. I told her I was sorry, too." Em ran her fingers through her hair. He waited, knowing there was more to tell. "She seemed changed somehow."

He imagined it was from Bette Davis to June Allyson. He tried not to laugh. "How do you mean?"

"Warmer. Gentler. I think she's feeling sad because she doesn't know me better. We're going shopping for clothes Sunday afternoon. That'll be fun."

"Your Mom is a good person inside, Em. Otherwise, I wouldn't have fallen in love with her." At least he wanted to think so.

"When did you guys fall out of love?"

He glanced across at her, then back to the street. How could he say it really started when Em was born? How could he say he thought Bernice felt she was competing–even when Em was a little baby–with her for his attention? He looked straight ahead.

"Probably when you were four or five," he replied, trying to maintain a steady voice. "I was still upset from the war. Nervous. Depressed. Sometimes I'd go off on a drinking binge with some Nam guys. Not a pleasant story." He was telling half-truths. He hoped they were convincing.

"I always thought it was me somehow, you know? I got between you two, you know what I mean?"

"Yeah. No. Never think that, Em."

"Why didn't you get a divorce earlier?"

She was absorbing every detail of their conversation like the time he confronted his own mother about who his father was.

"We made an agreement. No divorce until you finished high school."

"Wow. That was a long time. Haven't you been lonely?"

"Sometimes." He tried to smile. "Not often, thanks to you. You've been the one bright star in my life all these years."

She teared up. "Yeah. Me, too. I wouldn't have made it without all your help. I love you so much, Dad."

"I love you, too. I'm glad you and Bernie were able to talk. You guys ought to make the most of the time you've got left."

"Bernie... I haven't heard you call her Bernie in a long time. Do you still have feelings for her?"

"To be honest, no. But I hope she and I can respect one another for all the good times we've had. No more of this gnashing and slashing."

"Hooray!" she said with a droll look. "I won't have to hear Mom shouting at you for being so damned stubborn." She laughed through tears.

"I hope not."

The sun was still bright and hot. Great white billows of clouds filled the blue sky.

"Days like this I wish we owned a convertible like Chuck's," he said, pulling into a parking space at dockside.

"Me, too."

They climbed out. He glanced around the parking lot, half expecting Bryan to be sitting on a bench staring blindly at his computer. Satisfied he was not nearby, he unlocked the gate. They went down the gangplank to the floating dock. QT2 was lying in the water with vibrant expectancy, lounging, shifting on gentle waves. Em noticed first.

"Oh, gosh, Dad..." She stood portside of their boat, pointing.

"Why? What..."

Then he saw. Eggshells were splattered across the deck, fore and aft, with bloody, featherless embryos lying scattered here and there.

"Fertilized eggs. Son-of-a-bitch! Sorry, Em."

"It's awful!"

He stepped closer and examined the dried blood and congealed fluid and tiny, dead bodies. They had been there long enough to get hard. Baked by the sun. They would be hell to clean up. Bastard! The entire deck would have to be refinished.

"Nothing we can do tonight except report it," he said to Em. "At least he didn't smash the hull and sink her."

They went to the pay phone next to the Winn-Dixie and dialed Bill Winters' number.

"Chief Winters' office."

"Florese? May I speak with Bill, please?"

"He's gone for the day. Can I help you?"

"Somebody egged my boat. Used fertilized eggs. I presume it was Bryan Cutler."

"Ugh! I can report it for you. Do you know when it happened?"

"No. Probably sometime last night or early this morning. Otherwise, Jim Carleton in the next slip over would've noticed."

"Any other damage? Signs of broken entry?"

"No... Maybe. I really didn't stay to look. Thought I might be messing up evidence."

"What's the address there?"

"Slip sixty-four, Municipal Pier."

"I'll try to get Sergeant Nelson and Corporal Schneck out there ASAP. Will you be there?"

"Tell them to call me at home before they leave. I'll meet them."

"Very good... I'm so sorry, Mr. Kaufman."

"Thanks."

They drove home in silence.

Chapter 25

Wednesday Evening, May 22.

When Jack returned to the dock, two cruisers and Bill's jeep were parked next to his slip. Jim Carleton, who lived aboard his schooner, was standing with Bill, watching as the two officers checked for evidence and damage.

Jim waved an arm. Bill turned. He was wearing civilian clothes.

"What're you doing here, Bill?" Jack asked.

"Florese called me. I wanted to see what that son-of-a-bitch did to your boat. Damage's limited to the eggs. No forced entry. He apparently stood in the parking lot and lobbed the damn things across the water."

"I heard some light splotchy noises in the middle of night," said Carleton. "I jest thought it was somebody rowing a dinghy. Sounded like oars striking the water. I was only half awake."

"Can you pinpoint the time?"

Carleton scratched his tattooed arm. "Had to be three or so."

"You didn't see anybody? No voices?"

"No. I'm used to noise. There's always something going on in the parking lot, now Winn-Dixie is open twenty-four hours. I don't pay much attention to noise unless it's close-by."

Winters turned to Jack. "Has this Cutler guy ever been on your boat?"

"No. I can't imagine how he knew we had one."

"When's the last time you came over to check it out?"

"Oh, two days ago, three. I was shooting pictures of the tall ship. You know, the Sea Siren? She was anchored right over there." He pointed to the larger wharf at the mouth of the channel. "After I finished, I came over and checked the hatch was all. I didn't go below. Haven't been below in months, I'd say."

Winters held his elbow in hand, other hand to chin, contemplating.

"Will you be taking Bryan in for questioning?"

"I'll call Chief Jackowitz over in Seagate. Maybe they can take him into custody. The kid'll deny he was within five miles of here. He'll drum up some alibi."

"Yeah. He lies well."

"It could scare him, though. Old Jackie can be pretty intimidating. Worth the exercise."

"Oh," Jack said, remembering. "One of Emily's friends–a guy she dates named Chuck–found a dead rat on the front seat of his car this morning."

"I talked with him. Chuck Hampton. He filed a report. Seems like a nice kid."

"Yeah. He and his buddies look after Emily."

"This crap has gotta stop," Winters said. "I'm trying to think of some legal way I can haul his ass down to Dade Psychiatric Center. They'd keep him under lock and key for observation... I feel sure they could find a good reason to commit him. Just don't know how I can do it without getting the juvenile authorities on my back. I might have another chat with Cutler's probation officer. Cute lady, huh?"

"Different," Jack responded, trying not to show particular interest.

"I'd like to count her freckles. Good Lord, she's a pretty thing," said Winters, turning to Carleton. "She's got the most beautiful red hair I've ever seen on a woman. A peaches and cream complexion, and all these damned tiny orange freckles thick as can be all over her face and arms and hands and neck. Lord almighty, she's cute. Incredible smile. Great body, too, and green eyes. Right, Jack? Am I exaggerating?"

He tapped Jack in the gut. Jack realized he probably had a silly smile on his face. "No. She's a knock-out."

"I've seen her around different places. Dates one of our firemen, Phil Henshaw. You know Phil, Jack?"

"No. Probably I'd recognize him. I've taken plenty of pictures of the fire teams. Which station?"

"Number three, down on the beach. He's a big sombitch. Used to be a light heavyweight fighter out of Jacksonville 'til some hot-shot took him out with a kidney punch. He quit after that and went to fire school."

"Yeah. I know who you're talking about now," he said, thinking Sally's taste in men could be improved. He was handsome enough, but he had the reputation of being a womanizer.

"Not to change the subject," Jack said, wanting to get back on track, "but is there any way I can get the court to put our case on the calendar? They haven't granted a Temporary Restraining Order because Suzanne hasn't served Bryan with notice. The process servers can't find him."

"Figures." Winters surveyed the top of QT2's main mast. "Know who the judge is?"

"No."

"I'll check around in the morning. See what I can do."

"Appreciate it."

"Will your home owner's insurance cover the damage to the boat, Jack?" asked Carleton.

"I've got a deductible. I'll have to cough up the first $500."

"Dang..." Carleton exclaimed. He turned to Winters. "Ain't no way this kid is liable for damage?"

"Not unless we can tie him to it. Could've been anybody. I'm sending Schnecky over to Grable's Hatchery in Baytown tomorrow. We may get some leads there."

Chapter 26

Thursday Morning, May 23.

At eight o'clock, the phone rang.

"Hello?"

"Ed Mumford here. I need to change your assigned weekend to cover a special training exercise. General Selby asked specially for you, Jack. The NASA photographer assigned to it has been in a car accident. You're number one on the general's list. I told him you'd help us out."

"Thanks for the good word, Colonel. I'd like to do it, but I have an emergency down here. I can't get away."

"Oh?" Mumford cleared his throat. "Can you tell me the nature of it? Perhaps we can help free you up."

"It involves my daughter. She may be in danger from a stalker. I've got to be here."

"Sorry to hear that... You know, of course, you have only one more shot at making lieutenant colonel before you retire..."

"I'm aware of that, sir," Jack replied firmly. Mumford was laying one on him, he thought. He could see it coming.

Stalker

"I'm gonna hafta ask Ted Phillips to take your place. It'll score some points for him. I hafta tell you, he's gunning for your slot."

A heaviness invaded Jack's chest. What a liar and hypocrite! Ted was Ed Mumford's prodigy. They were buddies. Mumford would like nothing better than for Ted to take over his position and push Jack the hell out. Damned peacetime military politics.

"Sure you won't reconsider, Jack?"

"I can't, sir. There's a guy stalking my daughter. I must be here."

"That's too bad... She's an actress and a model, I believe."

"Yes, sir."

"I guess that's part of the profession..."

"I don't follow you... How do you mean?"

"Attracting perverts. I read just the other day about some Hollywood actress being pursued. Had to hire a bodyguard..." He paused. "That's too bad. Well, we'll manage without you. See you on your regular weekend, Jack. Got another exercise, a smaller one, scheduled. You will be able to make that one, won't you?"

He calculated the weekends. Two more. "Oh, yes. No problem then," he lied.

"See you," said Mumford in a whisper, hanging up before Jack could reply.

Damn it all to hell. Cutler was jeopardizing his Air Force Reserve assignment and twenty good years.

The phone rang.

"Hello?"

"Bill Winters, Jack... I just talked with Sally. The jerk's been served, but Judge Donaldson still refuses to grant a TRO."

"What can we do?"

"No problem. We traded. No TRO for getting you moved up on the calendar. Donaldson and I go way back. We played football together at Florida State. He was a helluva tailback. Good in track, too. He's going to lean on the clerk and shift a few cases around. It'll rattle the chains of a few defense lawyers, but what the hell."

"Great!"

"Who's your attorney?"

"Suzanne said we didn't need one, since Emily is an unemployed minor and the case is straightforward. She's listed as an un-represented party."

"Oh, right..."

"Why? Do you think we need one? I can get Ray Stewart, the former D.A."

"Nah. Don't waste your bucks. Ray charges like he's F. Lee Bailey. When Suzanne says you don't need one, you don't. The lady oughta be a trial lawyer herself."

"Yeah. She's handling our divorce, too."

"When's the split official?"

"We legally separate June the twenty-fourth."

"I'll bet you'll be glad to get out from under... Been a terrible strain on you."

"On all of us."

"Time to think fishing, brother. Get the deck refinished. We need to do it."

"We will."

"Call your insurance agent?"

"Yeah. A claims adjuster is coming by."

"Oh, before I forget... There's another thing."

"What's that?"

"Just between us, the mayor and the police committee are planning an internal audit of my department. I'm gonna have to take the additional cruisers and our foot soldier out of your neighborhood. I've also removed the tap."

Jack's heart sank. What else could happen? The cops had been keeping Bryan at bay the past several nights. "You couldn't keep Nesbitt on foot patrol until the court date?"

"No, buddy. I can't afford to show special treatment."

"So when's the change to occur?"

"Effective today. The one assigned cruiser will continue making frequent rounds on Palm and Pitcairn and Eisenhower Park, so it won't be like you're on your own. The scrambler can stay in place. It's standard procedure to loan 'em out in cases like yours."

Funny. Just when he was beginning to feel protected, Bill was removing the safety net. "Are you under that much pressure, Bill?"

"My informants tell me Gottlieb has his own guy from Key Biscayne lined up to replace me as soon as they dig up the right dirt. You know how it is... New mayors want a clean laundry basket, so to speak."

"Sounds like my Reserve position. Because of Bryan, I had to turn down a training assignment. The generals are ticked off."

"A damn shame. You know? You work hard. Try to do the right thing. Put together a career. Then, wham! Somebody starts taking cheap shots. And I have just enough enemies around here to make Gottlieb's case for him."

"Too bad. Anything I can do, just holler."

"Thanks... Who needs this crap at our time in life? For two cents, I'd tell 'em all to go straight to hell and retire. Cindy wants me to."

"I hope we're talking on a clean line."

"Better believe it. I installed a dedicated line at my own personal expense. It's got an automatic detector on it. Anybody listening activates a warning signal. You can't tap it without setting off a red light."

"I should get one... Let me know if I can put in a good word, Bill."

"Thanks, pal. See you!"

Jack put down the receiver. So Gottlieb was out to get Winters. It didn't surprise him. Bill had ruffled plenty of feathers at City Hall over the years. He was too honest to be chief cop. Jack laughed at the irony of it. A new laundry basket, indeed. He gathered his camera equipment and started for the door when Bernice strolled in wearing bathrobe and slippers. It was too early for the queen to be out of bed. Only nine-thirty.

"Morning, Jack," she said sleepily. "I was wondering whether we could switch cars today."

"How come?"

"I'd like you to drive the Mercedes. See what you think. It makes a funny noise when I put on the brakes."

"Can't take it in?"

"No," she said, reaching in the refrigerator and pulling out a quart of orange juice. She poured some into a glass. "I've got to meet clients one after the other all afternoon. Tonight, there's an opening. I need dependable wheels."

It would never occur to Bernice, he thought, to get up early and drive down to the dealership and get a loaner. Jack went out the front door and unlocked her Mercedes. He retrieved her attaché case.

"That's awfully good of you," she said when he put her case down on the table. She leaned against the doorframe, sipping juice. "Emily and I have had some wonderful late-night chats. She's quite a girl."

"Yeah?" He carried his two camera bags to the front door. It was unlike Bernice to be this talkative so early in the day.

"Did she tell you that Jewish man, Harvey Gold, was standing in the parking lot when she and her gang came out of rehearsal last night?"

"No."

"He told her he was keeping an eye out for the Cutler boy. He said he wouldn't let him get near her."

Jack was surprised at Harvey taking such a personal interest.

"That's great. I've got to go now. I'm almost late for an appointment."

"Where are you going?"

"Construction shots of the new health services annex at the hospital."

"Have a good day, Jack," she said softly, a sad smile forming. As he walked down the front sidewalk, she called after him. "Did you reach the insurance man about the boat?"

"Adjuster's meeting me at three this afternoon."

"Good. See what you think of my car."

"I will."

"Be careful, Jack. Don't tangle with that boy."

"I won't."

He hauled the equipment to the Mercedes and piled it in the back seat. It was like Bernice did not want to let go of him this morning. It appeared she was becoming human again. Thank God for Emily's sake. He started the motor and retracted the overhead hatch. The car needed air. Too much perfume and cigarette smoke. Sunlight bathed the interior. He put down all the windows, backed out, and swung the car into drive. She felt tight and good. The rush of air cleared the odors, replacing them with the sweet scent of fresh leather. No wonder everybody always thinks of good cars and boats as females, he thought.

224

Jack pulled into traffic on Seaview, listening for the odd noise Bernice described. He could not hear it. When he applied the brakes at the light, however, there was a slight thumping sound as though something were loose. It continued briefly as he kept his foot on the brake pedal waiting for the light to change. There was definitely a slight vibration. Bernice needed to take it to the garage and have it checked by a mechanic. Be damned if he would do it for her. It was her car and her responsibility.

He switched on the radio and was immediately slapped with voices arguing about abortion rights. A local talk radio station. He changed the dial to a jazz station and pushed back in the leather seat. Art Tatum was a tonic. Unfortunately, he was too distracted by the possibility of seeing Bryan to enjoy the music. And thinking about Bryan brought Harvey to mind. He had gone out of his way to protect Emily. He should invite Harvey out to dinner.

Chapter 27

Thursday Evening, May 23.

Harvey Gold insisted that Jack come to his place for dinner rather than eat out. At seven o'clock, Jack followed Harvey up the steps to the apartment above the Bagel Shack. The place was filled with rich aromas of spices and herbs.

"Two bedrooms, a living room, dining area, and kitchen. What do you think? I designed it myself."

"Very nice, Harvey." He glanced around at the sparse furnishings as Harvey led him into the living room. The living room contained a green velvet sofa, a brown recliner to the left, and a television. Next to the chair was a small table with a strange looking black leather box with ribbons and a worn copy of the *Torah*. He leaned down to study the leather object closer.

"You never see one of those before, Jack?"

"No. What is it?"

"That is what we call a tefillin. I tie it to my left arm during prayers. It is quite old." He handed it to Jack and tapped on the top. "The box contains quotations of Hebrew scriptures written on small pieces of paper. Here. I show you how it works."

Stalker

Harvey took the box and laid it on his arm, wrapping the attached ribbons around until they held the box tight against his forearm. He then tied the ends securely.

"See? Now, I sit down and open my Torah each morning with a reminder that I should concentrate on the spiritual."

"Interesting. Do all Jews do that?"

"Mostly Orthodox. Ha! I do not know why I still do it, since I am a very poor worshipper. But I do it because that was how I was taught as a boy."

Harvey untied the tefillin and replaced it on the table.

"You've managed to keep it all these years?"

"No. I got it while in Dachau. I hid it until we were rescued. The person who owned it worked with me until he died of pneumonia."

"I see."

"Come! Let us not dwell on this. I have good things for us to eat and drink."

The table was neatly set for two with white linen napkins, a blue tablecloth, and plain white plates.

"Could I offer you some wine?"

"Sure."

Harvey retrieved two German-style wine glasses with green stems and a bottle of Manishevitz from the refrigerator. He placed the glasses on the table and poured. He handed one to Jack.

"Probst!"

"Probst!"

They sipped the wine. Jack's eye was attracted to a large corkboard next to the cupboard. There were clippings and photographs from old newspapers and magazines. Many were written in foreign languages. He recognized some of the people dressed in Nazi uniforms and civilian clothes.

"War criminals?"

"Ya. My little hobby. I watch for them still. You never know when one will pass through here."

"Really?"

Jack thought it was unlikely that old Nazi war criminals would be traipsing through Florida so many years after their escape from Germany. And yet, now and then you read about some of them living in places like Cleveland and Detroit.

"Oh, yes. Florida is a favorite tourist attraction of Germans. I wait and watch. One will come along some day I will recognize."

"Who would you alert, the FBI?"

"Ha!" Harvey's eyes flashed at the thought. "I have my own remedy."

"Yeah?"

Harvey went to a closet near the stairwell and pulled a brown wooden box from the top shelf. He carried it to the table and placed it in front of Jack.

"Open it, please."

Jack opened it carefully. The box gave off a mixed scent of old leather and corrosion. In it was an automatic pistol in a black leather holster on a belt.

"Pistolen-08."

"What we call a German Luger?"

"Ya! So often in factories and the camps I see officers pull them out and for no good reason shoot a Jew dead on the spot. They sometimes did it for sport, to show off."

Jack unsnapped the buckle and opened the leather flap on what he recognized as a 'hardshell' holster. He carefully removed the Luger. It contained a clip.

"How long has the magazine been in here?"

Harvey shrugged. "1949? 1950? I loaded it after coming to America, but I never shoot it."

Jack managed to pull the clip out of the handle. It was filled with seven corroded green cartridges. He pulled the breech back. The extractor held a live shell that had been in the chamber, but would not release it. The thick corrosion in the chamber looked like blue cheese.

"How come you keep it loaded?"

"Ach! You never know!"

"I think your pistol needs a thorough cleaning and some new rounds, Harvey. If you tried to fire it, the whole thing might blow up in your hands."

"Oy vey!"

"Yeah. I'd do it soon. Too fine a weapon not to keep it clean and safe. It's worth a lot of money."

"I've thought about having it cleaned professionally."

"I'd be glad to do it for you. I could check out the firing mechanism, too."

"Ya? You know about such things?"

"I do."

"That would be kind of you. I'll pay you to do it."

"Nah! Like to do it. I notice the stripping tool is still in the holster." He removed it and held it up.

"So that is for stripping? What is stripping?"

"Taking the pistol apart. Field stripping. Each weapon has a special tool for the job."

"I see."

"Mind if I take it home with me tonight?"

"Not at all."

"Where in the world did you get it?"

"An American Army officer. He confiscated it from a German officer who was attempting to smuggle it out of Germany."

"Oh?"

"Ya. After spending a few weeks in hospital, I was offered a job by the Americans. I worked as a translator at a refugee processing center up in the mountains above Strasburg."

"Wow!"

"What made me important to the Americans was the fact I had spent five years in various concentration camps—Birkenau, Treblinka, Dachau– and could recognize some of the worst Nazis on sight."

"Really?"

"Ya. Really!"

"How come you were in different camps?"

"Who knows? Sometimes it was to keep us away from the Russians late in the war. Other times, they open a new factory and need strong men like me."

"You are amazing, Harvey."

"So, I worked with OSS from 1945 until September 1946."

"Intelligence."

"Ya. I worked under a lieutenant colonel named James Wafford. A really nice man. He'd give me oranges and coffee from the Commissary, which you could not buy on the economy. I understand he was murdered back in the fifties by a German."

"No kidding."

Harvey laughed. "You think I am kidding?"

"I'm sorry. No. It's just that I never would have suspected."

Jack slipped the Luger into its holster, placed the magazine next to it, and closed the box.

"No. You wouldn't have. But that is my story. Colonel Wafford made sure I had papers for the Pistolen. I had no trouble bringing it to America."

"When you were up on the mountain, did you ever catch any of the more notorious criminals?"

Harvey reached for a dishcloth and leaned against the counter.

"Oh, sure. But they would not be what you call 'household names' here in the states. I once identified three who worked for Dr. Mengele. You know of Dr. Josef Mengele?"

"The guy who performed all those horrible medical experiments, such as trying to see whether people could survive on seawater and the like?"

"Ya. He killed thousands."

He nodded at the bulletin board.

"That is Dr. Mengele."

The largest photograph in the center of clippings showed a dark man in a suit and tie. He had wide-set eyes and an unusual space between his front teeth. Jack guessed his age at 35 or so.

"I was nearly one of his guinea pigs. The only thing saving me was my strength. Most of my friends who became exhausted from the heavy labor were sent to Mengele. Anyway, I identified three of his assistants who were tried and convicted. They are serving life sentences."

"As I recall, Mengele himself was never caught."

Harvey went to the oven and turned it off. He used the dishcloth to remove a baking pan sizzling with brown meat. He spooned meat, potatoes, onions, and gravy onto the two plates.

"Mengele is believed living in South America. Possibly Brazil or Paraguay. He of all people I would personally like to kill. I would give anything to use that Pistolen on him."

"Well, you picked a good weapon to shoot him with."

"Ha! I would not want him to get off so easy… I would use the butt to beat him to death slowly… But enough of this. Let's sit down and enjoy our supper. I hope you like veal and potatoes."

"Very much."

Harvey poured more wine and handed it to Jack.

"To your daughter Emily! May she enjoy a long and happy life."

"To Emily."

They raised their glasses and drank the wine.

"God and I have had so many conversations, arguments and prayers over the years… I only have one prayer left that I can think makes sense… If you will join me."

Harvey reached out his hand and Jack took it. They bowed their heads.

"Dear God… May thy will be done. Amen."

"Amen."

"Now, please sit."

Harvey poured more wine. They sat down across from one another and began to eat in silence, the German Luger in its box still on the end of the table.

Chapter 28

Later Thursday Evening, May 23.

"You won't believe this, Jack," Bernice said excitedly as she stepped into the studio for the first time in years. Jack glanced at the cigarette in her hand.

"Oh, sorry," she said, backing away. "I'll put it out." She reappeared without cigarette, looking contrite and nervous.

"Have a seat." Jack pointed to the sofa.

"It's that boy..." said Bernice in a low voice. "I came out of the Ellis Building to get in the car to come home. Charley Brooks was with me. I looked across the street and there he was."

"What time?"

"An hour ago, maybe? Charley and I stopped at the Flamingo for a drink. He's signing a long term contract with me to handle his advertising."

"What was he doing?"

"Bryan?"

"Yeah."

"Leaning against his bike. He had on a knapsack. Looked absolutely terrible."

"In what way?"

"Unkempt hair. Unshaved. He was filthy. He seemed surprised when he saw me."

"What did he do?"

Bernice threw out her arms from her sides. "Hopped on his bike and trundled off. He might have looked back once is all."

"Let's see..." Jack sat back in the swivel chair, locating the Ellis Building in his mind. "The cross streets are..."

"Church and East Main," Bernice responded, crossing her legs.

"Church runs through to Seagate... Near where he lives."

"Coincidental?"

"Probably. He was on his way home and spotted my car. Decided to wait 'til I came out so he could play his game with me. Instead, you showed up. It probably shook him up as much as it did you."

Bernice put her hand on her heart. "It really gave me a fright, Jack. Even with Charley there."

"He's got us all conditioned. Sometimes, just the thought of him sends a chill down my back. What direction was he headed when you last saw him?"

"Toward Seagate."

Bernice got up and went over to the Nam photos on the wall. "Still have the same pictures up, I see."

She leaned in closely and examined the one of the patrol preparing to go on a search and destroy mission.

"So many young faces. Which did you say made it?"

"The three guys on the front row, left side."

"My word," she whispered, putting a hand to her cheek. She turned back to him. The front door slammed. Emily burst through the doorway, looking from one face to the other.

"Hi, guys. What's up?"

"Your mother spotted Bryan across the street from the Ellis Building tonight."

"Not cool! What did you do, Mom?"

Bernice walked to Em and lifted her shoulders in a shrug. "Nothing. I got into your father's car. Bryan hopped on his bike and was gone."

"Weird."

Jack slid a thick envelope across the desk toward Em and Bernice. "This was waiting for me when I got home."

Em picked up the envelope. "It's addressed to you."

"Yeah," Jack responded, pulling his arms back and lacing his fingers at the back of his head. "He's received my letter to his mother and a copy of the Order to Show Cause. You might say he's a little peeved with me..."

Em read through the pages, handing them one at a time to Bernice.

"Oh my God," exclaimed Em. "He says he didn't do any of the stuff mentioned in the court papers. It's like... he's in his own little world. We've got proof of what he's done. He admits it in his own letters."

"All the obscenities," Bernice whispered. "This is so filled with hate. I don't care to read anymore of it. It's all the same crazy stuff repeated over and over." She dropped the pages on the desk and clutched Em's arm in hers. "I don't see how you've stood up under all this."

She pulled Emily close.

"It hasn't been so bad. Between all my friends and you guys, I feel pretty safe."

"Would you like to share a Coke?"

Em looked from Bernice to Jack with a puzzled face. "Yeah. Sure."

"I'll take this letter and your new notes over to Suzanne tomorrow," Jack said as he put Bryan's letter back in the envelope. "She can send an addendum to the court papers and include the latest rhetoric. I'm sure Judge Donaldson will be amused."

Bernice and Em went into the kitchen.

"Can I get something for you, Jack?" Bernice called out.

"Just a glass of ice water. I'm going to develop some film. I'll be in the lab." The sweetness and light of Bernice was almost too much to bear. Miss Domesticity herself. He was heading toward the lab when the phone rang. "Hello?"

"This is Ed Mumford, Jack. The general's uptight and wants to know whether you'd change your mind and help us out this weekend. Two senators and some congressmen are flying in tomorrow. We need you here..."

"Any other time, I'd come. You know me, Ed. I don't shirk responsibility. But I have to deal with a predator here."

"Suit yourself, Jack. Enjoy your weekend."

He hung up. Enjoy your weekend? The bastard thought he was making this up. No. That wasn't it. Mumford called knowing he would turn him down. Now, he could write another report to the general noting that Major Jack Kaufman was being most uncooperative. The second strike against him.

Em came in with the ice water. "Who was on the phone? Not the dark phantom, I hope."

"My boss, Colonel Mumford. He wanted me to do him a favor."

"Are you?"

He took a sip of water before setting the glass down. "No. I can't."

Her face brightened. "Guess who I spoke with at school today?"

"I don't know... Who?"

"Bryan's parole officer. Sally Brand. We met in the counselor's office."

The image of Sally and Em together caused a warm sensation in his chest. "How'd you like her?"

"Really a neat lady. I liked her a lot."

"What did she ask you? Start at the beginning. Tell me everything."

"She told me how impressed she was with the log stuff."

"Good."

"She questioned me about Bryan's behavior when we dated."

"Yeah? And what did you tell her?"

"I said we'd held hands. He tried to kiss me, but I didn't let him. That's about it... And, oh, she asked if I'd be comfortable testifying against Bryan in an open hearing."

"And are you?"

"I think so. She explained what the judge would ask me... I feel better knowing what will be coming down, you know?"

"Always nice to know what's ahead. How long did you talk?"

"Fifteen minutes or so... Know what she told me?"

"No."

"She wanted to be an actress when she was in high school."

"Interesting. How come she didn't pursue it?"

"Her dad was a police officer in Miami. He was killed by a teenager high on drugs."

"Oh?"

"She said that changed her whole life. She was sixteen when it happened."

"Too bad."

"Yeah. She said she knew she would have to find a profession where she could help kids. She chose to become a juvenile probation officer. Graduated from Florida. Said her first job was in Jacksonville."

"How long has she been here?"

"Six years."

"Does she have children of her own?"

"I don't think so. She didn't talk about being married. There were no rings on her finger."

"Maybe you ought to consider photojournalism... You're so observant and a good listener."

"Never know, Dad. With all you taught me, I'd enjoy interviewing people and taking their pictures. Like, it's fascinating to me how Sally's father's death instantly changed her whole outlook on life, you know what I mean? I love to talk to people like her who have something meaningful to say."

"Gives you a deeper perspective on acting, too."

"For sure. Well, good night, Dad."

"Good night. Sleep tight. Don't let the bedbugs bite."

He entered the lab feeling mellow, warmed by Sally's sharing with Em. She had reached out and snagged another admirer.

Chapter 29

Friday Morning, May 24.

"I thought you were against having guns in the house."

"This is a vintage World War II German Luger, Em, one of the classic pistols ever made. I'm cleaning it for Harvey."

Parts of the weapon lay strewn across the workbench on newspaper. Em picked up several small pieces, examining them closely before putting them down.

"Why does Harvey keep it?"

"He thinks he might use it if a Nazi war criminal shows up."

"Harvey's too nice to kill somebody."

"Given the situation, you never know."

Chuck's car roared up to the curb.

"See you, Dad!"

"See you…"

He wondered what she would think if she knew he had bought a Colt .45 and had it stashed in his raincoat. He ran a cleaner back and forth in the barrel, eyed it, and began reassembling the Luger. Unlike many he had seen, this one had hardly been used. Its owner must have been lucky and had a desk job throughout the war.

He had gone to The Arsenal just after breakfast and bought a box of new 9 mm. cartridges and turned in the corroded bullets for disposal. He loaded all three clips and placed two of the magazines in their leather pockets. The third clip he placed in the wooden box rather than back into the Luger. He did not want Harvey to accidentally fire the weapon. At least now Harvey could either beat hell out of the war criminals or else shoot them without blowing himself sky high. He replaced the stripping tool in the holster.

He slid the Luger into the its case and buckled it. He hoped Harvey would not mind that he had made arrangements with Sam at The Arsenal to test the Luger and give Harvey a quick lesson in how to fire it. According to Sam, the "G" marking on the weapon indicated it was made in 1935. When Sam saw the Luger, his mouth watered. He was willing to buy it on the spot. He had immediately checked out the marking and serial number in one of his many gun books and was amazed that the Luger was practically in mint condition. If Harvey were wise, he would sell the damned thing to Sam and be rid of it.

Chapter 30

Saturday, May 25.

Jack was sitting in the Bagel Shack with Bill Winters and Harvey Gold having coffee and cherry blintzes.

"You hear about the Russian deserter," asked Winters.

Jack and Harvey shook their heads negatively.

"On the television this morning. Seventy-four years old. He'd hidden in a pigsty 41 years."

"Oy vey!"

"The poor guy's wife brought food to him until she died last week."

"Really?"

"He came out because he was starving. Can you believe a guy would hole up in a pigsty 41 years? Oh, by the way, Schnecky is…"

Harvey touched his sleeve and pointed out the window. Bryan Cutler pulled up at the door on his bike. Jack barely recognized him. His hair was long and uncombed. Bloodshot eyes. And his black shirt and pants looked like he had slept in them a week.

"Talk about somebody living in a pigsty…" Jack muttered.

"Looks like a damned bum," Winters commented.

"I never see him looking like this," said Harvey, tapping his finger on the table.

Bryan looked in the window for a second, turned abruptly, and pumped his bike into movement, heading east on Magnolia.

"How does he know where I am," Jack asked.

"The guy's got radar," said Winters, watching Bryan disappear around a corner. "I'm convinced of it."

"You started to say something about Corporal Schneck."

"Ah. Schnecky. Yeah. I was about to say he visited the hatchery and talked with Jim Gable. He couldn't verify any flats of fertilized eggs were missing. However, it would have been a cinch for Cutler to ride over there and get some. Seems they stack the crates of dead embryos on the freight platform overnight. A truck hauls them to a rendering plant every morning."

"He'd have to know they were there," Jack said. "Any record he ever worked for Gable?"

"Nah. Schnecky checked the full and part-timers. They hire some kids over sixteen. Gable's never heard of Bryan Cutler."

"No other hatcheries around here?"

"There's one up river ten or so miles from here. I don't see Cutler going ten miles to steal eggs. Only explanation I can figure is the Biology instructors at Ocean High and at the college use fertilized eggs for dissecting in their classes. Cutler coulda found some stored right on campus. He wouldn't have to bike out to Grable's."

Harvey nodded. "Ya. More likely"

"Is it worth investigating," Jack asked, realizing some missing eggs in the Biology lab wouldn't prove anything.

"Not unless it happens again, which I don't see Cutler repeating. Right now, he's enjoying pulling our strings by random acts of stupidity. I'd check your car to see he hasn't slashed your tires. I wouldn't be the least surprised if you come home some night and find roofing nails all over your driveway."

"Why is he resorting to petty stuff?"

Winters scratched his chin. "We've got him confused. His target, Emily, is surrounded by people who are willing to protect her. The cruisers and foot patrol have pretty much kept him scared. He gets served with court papers. He's unsure how to get at Emily. So he gets at her indirectly by dumping a dead rat in her boyfriend's car and egging her father's boat. I'd say he's biding his time, trying to figure his next big step."

Harvey and Jack gazed at one another, knowingly.

"One of his letters threatened to sue me... for violating his freedom."

"So much bullshit," said Winters. "Oh, before I forget it, I have word through the grapevine that you'll be getting a court date in your mail today."

"How soon are we scheduled?"

"Next Thursday. It was the best Donaldson could do."

"I appreciate it, Bill"

Winters pushed his chair back as if to rise and stopped like he was struck by an idea. "The jerk's letters mention a gal named Jean. Does the name ring a bell with either of you?"

Harvey shrugged. "Lots of Jeans I know."

"I asked Em about that," said Jack. "She doesn't have a clue."

"He says he works with her. Any ideas who would hire Cutler?" Harvey and Jack shook their heads negatively.

"I figure it must be a packing or fabricating place. Maybe an electronics plant or a supply house. I'm having Schnecky and Nelson come up with a list. Who knows? Maybe this gal Jean is in greater danger than Emily right now."

Chapter 31

Sunday Afternoon, May 26.

Sam locked the front door to The Arsenal and took Harvey and Jack back to the range.

"Lou," Sam said, "this is Mr. Gold, the man who owns the Luger. Could you check it out for safety? It hasn't been fired since World War II. And you remember Mr. Kaufman?"

"Sure." They shook hands. "Nice to meetcha, Mr. Gold."

Lou opened the brown wooden box.

"Never seen one of these boxes."

Lou unbuckled the holster and removed the Luger.

"Wow! That's a real beauty."

He checked the open magazine chamber, pulled the breech back, checked the tension, examined the extractor, slid the breech forward, and clicked the trigger.

"Tension's fine. Don't need no new springs. Truly a beauty."

"Wouldn't want to sell it, would you," asked Sam. "That there weapon is worth considerable money to a collector. I'd give you top book dollar for it."

Harvey shook his head. "No. I keep it."

Lou checked each of the three loaded clips, removing the eight rounds and examining the springs.

"Magazines are fine. Did a good job, Mr. Kaufman. She's ready to fire."

"Since I'm the one who cleaned it, I ought to be the one testing it," Jack replied. "I read where these can malfunction from time to time." "Only with dirt or corrosion," said Lou. "There shouldn't be any problem with this one. They're supposed to last at least a 100 years."

"That so? Hadn't heard that one before," Jack responded.

"Better put on the muffs," Sam said, pointing to the four pairs resting on pegs.

Jack put on the ear protectors and took the Luger and clip to the firing room. He slipped in the magazine, snapped it in place, and loaded the first round in the chamber. He lifted his arm high and slowly dropped it over the target. The sound of the explosion was different from the Colt .45, yet the recoil felt similarly solid. He liked the alignment of arm, pistol, and target: totally straight. He repeated the process eight times before dropping his arm.

"Now it's your turn, Harvey. Lou will show you how to do it."

Lou retrieved the target.

"I'm surprised," said Lou. "Not as good as with the .45, but better'n 99% of the shooters that come here. Seven bull's-eyes and one in the eight ring. Most do better with the Luger than with a Colt."

"It felt really fine," said Jack.

"Come over here, Mr. Gold. I'll give you some tips on safety as I show you how to shoot."

Sam beckoned to Jack.

"Got somethin' I wanna show ya."

Jack followed to where Sam unlocked a glass case.

"This here's a favorite with criminals. Just came in… It's called the MAC 10."

He lifted what appeared to be a machine pistol from the case and laid it on the counter.

"Ever see one of these?"

"No."

"That pan fills up with heavy slugs. It can fire 1200 of 'em every minute. It can destroy a concrete wall in seconds."

"Jeez! You're kidding!"

"No, sir. I'm not. Like to buy one?"

"Probably not today… Do you think you'll have customers for it?"

"Oh, yes. They're selling big in Miami. Ya only have ta fill out a form, pay the price plus $200 tax, and you got maximum pertection."

"And they're legal to own?"

Legal to own, yes siree bob!"

Chapter 32

Monday Morning, May 27.

Jack awoke early and went for a jog. There was good air at 12 to 15 knots. The refinishers were coming again today to put the final coat of sealant on the deck of QT2. They were doing a great job, he thought. Oh, to be sailing again! When he got home, there was a message from Harvey to call him.

"Harvey?"

"Morning, Jack. I wanted to know whether you would like to go over to The Arsenal with me after lunch?"

"Any other time I would, but the guys are finishing up the new boat deck today. I've got to be there. Why? Something important?"

"Ach, no. I feel a desire to become good pistol shot. That is all. I want to go there and practice today..."

"You liked it, then?"

"What do you mean?"

"You like the feel of it when the gun goes off?"

"Ya... I suppose I do... I hadn't thought of that... Strange, isn't it?"

"What?"

"I feel now the power of a Nazi!"

"Yeah. That is strange, Harvey."

"See you."

Jack also had a strange feeling. Yeah, he thought, anybody could become a Nazi with a Luger in his hands…

Chapter 33

Saturday Evening, June 1.

There had been no sign of Bryan since he showed up at the Bagel Shop the previous Saturday. Given his seedy appearance, there was speculation that he was staying high and could be dangerous. But every effort by Ocean City and Seagate police failed to locate his whereabouts.

Meanwhile, Em's senior play, "Autumn Drums" opened Thursday night to a full house. The Friday performance was even better. The final night of the play, Saturday, the Civic Center was packed to overflowing despite a vicious thunderstorm. Practically the whole city was there. The cast responded by giving its best performance, Jack thought. Em had nailed her big scene with superb underplaying of her character, using subtlety and nuance in ways he hadn't noticed before. The final curtain brought everyone to a standing ovation. There were seven curtain calls.

Jack felt like the proudest parent on earth. Bernice was so excited she turned and embraced him. The fire whistle sounded. Five times. Everyone laughed and applauded more, thinking the whistle was the firemen's tribute to the players just like they did when Ocean City took the regional football championship two years ago. Jack and Bernice went backstage to congratulate Em.

Another storm was moving over. Loud thunder rolled and cracked and shook the building.

It was a mob scene. Harvey had managed to get to Em and was giving her a big hug. Standing next to Harvey was Sally. She looked so different out of uniform. The white silk blouse accentuated her beauty, making her face and shoulders smaller somehow. She was saying something to Em as they approached.

"Thanks," Em said, waving to her parents. "Sally, have you met my Mom?"

Sally glanced at Jack and then at Bernice.

"This is Sally Brand, Mom. Sally, this is Bernice."

The two smiled politely and grasped hands momentarily. Jack felt self-conscious in a strange way. Bernice and Sally seemed to be sizing each other up.

"We so appreciate all your help, Sally," Bernice said, using her very best Bette Davis business voice.

"Wish I could do more," Sally replied softly.

"What a wonderful performance, darling," Bernice exclaimed in her Bacall voice, turning her full attention to Em. They hugged. Bernice planted a lipstick kiss on Em's cheek. She whispered something in Em's ear.

"Super play," Sally said to Jack while watching Em. "Super gal. She's total magic on stage."

"Her passion," he added, smiling as Em winked at him.

Em reached a hand out towards Jack. He grabbed it. She pulled him to her. He kissed her on the cheek.

"You nailed it again, kid!"

"Ya think so?" Her face was full of emotion. Her heavy make-up could not hide tear-rimmed eyes.

"Yeah. I know so."

She embraced him again. "I love you so much, Dad."

They both knew it was all coming to an end. An important, wonderful time of their lives had come to a close with the final curtain. Twelve years of rehearsals, plays, musicals, dance lessons, music lessons, modeling. Hundreds of chats over hot chocolate and tea about interpreting characters, fictional and real. Pretending they were buccaneers sailing a pirate ship. Walks along the beach at daybreak. Thousands of miles driving her back and forth, listening to her latest happenings. Hundreds of performances where he stood bursting with pride. And now, it was over. The home town, friends, Dad and Mom, would recede into the background, a memory of what once was and could not be again–ever.

It was all Jack could do to hold back the tears. He already felt bereft. He had lost her to the world. She no longer belonged to him. Truth was, you didn't own a child. You were given the gift of sharing her life for a while, nurturing her, helping her grow, until she becomes a lovely creature. And like a beautiful, precious butterfly, she flies away.

"You'll always nail whatever you do," he said, searching to find words that were safe. He realized many people were waiting to see her. "I'd better step back and let you enjoy all your admirers."

He pulled away. David embraced Em and they held one another, rocking from side to side. She in her lovely blue gown and he wearing an 1860's Rhett Butler suit with vest. Sally had disappeared in the crowd. He and Bernice made their way toward Chuck, who had been transformed into a dashing cavalry officer with red sash and sword and fake mustache.

Stalker

"Is Harvey Gold here," called a loud voice Jack recognized as Mr. Enright's.

"Here," cried Harvey from across the hall, waving an arm above the crowd.

"You have an emergency telephone call," Enright shouted. "Come to the office at the front of the theater."

Harvey brushed past, a look of uncertainty on his face. Jack could not imagine the nature of the emergency. Harvey had no relatives. No ties, unless it was an employee who needed help. Perhaps there was a break-in.

After Jack and Bernice had congratulated the cast and were about to leave, they overheard someone mentioning Harvey. "Yeah, Harvey's Bagel Shack," the voice said.

It was Jake Timmons, the tire dealer, talking to Dave's father.

"Bad," asked Dave's father.

"Don't know," answered Jake. "Thought I'd drive up and see."

Jack approached. "What's this about Harvey's shop?"

"A fire," said Jake. "His place is on fire. Probably lightning."

Jack grabbed Bernice's arm. They hurried to his car. The night was pitch black. The rain had stopped. The air was cooler. A low rumbling of thunder came from over the ocean, followed by brief orange flashes of lightning against dark purple clouds.

He took a shortcut through Wesley Beach subdivision and pulled out on Seacliff Boulevard. Ahead, flashing red and blue lights reflected off the wet asphalt. They parked and walked to the scene. There were probably two hundred people watching from across the street at the high school. They edged close to the crowd standing next to a red pumper. The sidewalk was cordoned off, and an auxiliary policeman was keeping people back.

The building seemed okay. All the lights were on. He saw Harvey and firemen inside. Chief Jenkins and Morley, the fire inspector, were talking with Harvey. No signs of smoke. Searchlights on the pumper and another engine played moving circles of light on the roof. He could hear other trucks and activity behind Harvey's in the alley.

"Was it a fire or just a false alarm," he asked a bystander he did not recognize.

"They got it out. A fire in the back storage room, they say."

"Anybody hurt?"

"None I know of."

"Good." He took Bernice's hand. "Come on."

They went back down the street to the drive-through at Kessler's Dry Cleaners and entered the alley. They ventured in a little way and saw that the alley was cordoned off several hundred feet away from Harvey's. A bolt of lightning flashed, followed by booming thunder and it began to rain.

"Might as well go home, Bernice. Nothing we can do except get soaked." They dashed for the car and made it just before the sky opened and a heavy downpour pelted the roof and windows. There was no point in trying to drive until the heavy rain subsided. Bernice took a tissue from her purse and patted her hair and forehead lightly. She checked her make-up in the lighted mirror behind the visor. He watched her apply fresh lipstick, wondering why she was so fastidious about how she looked when there was no one to impress.

"Are you thinking what I'm thinking, Jack?"

"Yup. It's too coincidental. The whole town was at the Civic Center. Perfect time for Bryan to commit another act of revenge."

She pressed a tissue to her lips, removing the excess lipstick and checking the results in the mirror.

"Can't the police do anything?" She slipped the lipstick into her purse and switched off the mirror light.

"Sally says Seagate Police pulled Bryan in for questioning about the dead rat in Chuck's car. He denied having anything to do with it. They had to let him go."

"She's very pretty," Bernice said, pulling a cigarette from her purse. "Oh, I forgot... Sorry."

She replaced the cigarette in the pack and put it in her purse. The sudden downpour had stopped. She looked at him as he started the car and pulled out.

"Did you hear what I said?"

"I was thinking of Em...how beautiful she was tonight," remembering Sally and Em talking together backstage. "You're right. She is pretty."

"You don't see hair like that every day."

"No, you don't."

He looked straight ahead, feeling Bernice's eyes studying him.

Chapter 34

Sunday, June 2.

"My enemies call this 'Jewish lightning'," exclaimed Harvey, throwing out a hand toward the burned out storage room. "I do not need insurance money so bad that I would do such a thing to myself... Still, some will wonder."

Jack ducked under the yellow police tape, walked amongst the sodden ashes and peered inside the gutted interior. There was a mound of broken glass, blackened five gallon cans, charred roof shingles, burnt timbers, and large piles of darkened flour.

"Arson instead of lightning?"

Harvey squatted down, showing Jack the flash point, an area just inside the door.

"It is so hot, you see, it turns these blocks almost to dust. This is where fire begin... Fire Inspector Morley believes a person broke the lock, poured olive oil on the floor from one of those cans, added kerosene to it, and, puff, a big fire he start."

"Bryan?"

Harvey nodded. "Ya."

"But why? What have you ever done to Bryan?"

Harvey pushed against his knees and stood. He wiped a thick forearm across his mouth in disgust. "Ach! You want to know the truth?"

"Sure."

"Bryan calls me one night not long ago. Wednesday, it was. I can tell the man is drunk. I don't recognize his voice. I say, 'Who is this?' He answer, 'I thought we were friends. You turn against me... like all the rest.' I still am not sure because the voice is unsteady. I ask, 'Is this Bryan Cutler I am speaking with?' He replies, 'Yes, you Goddamned Jew. I hate you, you fuck'n Jew! ' So I ask, 'Why, Bryan? Why do you hate me?' And he answers, 'You protect that bitch. You hate me. I've seen you hanging out in the parking lot. Watching out for me. You are a kike turncoat. I hate all you Jews!' That is what Bryan say to me."

"You tell Bill Winters? File a report?"

Harvey leaned against the blackened wall, realized what he had done and pulled away, brushing the seat of his pants. "Words? What are words to me? They mean nothing. I am used to far worse insults. There's nothing I should report."

"Still, it's another bit of evidence." Jack pointed to the ashes. "A report on file together with this makes a pretty convincing case against Bryan."

Harvey was not listening. He was gazing at a broken hinge attached to the charred doorframe. He took his fingers and turned it slowly back and forth as though learning how it worked for the first time. He stopped and turned. His eyes were filling.

"Except... you know Jack, when Bryan used those ugly words... they are like knives stabbing me. It hurt like hell. It is like God is punishing me for not helping Bryan."

"Did you know he was anti-Semitic?"

"Never! He was always polite. I do not believe in his heart that he hates Jews. He once gave me a present at Hanukkah. I sometimes would tell him stories about Jewish holidays. We would sit together at table and I would tell him about Mesada and how I talk to God every day. He would ask me questions and sometimes want me to repeat stories I have told him...." Harvey nudged broken bottles in the ashes with his foot. "I am thinking about these things all night when I go to bed. I think someone else set this fire. Then, I remember Bryan's anger and know it is he..."

"It's a wonder it didn't catch the whole place up."

"You see here?" Harvey pointed to crumbled materials along the wall nearest the kitchen. "I double insulate the storage room. Almost like ice house, it is. Maintains almost same temperature summer and winter. The insulation I put here saved my restaurant, Morley says."

Harvey shrugged his shoulders. "Ach. You don't mind I do some work while we talk?"

"No, not at all."

They entered the back door into the kitchen, and Harvey poured two cups of coffee. He handed one to Jack. Jack sat on a stool watching as Harvey put on his white apron and set about preparing for the day. He noticed Harvey was moving about in slow motion, like a zombie, without his usual energy. He suspected Harvey felt today like Jack had been feeling lately, defeated and saddened by what Bryan had done to him. Mary and the new kid, Alex, were already making salads and slicing lunchmeats.

"I'm sorry I got you into this, Harvey. You don't deserve any more grief in your life."

"This," he pointed a thumb over his shoulder, "is nothing. I am lucky. I have still a nice bagel shop. No smoke damage. Some water damage here and there. It is nothing. No problem. A little higher flames and maybe the roof of my apartment catch fire. Then, I wouldn't be so lucky. The whole place would burn up. No more shop. Kaput!"

"It's like he wanted to make a point without totally destroying you."

Harvey scratched his chin. "Yes. Morley agrees. He could just as well have broken the kitchen lock and done the same here. Made one helluva fire with these wood walls."

Jack finished the coffee as Harvey started up a large mixer and poured in the contents from a plastic bucket. "See you, Harvey," Jack shouted over the noise of the machine. "Thanks for the coffee!"

He went out the back door, stopped and looked at the ruins of the storage house. Bryan was still crying for help, being careful not to do something that would get him into worse trouble. He was walking a fine line, but it was only a matter of time before he stepped over it and would not be able to pull back.

Chapter 35

Wednesday, June 5.

Bryan Cutler evidently remained in hiding or had fled elsewhere. It was as though a good genie had come along and magically swept Bryan away to some distant land where he could not do anyone harm. Em, Bernice and Jack sensed it was a calm before the storm. So did Sally and Bill. Yet, everyone was feeling lighter, enjoying the respite.

Em was busy attending one party after another. Guys of all ages were calling her and leaving messages, wanting dates.

Bernice softened. She took stickers off several items throughout the house, including Jack's favorite box of chess pieces and an inlaid chessboard he had bought in Japan. She decided Em should have whatever she wanted from the house. Jack could not have been more pleased.

Harvey speculated that Bryan and his mother had gone to stay permanently with an uncle in Jacksonville. Sally wasn't buying it. She had confirmed with the landlord that Adelia Cutler continued paying rent and that their personal belongings were still in the apartment.

Jack invited Sally to lunch at Marco's, a popular eatery specializing in Cuban sandwiches. To his delight, she accepted. As he drove down Church Street toward the restaurant, he felt a keen sense of elation. He was not sure why he had asked her... or was it that he did not want to admit how much he was attracted to her. He pulled into the parking lot. She was there, sitting in her car dressed in uniform. He swung in next to her, came around to her door and opened it for her. She got out and extended her hand. He held it. Her face was serious.

"Is this about Bryan," she asked as he let go of her hand.

He attempted to be nonchalant. "Not really. We haven't seen or heard from him since the last letter I sent over. No, I just wanted to share lunch with a pretty lady."

"A nice surprise." She seemed pleased.

"In or out?"

She beckoned to a corner table on the patio. "Out."

"Do you realize it is the hottest day on record—99 degrees—and you want to eat outside?"

She grinned. "I like it hot."

"I guess I do too," he said sheepishly.

They ordered and sat beneath a red and white umbrella advertising dry Vermouth.

"This is special," she said, a mischievous smile playing about her mouth and green eyes. "Not often I get taken out by a handsome photographer. In fact," she licked her lips, "this is my very first time."

A big smile broke involuntarily across Jack's face. "Me, too. I've never been out with a probation officer before."

Her face turned a bit serious. "I've been talking with the detectives about Bryan this morning..."

"Oh?"

"They've been wanting to question him about the fire. He's in hiding. They're laying odds he won't show up for the court hearing tomorrow."

"How come? He claims in his letters I'm the one at fault."

"It would interrupt his fantasy life... Bring him into reality for a few minutes. He doesn't want that. Lieutenant Maynard is working with Bill Winters to figure some way to pick him up for psychiatric observation. They're hoping Bryan will show at the courthouse so they can provoke a scene and cause him to react."

"You mean, cause Bryan to do something dumb?"

She leaned in close and whispered. "That's the plan. You're not supposed to know it, so I didn't tell you. I just thought you'd like to know."

He could smell her warm scent, fresh and clean. A bit of swelling, whiter skin with orange freckles showed at the top of her open khaki shirt. He wanted her to stay close to him. She moved away slowly.

"Anything I should do?"

She pressed a hand to his wrist. "Ignore any police presence and stay clear of Bryan. Let our guys and Winters do their thing." She patted his wrist. "Enough business. Let's talk about something pleasant..."

"Like what?" She had a special gleam in her eyes. Jack looked away, thinking that was how the couple at Harvey's looked the other night. He should not feel like that. He was still married.

"Like, tell me how you raised such a wonderful girl."

"She is, isn't she?" He pushed back his chair so he could stretch his feet. "We've been very close from the time she was born."

"It shows. You've given her confidence and a terrific sense of who she is... I can't imagine a more together teenager."

"You have kids?"

Sally looked toward the orange stucco and blue doorframe. "Always wanted some... Seems like my career took me in another direction."

"Em told me about your father. How his death changed your goals."

"I've never been sorry for my decision. Every day I honor my father's memory by trying to keep kids from shooting up and killing somebody."

"I admire that, Sally. I can't imagine a more worthy calling. So... you never married?"

"No. When Dad died, I had to take care of Mom. She had Parkinson's disease from the time I was eleven or twelve. After Dad was gone, I had to pitch in."

"You went to work?"

"Yeah. I worked after school. We lived in a big ole three-story house, so we tried renting out rooms. That didn't work too well. One guy tried to rape me one night. You know how it goes. So I convinced Mom to sell it, and we moved into an apartment until I graduated from high school."

"Then what?"

"I moved Mom into a nursing home in Fort Pierce so I could go to college."

"Where?"

"University of Florida."

"And majored in Criminal Justice?"

"Psychology. I took additional courses in Criminal Justice."

"I see."

Sally leaned closer again. "You mind a personal question, Jack?"

"Shoot."

"What are your plans after your daughter goes to Spain?" She squirmed a bit in her chair. "I mean, from what I gather, you'll pretty much be able to do what you want..."

"Well," he hesitated, rather taken aback. "With Bryan on the loose, I haven't really given much thought about what I will do. I was thinking of renting out my house. I figure I can live on my sailboat, once I set up a dark room. That way, I could have additional income. It'll be cramped, but I can manage."

"You get to keep the house, then?"

"I get to keep it until I decide to sell. Bernice will eventually get half the proceeds."

"I see."

She was definitely curious. Wheels were turning beneath that lovely flaming red hair. It was difficult for him to see her all at once... Her hair. Her green eyes. All those freckles. Her mouth. Jack's eyes wandered over her features, not knowing where to concentrate. She seemed to sense the intimacy and shifted self-consciously in her chair. She licked her lips.

"What's your boat like, aside from fertilized eggs?"

"Actually, the deck's refinished. It looks great. It's a fifty-foot ketch. Sleeping berths fore and aft. Nice galley. She's fast and reliable. Why? Are you a sailor?"

The freckles on her face seemed animated, like her eyes. "Always wanted to learn. My Dad was into sailing. He was navigator a year or so for a racing team. Never took me out, though."

"Too bad. Sailing is neat for kids."

Sally crossed her legs. Her foot began to jog in a slow rhythm. "I'll bet Em knows how to sail."

"Yeah," he acknowledged, liking how she said 'Em' instead of Emily in a natural, unforced way. "We've sailed together all her life. She got to where she could handle the boat in heavy weather... Until her acting became first priority. She hasn't sailed in a while."

"Could I invite myself on a sail with you one of these days?"

He felt a definite tingle.

"Once I get her cleaned up."

"Could I help?"

"You're the second volunteer. Bill Winters is antsy for me to take him fishing. The boat's been so neglected, I'm embarrassed to have anybody aboard."

"Bill and I can help. What needs doing?"

"I've got some heavy duty work down below."

"Like, stuff I couldn't do?"

An image of working below deck with Sally brought all kinds of fantasies to mind. They all ended up in the same double berth, both of them naked, with Jack kissing all her freckles.

"Cleaning wood, brass, fixtures, surfaces, mostly. I've got some mechanical jobs, too. I think I'll have to repair the bilge pump before I take her to sea."

"Well, I'm available if you need a first mate."

"Second?"

They laughed and gazed at each other. Their sandwiches and drinks arrived. He wanted to reach over and kiss Sally on the mouth: one of those slow, soft-turning-to-hard kisses. Taste her taste. Touch his lips to the soft white place at the nape of her neck where the freckles were gathered like tiny eggs in a nest. He hungered for her. He wanted her arms around him. God... it's been so long. Was he lusting or loving, he wondered? Whatever, it was grand.

Chapter 36

Thursday, June 6.

Em, Bernice, and Jack arrived early at court. They crossed the asphalt parking area, already hot from the morning sun. Chief Winters and a cluster of men dressed in civilian clothes stood at the bottom of the steps leading to the courthouse. At their approach, Winters turned his back to them, avoiding any opportunity to exchange greetings.

They climbed the steps and entered the foyer where the black and white marble floor caused every step to echo and voices to resonate. They went through the swinging doors and discovered most of the seats were already taken. Em glanced about. All three of them, he thought, were dreading the confrontation with Bryan. They found seats near the back. Sally was sitting in the second row. She turned and waved at them. Em and Jack waved back.

Em sat between Bernice and Jack, holding their hands. They were here as a family, he realized, united possibly for the last time. His fantasy was that the judge would somehow find a way to announce to everyone that in the pending case of Bernice Kaufman versus Jack Kaufman, the divorce was granted. He could almost hear the judge saying, 'You are forever split asunder. Lose and let go. Part now. All three of you go your separate ways, never to be joined again.'

The place was packed and noisy. His attention fell upon Sally's wavy, red hair, as though he had never seen it before. It was at once sculpted, feathery, and stunning.

A hush came over the crowd when a side door opened and the bailiff, a heavyweight with most of it hanging over his belt, announced in a loud voice, "Everyone please rise. Court is now in session. Judge Donaldson presiding..."

Judge Donaldson, looking like a tall, angular jogger in his fifties, strode across the chamber and dropped into his chair. Chief Winters said their case would be the first on the docket.

The clerk called out, "Case Number 20482-422. Emily S. Kaufman versus Bryan R. Cutler."

The clerk explained the petition to the court. The judge called Jack's name, then Em's.

"Will you both please stand and state your full names and places of residence?"

They rose. Jack stated his name and address. He felt added pressure from Em's hand as she took a deep breath and delivered her lines like the good actress she was. Her voice was clear and resonant.

"Bryan Raymond Cutler, will you please rise and state your full name and address?"

Silence. Everyone looked around. The bailiff took a step forward and searched the audience.

"Bryan Cutler, are you present in the court," the judge asked in a loud voice.

The judge whispered something to the bailiff and the clerk. The clerk waved a wad of papers she was holding. The judge nodded his head, took the papers, and addressed them.

"Miss Kaufman, can you tell us in your own words why you are here this morning?"

Em gripped Jack's hand tighter. "Yes, your honor. I am here to request you to keep Bryan Cutler away from me and my family. He's been stalking us, you know?"

"Are you frightened of him?"

"Yes, sir."

"Thank you, Miss Kaufman. Petition is granted. Mr. Cutler shall be so informed." The judge rapped his gavel. "Next case."

They slipped out of the courtroom, followed by Sally. She and Bernice conversed as they walked down the courthouse steps. At the bottom step, Sally announced she had to get back to her office. She caught Jack's eye.

"Any chance you can come by later, Jack? It's important."

"Sure."

They headed toward their car.

"Glad that's over," said Bernice, patting Em on the back. "I was very proud of you."

"Thanks, Mom."

"He's not to come within 1500 yards of the house," Jack explained. "That would keep him out of the park, too."

"It'll be so nice not to have to worry anymore. I can enjoy the graduation parties and seeing friends... feel normal again, you know?"

"I know, dear. Me, too." Bernice gave her a squeeze.

Jack wanted to think that, too. Unfortunately, there was doubt playing at the edges of his mind. Sally seemed anxious that Bryan didn't show.

Stalker

He dropped Bernice and Em off at the house and drove over to the Seagate police station. Sally was sitting in her office sorting through a stack of files. She looked up as he knocked on the doorframe. She pointed to the nearest chair.

"Come in, Jack. Have a seat."

Bryan's file lay open before her. There was no reaching out, no touching of hands. He sat and waited. She spread her freckled hands, exposing smooth, un-freckled palms. "Bryan's latest no-show has me concerned. I've got paperwork requesting he be picked up and brought in."

"Harvey believes he's gone to Jacksonville."

"Let's hope he has, but I don't think so."

"Oh?"

"I think he's here, hiding out." Freckles gathered at the corners of her pretty mouth in creased clusters. "I'm afraid Bryan's chosen the path of no return. Nobody has seen him in nearly a week."

Sally reached for a pencil. She tapped on the blotter with the eraser. He watched the rhythmic tapping. She drew in breath, expanding the shape of her breasts beneath the khaki shirt. "I got the impression from Bernice this morning that you guys think there's no more problem after the judge approved the restraining order. I hope you aren't thinking this is the end of it, are you?"

He blinked. "Wishful thinking?"

She nodded and shifted her eyes to a potted violet sitting on the corner of her desk. She reached over and plucked a dying leaf from it and twirled it between thumb and forefinger. The flat part of the leaf made a little flapping noise in the hollow of her hand. He had never seen Sally nervous before.

"Bryan's lost it. There's no doubt in my mind that he'll come after any one of you–Emily, Bernice or you. He will do violence this time... when you least expect it. You must take extra precautions. Can you find another place to stay for a few days? In Monroe or Harbor Town?"

"Is it that critical?"

She dropped the leaf into the wastebasket. "Yes."

"I guess we could make arrangements with friends."

"Can I tell you some things in strictest confidence off the record?"

"Sure."

"You won't repeat this to another soul? Not to Chief Winters or to your family?"

"You have my word."

She got up and closed the door and sat down again. She looked at him without moving a feature. Then her mouth opened slightly and she began. "You're daughter isn't the first person he's become obsessed with. Four years ago, Bryan and a friend whose name I can't share got into playing Dungeons and Dragons nights and weekends. You familiar with the game?"

"I've heard of it. How old was the girl?"

"This is a boy friend I'm talking about, not a girl."

"You mean a gay relationship?"

"No. They were just pals as far as I can tell. They got so deeply involved in the game that they played it almost continuously from Friday night 'til Sunday night. Sometimes, they'd play as much as thirty hours straight. When the friend decided he'd had enough, Bryan wouldn't let him leave. He threatened the kid unless he stayed. This happened on several weekends.

"Finally, the kid gets really frightened of Bryan and tells his parents what's going on. They try to keep Bryan from seeing their kid. He won't let the kid alone, like with Em. He stalked this boy and made more threats. When I heard about it, I didn't know much about stalkers. I sought help from social services. They put me in touch with a psychiatrist, Ann Radcliff."

"I've heard of her. She's got a book out on predators."

"Right. She was the first one to tell me Bryan could become a dangerous predator. There was one incident where he actually beat the kid up. He was arrested for assault and battery."

"How did it end?"

"Oh, it would have gone on indefinitely, except for the car accident involving another boy. That took all of Bryan's attention."

"The involuntary manslaughter conviction Bill told me about?"

She looked at him through half closed eyes, tapping her pencil on the blotter. "Let me put it this way... There are some people around here who believe it was no accident."

"God almighty!"

"Bryan knew the boy who was killed. They were the same age, went through junior high together. The police officers investigating the accident described Bryan as showing little if any remorse at the scene or later. When he was questioned, it was like nothing happened. One officer said Bryan acted like a psychopath."

"You mean he might have done it for the thrill?"

"We don't know. The investigators found no proof of any problem between the two. They had been good but not close friends through eighth grade. After that, they split. Bryan attended Ocean City High School; this other kid went to St. Francis here in Seagate. No evidence of a vendetta or grudge."

"Unbelievable!"

Sally rocked back and forth, nodding. "If you were to talk with certain officers around here, I believe they'd tell you Bryan hit the guy intentionally." She paused, tapped the pencil again. "There were no tire marks."

"Damn! How old was he?"

"Bryan?"

"Yeah."

"Sixteen. He'd just gotten his driver's license."

Jack looked at the palms of his hands as though he might find answers to all his questions in the lines and calluses.

"You couldn't have told me all this earlier?"

"No... I'm sorry. I shouldn't be telling you now..."

"Thanks... No luck locating Bryan's mother?"

"None. She's vanished. I just hope Bryan hasn't killed her. I'm checking with the Fed to see whether her Social Security checks are being cashed."

"Can't the police break into the apartment? See if she's there?"

"Until his no-show at court, we've had insufficient cause. There's a class action suit pending against the department for using excessive force against a tenant over there. You probably read about it in the papers. The chief has wanted to avoid any high profile activity unless he's got a court order. You have to remember, this is an election year."

"Yeah. So I hear..."

"As it stands, we know neither Bryan nor his mother has entered or left the apartment since last week. Jackowitz will issue an APB on Bryan as soon as he obtains a warrant. Once he gets the warrant, they'll search the apartment."

"Will they put out an All Points Bulletin on Mrs. Cutler, too?"

"I'm sure... In the meantime, you, Em and Bernice must stay away from your house and change your routines."

He looked out the window. The sunshine and new leaves on the water oak looked so inviting. He, too, wanted to escape. He would like to climb into that tree outside the window and hibernate. Take Em and Bernice up there in the thick leaves where nobody could see them.

"Your wife needs to take extra precautions. Her evening meetings make her quite vulnerable to attack."

"How'd you know about Bernice's night activities?"

Sally tilted her head, a little grin forming, pushing freckles into unusual patterns. "I had to check you and your wife out through PD. It's routine on probation complaints. I checked a little further when I found out she was divorcing you. We try to determine whether the people filing the complaints are mentally stable."

"I see."

"Something else you won't want to hear..."

"Yeah?"

"The four page letter you faxed me... the one that's barely legible where he talks of killing himself? That tells you where Bryan is right now..."

"Where?"

"He hasn't left town... He's freaked out on dope. He's sky-high some place. Probably staying within a few blocks of here... waiting to make a move."

He tried to rationalize. "Maybe the drugs have immobilized him."

Sally leaned back in her chair, pushing an index finger into her cheek. They gazed in silence at one another. She dropped her arm and shifted forward. "Our guys are trying to get a lead on who this Jean woman might be. Any ideas?"

"No. Winters has a couple of cops working that one, too." He felt helpless again. He looked at Sally for consolation. There was none. She closed Bryan's file. He got up wearily.

"I felt pretty good when the judge granted our petition... Now? I don't feel so red hot. More like I've just been kicked in the stomach again."

"I know..." Sally said, wincing. "Just don't let up. Bryan is like a wounded animal. He wants to hurt back. And he will..."

Jack recalled Harvey's words about Jack being smart enough to trap Bryan. Images of Bryan attacking him played in his mind. He blinked to clear them away. Bryan's face kept reappearing, his eyes filled with hate. "Any final words of wisdom?"

Sally reached for his hand and grasped it firmly. "Stay alert. Change your daily patterns. Move out of your house. Be watchful twenty-four hours a day. That's my advice."

"Appreciate it. I've got Reserve duty this weekend. Perhaps I can get Bernice to take Em to the cabin rather than stay at the house."

"Super. I assume Bryan doesn't know where the cabin is."

"I don't think so. It's on the river up near Adams' Crossing."

"Um... Take care."

He held her hand, feeling her warm strength before releasing it. "See you, Sally."

Chapter 37

Thursday Evening, June 6.

"You really think we have to leave the house," Bernice asked.

"Yeah. Sally says Bryan's over the brink. He'll be coming after us big time. I was thinking you guys might spend the weekend at the cabin. Next week, we can figure something more definite."

He studied Bernice. There was a strange look on her face, a bittersweet softness playing at the edges of her eyes and mouth. She took a long draw on her cigarette and blew smoke across the room, keeping her head raised in contemplation. She seemed to be struggling to tell him something. He sat down across from her. It was almost like old times, when they were close and read each other's thoughts.

"What're you thinking," he asked gently.

Her eyes narrowed and fixed upon him. There was both affection and sadness in them. She put her cigarette down. She reached across and he gave her his hand. She examined it, stroked it. A tear fell upon the back of his hand. She brushed her tears away. "Sorry," she whispered.

Jack reached across and embraced her. He was doing it without any particular emotion. She clutched him to her and cried softly against his chest. She finally pulled away and sat upright in her chair, dabbing at her face, trying to smile.

"Well! I certainly can make a spectacle of myself, can't I?"

"No problem, Bernice," he said, angry with himself for sympathizing with her.

"Excuse me for a second." She went into the kitchen and blew her nose. She returned to her chair, more composed, looking at him.

"I guess it's no secret, Jack. I do have another man in my life. You knew that, didn't you?"

She delivered the lines using her best Greer Garson sadness. Jack put elbows on knees, playing out the charade, and nodded a yes. He pretended to be Humphrey Bogart. "I figured that out a long time ago."

"His name, in case you don't know, is Michael Breslin. He's from Fort Lauderdale."

He nodded again, more surprised than he showed. He attempted to keep a game face. What could he say? The name was more than familiar. Breslin Yachts. A wheeler-dealer yacht broker down there. His name and face were everywhere: on billboards, in the yellow pages, on TV commercials. A red-faced, potbellied, gregarious, down-country type who probably started out selling used cars. His Bogart role evaporated. "How'd you meet him?"

Bernice mashed the cigarette out and lit another.

"Oh, I did some promotional pieces for the boat show three years ago. We became friends. I developed some ads. Next thing, I took the Breslin account away from Mariner Advertising."

She looked at the ashtray where she was flicking ashes deftly now, not missing her mark. "Soon, it was more than being friends."

It is funny, he thought, how honesty could connect people again. An involuntary flash of the warmth he used to have for Bernice rushed back, if just for a split second. At least she was finally being half honest with herself. He mustered appropriate words for the occasion. "I'm happy for you, Bernice. You planning to get married?"

"Mike's going through a nasty divorce right now." She threw up a hand. "Not because of me, Jack! They've been separated over four years."

He nodded.

"We'll get married eventually. Meanwhile, I'll live on one of his boats. He'll stay in his condo."

Jack reached over and took her hand and gave it a squeeze. That was the least he could do. He shifted back into his role as Humphrey Bogart, seeking the words Bogey would say in such a situation. "Thanks, Bernice, for telling me. It makes a helluva lot of difference. There's a place inside me that will always love you."

Tears trickled down her face. The sadness was mixed with equal portions of petulance and relief.

"Me, too."

They stood and embraced. The scent of tobacco smoke and perfume in her hair repelled him. He held her back from him, looking her in the eye, like Bogey might do.

"That was a brave thing... telling me. I truly respect you for it."

She gave him a hug before taking out a tissue and wiping her face. "Well, I just thought maybe we could pull together one last time for Emily's sake."

Yeah, he thought, one last time for the Gipper. "Sure."

He pretended Em had told him nothing. "Have you told her?"

"A couple months ago. I thought she might like to meet Mike and see where I plan to live."

How sweet, he thought. He kept his game face. "Has she met him?"

"No"

Jack figured the truth of the matter was that Em had been finding excuses not to meet the guy. He read Bernice's mind. "So..." he said with Bogart's tone, "I guess you plan to take her down there to meet him this weekend while I'm on Reserve duty?"

Bernice glanced up. A flutter of eyelashes said she was counting on him.

"Only if you agree," she whispered huskily.

He shrugged, wishing he had a cigarette to flick like Bogey used to do.

"Why not? When will you leave?"

"Tomorrow night? After traffic lets up? Emily doesn't have plans."

"Sure. The sooner the better."

She embraced him again, taking on an Ingrid Bergman look right out of *Casablanca*. "Thanks for being so understanding, Jack. You've always been a good man. And I know I've been terribly hateful these last months."

"I've done my share, too," he replied, looking over her shoulder, fully expecting Claude Raines to be there. "It takes two to tango."

She gave him one of her smiles that used to make him believe two people could never fall out of love. He had forgotten how pretty she could be. Her face was open, almost young again except for the crinkles around her eyes and below her chin. In her mind, she had patched things up with old Jack-the-Ripper Kaufman and was chomping at the bit to be off to see her new beau. Well, goody! All's well in Bernice's La-La-Land.

"I've got to pack," she said with finality, moving towards her bedroom. There was a new lightness in her stride.

"Fine," he lied. The lie made him grin for no apparent reason. He supposed it was the stupidity of this final charade with its false honesty and soap opera quality.

He went into the studio, leaving the door open. He felt happier than he had in a long time. And he had Bernice's transparent make-believe honesty to account for it. Not that he had any misgivings. Breslin. What was his problem? The Breslins of the world usually picked out twenty-two-year-olds for their little flings. Chain-smoking Bernice must have found a way to turn old Breslin on. The guy must be fifty-five or so. Well, that would fit. Fifty-five year old yacht impresario takes on forty-year old wine chick with nice jugs. What did Bernice have that she had not shown him? Had she come up with new tricks to make an old dog like Breslin a happy boy? 'Not nice, Jack,' he whispered through a silly smile. Maybe it was the other way around. Maybe Breslin had ways to turn Bernice on which had not occurred to him... His fantasies on that one were running wild.

He set about emptying his smaller equipment bag. He would need three cameras and several lenses for the space launch exercise. He reached for the 400mm lens on the shelf, sensing someone was nearby. He turned.

Bernice stood in the doorway. "Don't mean to bother you, Jack, but I was thinking... It might be nice if the three of us had dinner together tomorrow night before Emily and I head out. Have an early supper. Want to?"

Bernice had gone through a metamorphosis, from angry caterpillar to pretty butterfly. Her voice was soft. She looked radiant. She was warm and polite.

"Yeah," he said, dismissing her silly expression, thinking it would be special for Em. "I'd like that."

"Around six? Honey-mustard chicken on the grill?"

He smiled involuntarily. It used to be their favorite summer dinner years ago. He was willing to play the part of the cuckolded husband, content to prolong life at Dingly-Dell for Em's sake. "I'll need to see if we have any charcoal."

"Let me know. I'll shop for dinner."

She returned to her bedroom. Just like old times. He zipped up the camera case and put it next to his attaché case. It was truly a shame Bernice could not have done this months ago. He would have enjoyed playing the role of Kindly Sap married to Sugar Daddy's Sweetbuns. Still... he felt it was remarkable she did tell him even the varnished truth. He had to give Bernice a little credit.

Jack entered his bedroom. He stripped off his clothes and put on running shorts and a tank top. He laced up his running shoes and called over his shoulder, "I'm going jogging, Bernice. Be back in half an hour."

"Okay. I'll lock the door after you, so take a key."

He took a key from the top of the dresser in the hall and slipped it into his pocket. He couldn't wait to run off some of his latest frustration. Deep down, he felt jealous that Bernice would fall for a guy like Breslin. And at the same time, there was a warm and growing sense of elation, knowing Bernice had decided to confess and get off his back.

He ran down Pitcairn past Eisenhower Park, picking up a faster cadence as he watched for Bryan all the while. Hell, it was no fun running with Bryan on his mind. He turned onto Seaview and ran several blocks before turning off at Crescent and returning by the same route.

The moist, 80-degree air descending at dusk was like medicine to him, a lubricant for his muscles as well as his soul. He cut through Park Drive and crossed the soccer field, feeling lighter on his feet than he had in weeks. He swung around the chain link fence and turned the corner to Pitcairn in time to see Bill Winter's Jeep pull up in front of the house. He waved. Winters sat behind the wheel as Jack approached. Jack crouched slightly next to the open window.

"Come on in, Bill. Have a drink while I clean up," Jack said before noting Bill's dour expression. "What's up?"

Winters tapped his fingers on the steering wheel. "I'm on my way over to Seagate. Cutler raped a woman about two hours ago. He's on the loose somewhere north of Luko's Fish Packing Plant."

"Is she still alive?"

"She's lucky. Two guys fishing in the lagoon heard her screams. They shouted and Cutler took off."

"Guess I don't have to ask... Was she Jean?"

Winters nodded agreement. "Jean Weston. A student at Ocean State. She worked with Cutler at Luko's 'til Cutler was fired last Friday. He's been stalking her the past several days, apparently."

"Where is she?"

"Seagate General. She's given a statement. Talked with Seagate detectives and Jackowitz. We've got a positive ID from her and the fishermen."

"Anybody make contact with Bryan's mother?"

"Not yet. Jackie's searched the apartment on Harlan. Found all kinds of gadgets and computers. It appears both of 'em haven't

Stalker

used the place for at least a week. Seagate P.D. had it staked out. Anyway, buddy, I gotta be going. Jackie and I are having a strategy meeting with the State boys and Sheriff's office. See if we can't nab the sombitch before he strikes again."

Jack straightened, still dripping wet from running. He looked down toward the park. "Think he'll be coming this way tonight?"

"No way he can double back... He's somewhere north of the lagoon in that mess of live oaks and pine groves, more than six miles from here. If we don't get him, a moccasin will. Would you feel better if I assigned Nesbitt to guard your house?"

Jack shook his head. "No need, as long as he's that far away. We'll be fine."

"You sure? This kid's slippery, Jack. No point in taking a chance."

"We'll manage."

Bill nodded, started his Jeep, and roared down the street. His tires squealed as he turned on Palm. Jack didn't know what it was, but he suddenly had an irresistible urge to deal with Bryan himself. And his gut told him he would have that opportunity.

When Em returned from her date with Chuck, the family went into a huddle. Jack explained the latest development. They turned on the ten o'clock news. A photo of Cutler from the Ocean State College yearbook flashed on the screen. The announcer said Cutler was still at large and considered dangerous. This was followed by an interview with Chief Jackowitz and another with a physician at Seagate General who said the unnamed rape victim was in stable condition but was still traumatized by her experience. A spokesperson for Luco Seafood read a statement saying Cutler had been fired after several complaints of sexual harassment had been made by the unidentified female employee and subsequent victim.

They watched in numb disbelief. The phone began to ring. First Chuck. Then David. Sue, Julie, practically the entire cast. Everybody wanted to come over to keep Em company for the night.

Bernice looked at Jack. "Wouldn't hurt, would it?"

"Chief Winters says there's no danger... As long as it's okay with their parents. It's a school night. And on condition everybody stays inside the house with the doors locked. No sitting outside on the patio or out front."

"We won't," Em promised.

Em got on the phone and invited her friends over while Jack cleared out the den. Bernice ordered pizza and emptied her ashtrays.

By ten-forty-five, the kids arrived, carrying sleeping bags, stuffed animals, soft drinks, and snacks, and settled into a half-circle around the television to watch the latest developments. After the eleven o'clock news, which was a repetition of earlier tapes, they turned off the TV. They were subdued, for a change, and spoke in gentle tones about what had happened. They speculated about how it all would end with most believing the police would shoot Bryan dead before the night was out.

Bernice retired to her bedroom with a glass of wine. No television for her this evening.

Jack called Sally, but there was no answer. He left her a message not to call him back. He would check with her later.

He entered Em's room with ice water, two cameras set, and a softball bat poised nearby. His folded raincoat and Colt .45 lay on top of the dresser behind him. Another night watch. Not that he didn't trust what Bill had told him, but his gut said Bryan would outwit the police. He sat listening to the young voices. Em was surrounded by trust and friendship. Thank God. Around one o'clock, there was a steady line of kids in and out of the two bathrooms before the house settled into whispering quiet.

Jack stretched his legs in the swivel chair and found no difficulty staying awake. He could not believe Bryan would rape and nearly strangle a woman. Yes you can, he argued. You've known he could rape and kill from the very beginning. You simply didn't want to admit it...

His peripheral vision picked up movement outside the window facing the street. He recognized the uniform. Nesbitt or one of his buddies was back on foot patrol. Overhead, he picked up the faint swishing sound of a Huey, moving slowly northward at a very low altitude. So often had he ridden Hueys at treetop range at night or in early morning, looking through infrared devices, attempting to spot the enemy moving on hidden jungle trails. The night was filled with Nam sounds, it seemed, and he was as alert now as he had ever been overseas.

Chapter 38

Friday, June 7.

Six o'clock, it was bedlam at the Kaufman house. Kids came awake and headed home to shower before going to school. Jack turned on the local news at seven. Bryan was still at large. The search had widened. Police reserves had been brought in as well as county sheriff's deputies. They were deployed in a line along the north side of the river and moving northward on a wide front.

The phone rang.

"This is Jack."

"Hi..." It was Sally. She sounded dead tired. "Thought I'd check in."

"I tried to call you last night. I figured you must be working with Jackowitz."

"All night. I'm bushed. Jackie had me on the bullhorn, pleading with Bryan to give himself up. I'm hoarse from shouting. How're you doing?"

"We're fine. Em's friends rallied round. Six of them spent the night over here."

"Terrific! Well, I'll call you after I've had some sleep... Okay?"

"Sure. Appreciate you checking in."

"Bye."

After driving Em to school, Jack stopped by the Bagel Shack. Harvey's help was busily preparing for the lunch crowd, but Harvey wasn't there. Mary pointed to the closed door of Harvey's office.

"He's been in there all morning," she said solemnly. "I'm worried about him, Mr. Kaufman. Ever since the fire, he's been kinda out of it, you know? And now with the rape and all, he's like... like a different person. I hope you can talk him into going to the doctor. Alex and I think something bad is wrong with him."

He looked toward the office door.

"I'll have a talk with him."

She returned to the kitchen. Jack knocked on the door.

"Harvey? Got a minute? It's Jack."

"Not a good time..." came a voice he hardly recognized. "Come back tomorrow or next day."

"Harvey, it's no good fighting alone. Let's face it together. Please."

Silence. He knocked lightly.

"We both understand what's going on, Harvey. Come on..."

"I do not wish you to see me like this..."

"We see each other like this... Who are we kidding?"

Another silence, then some rustling sounds of a chair scraping the floor.

"Come in, then, if you must..."

His voice sounded flat, old, out of choices. Jack opened the door and stepped inside, closing the door behind him. Harvey's normally jovial round face was ashen. He sat slumped in his office chair, legs askew, his left arm resting on the cluttered desk. His eyes were bloodshot and forlorn. Harvey apparently had spent the night there. Jack removed some files from a chair and sat down. Harvey looked away and stared at the wall where Little League plaques were arranged neatly in two rows on shelves. He drew a hand up and wiped roughly across his eyes. Jack noticed for the first time the brown wooden box containing the German Luger was resting on a shelf immediately behind Harvey.

They sat for several minutes without a word, without Harvey looking at him. Jack waited, knowing the demons were gnawing him, tearing his insides to pieces, forcing him to acknowledge their power over him. Finally, Harvey's hand clenched into a fist, and he banged it down upon the desk, scattering papers. His head turned and watery red eyes showed a mixture of sadness, guilt, disgust, and rage.

"So many days I have chance to help him..." he whispered. "I fail..."

What could he say? They'd both had their chances.

"Can't take it personally, Harvey," he said in a soothing tone. "All the pros say nobody can help him... Even you said it..."

Harvey lifted his fist to his chin and tapped lightly. "Now... they hunt him down like the animal he is... and will kill him, which he deserves..."

"Yeah... They probably will shoot him, which will be as good or better than his spending the rest of his life in a cell. I don't see him giving up, do you?"

Harvey peered out of his bloody eyes, studying Jack. "I tell you something..."

He paused and looked at the wall for a moment and then back.

"You will not repeat this to another person what I tell you?"

"No." Jack noticed for the first time that Harvey's hand was shaking. He had seen it often in Nam. Hell, he, himself, had shook like that many times, even recently.

"I knew in my soul Bryan would come to this... It was God's will. And in my conversations and prayers with God, I felt it was my duty to keep Bryan from such awful acts as rape... And I did not do that which God told me to do in order to prevent it..."

"What could you have done?"

Harvey wiped his fist across his mouth, removing beads of perspiration.

"I should have killed him... That is what God wanted me to do..."

"That's crazy, Harvey. You couldn't sacrifice your life by killing him. I don't see God saying a person oughta kill another and spend the rest of his life in jail for it..."

"Did God himself not sacrifice his Son, according to Christian belief, so everyone might live forever?"

"Yeah, but..."

"By my not killing Bryan when I have opportunity, he causes a woman to almost die and changes her life forever. Don't you see that, Jack? She, too, will now have demons like you and me and Bryan. Her life is forever different, forever damned because I failed to stop Bryan."

Harvey's life had come apart and he could not glue it together again. And when Jack thought about it, he had felt similar thoughts many times: would it not be the right thing to put Bryan out of his misery? Hell, he had made up his mind that he would have an opportunity yet... Why else had he bought a Colt .45?

To make matters worse, there was a news story this morning on the front page announcing that Josef Mengele had probably drowned in Brazil back in 1979. They were going to exhume the body and compare dental records. Yeah, Harvey would be horrified to know Mengele had lived a full life on a farm down there under the name of Wolfgang Gerhard while Harvey spent every night of his life demonized. He wouldn't be able to bear it on top of everything else.

So they sat, deep in their own thoughts, occasionally glancing at the other, but mostly staring into space. At times, tears trickled down Harvey's pink face. At other times, he was composed and detached, looking like he was putting himself into a deep trance. Jack reached over and grasped Harvey's hand. He responded with his own grip upon Jack's fingers. Jack, too, succumbed to tears. They rimmed, then tumbled hotly down, dripping onto his shirt, making tiny sounds like falling snowflakes on frozen ground. It was a helluva thing, he thought, feeling like a witness to a death, yet he was not sure whose.

It was difficult to know how long they sat together, feeling the pulse of the other across the desk. It was at least an hour. Jack heard a few voices, then more, until there was a crescendo of words, laughter, whoops, and giggles. He gave Harvey's hand a squeeze and pulled away.

"Harvey… It's lunchtime. Mary and Alex need your help."

Harvey's eyes opened wide, blinked, and he snapped alive. "Yes… Lunchtime. You are right." He got up heavily, rubbed his eyes and face, took a deep breath, and beckoned for Jack to open the door. He pushed the chair back and got up. Harvey came around the desk and put his hand on Jack's shoulder. "You are the best friend I have, Jack. You understand how I am…"

"Yeah… And you are my best friend, Harvey. Always know that. I am here for you."

"Thank you…"

Stalker

He watched as Harvey brushed past him and waved to the crowd, moving through the line of kids to the counter. Jack suddenly felt a deep sadness and loss. He was unsure he understood anything, except at that moment he felt a deep and abiding love for Harvey. He slowly moved through the crowd and out the door into the bright light.

He spent most of the day clearing out cabinets and rearranging files in the studio, waiting for Sally to call. He could not dispel the feeling of dread about Harvey. It was like he was identifying himself with Bryan now, feeling Bryan's pain, sensing the end of both their lives as the hunters searched him out. Yes. Harvey believed he, himself, was a fugitive now, but from what? Our town? Our society? God? Did he truly believe he had run away from God and would be punished? For what crimes? Hell, Harvey had not committed crimes. Others committed crimes against him. The Nazis were responsible for Harvey's demons, not Bryan or anyone else. Yet... Jack, too, felt that bizarre attachment to Bryan. Jack, too, felt he was out there with him, evading, using his cunning to keep from being shot or captured. That's what it was about when somebody was after you... The phone rang.

"This is Jack."

"Hi! Oh, gosh, I feel so much better... I just woke up and took another shower... Any news?"

Sally's voice was clear, like a shower itself, cleansing his thoughts.

"No. He's still on the run. They think he may be headed west toward Three Oaks. The noon news said they've got bloodhounds on a fresh trail."

"I'll check in with the command center in a few minutes and get an update."

"Yeah, well, I think you ought to know Harvey's taking all this personally... He was in bad shape this morning. He may be suicidal."

"Oh, the poor dear... That bad, huh?"

"Yeah, well... He says it's all his fault. Had he done what God told him to do, none of this would be happening."

"You mean... How? What did God tell him?"

"I promised I wouldn't say this to anybody, but we need to help him. He told me God had commanded him to kill Bryan before Bryan did any harm..."

"Oh, how awful!"

"I tried to talk sense into him. But he's thrown up a wall, Sally."

"Tell you what... I'll drop by and see him. I know he likes me. We used to have some wonderful talks about Bryan. I'll see what I can do."

"Good."

"Maybe after all this is over, you and I need to take Harvey on your boat. Get him away from his shop. The poor guy works there day and night without a break. I can see him getting a little crazy."

"Let's do it."

He put down the phone, feeling some comfort in knowing Sally would find a way to bring Harvey back. He set about clearing a stack of file folders. Crises brought out the worst and the best, he mused. He would never have met Harvey or Sally had it not been for Bryan stalking Em. Now, they had become two of his closest friends. He imagined Sally and Harvey aboard the ketch, setting out to sea under sail on a bright, blue-skied day. He wanted it to be soon, very soon. Too bad he had the Reserve exercise tomorrow. He could be cleaning up the boat and getting it ready for sailing on Sunday. Oh, well, he reasoned, there would be other weekends.

Chapter 39

Friday Evening, June 7.

Jack relaxed on the patio near the lemon tree, basking in the last warmth of the day as the sun was setting. Small puffy clouds filled the sky, backlit billows of orange, pink and crimson. If only life were truly this peaceful, he thought.

Latest news: Bryan was still at large. State police located Mrs. Cutler in Jacksonville this afternoon. She had been ill and staying with a brother there. She returned to Seagate but would not appear on camera or make any statement. The rape victim's age was given as nineteen. She was a student at Ocean State, studying accounting. She had worked six months at the packing plant. Bryan had worked there less than a month.

Jack guessed that Bryan spotted his victim at college, learned where she was employed, and stalked her there until he could get a job near her. He got fired on Friday–the same night he probably planned the fire at Harvey's. Knowing it was only a matter of time before he got caught, he decided to act. Fortunately, he couldn't get to Em. He must have waited and watched his victim as she left work each day, hiding in the thick clump of palmettos next to the bridge. She had to cross the road to the parking lot there.

The crime occurred under the Second Street Bridge, at four o'clock, quitting time. It happened less than three hundred yards from the packinghouse. Jack could not imagine Bryan, as smart as he was, taking the risk of being seen by the seven or eight employees and passers-by. How could he think he could pull it off? Truth was, Jack figured, Bryan simply did not care at that point. He was so desperately obsessed that he was not thinking at all. Or, perhaps, it was his final cry for help. He wanted to be caught. Kind of like the time when he painted Salty the dolphin.

He didn't want to think about it. The rape reminded him of how close Em had come to being Bryan's victim. His mind switched tracks to the memory of Em and Bernice sitting at the dining table eating chicken and watermelon together.

Their "last supper" together went quite nicely. Despite the dark cloud of fear hanging over them, they managed some good laughs. The barbecue reminded them of happier times. Em said one of her favorite memories was when she was eight or so and, being the good Camp Fire girl she was, she had insisted they roast the Thanksgiving turkey on a spit over a campfire in the backyard. After five or six hours, the result was a blackened turkey with raw meat. Even Bernice laughed at that one.

Em and Bernice tidied up the kitchen, gave Jack a good-bye hug, and were now on the way south to meet the mighty television sales guru, Michael Breslin. He chuckled at Em's joking privately with him before she left.

"What color do you want, Dad?" she had asked cheerily. Her brown eyes were literally dancing with mischief.

"What color?"

"Yeah. I'll bring you a yacht back. Just tell me the color and how long you want it. Remember?" She started singing. "Come on down... Come on down the bay... to Breslin's... and get the best deal of the day!!!"

He laughed. That television commercial ran twenty-four hours, showing silver-haired Mike Breslin, a white toy poodle on his lap, sitting on the transom of a very fat looking motor yacht as a McGuire sisters sound-alike group sang in the background. It was probably Bernice's creation.

Em continued the ditty. "And Breslin's prices can't be beat!"

What would he do without Em's humor, he wondered? Most of the sky color was fading as he sipped the straw-colored Chardonnay. Bernice apparently had decided tonight was too special for the ordinary jug of wine. She had bought two bottles of a Wente premium. He stretched his legs out, feeling the residual heat radiating off the patio.

He finished the wine, sighting the door of the playhouse over the rim of his wine glass. Would he come tonight? Was he watching as Jack sat there? The last report had Bryan some fifteen miles northwest, according to the County Sheriff's office. No way in hell he could circle around and get here without being caught. Still, he had a suspicion that the police really did not have a clue as to his whereabouts. Nobody had actually seen him since the two fishermen described his flight. The bloodhounds lost the scent an hour after they were put on Bryan's trail. And there was no new evidence of his whereabouts, unless the police were not telling.

Jack carried the glass and bottle to the kitchen and checked the house. All was locked up except for Em's side bedroom window, which he had purposely left wide open. He drew the blinds and checked the two tripods and cameras to be sure they were aimed directly at each window. He double-checked the flashes and cords and the single remote trigger. It seemed silly now, with all that had happened, for him to think about getting a picture of Bryan coming through the window. What was the point? He was a rapist. A fugitive, wanted dead or alive. Jack started to dismantle a camera, then put it back. For some perverse reason, he decided to keep them where they were.

He thought about tomorrow and driving up to the Space facility. He did not look forward to doing Reserve duty after spending the whole night awake. Just for the hell of it, he filled a plastic grocery bag with glass bottles and jars and placed it on a shelf in Em's playhouse near the door. He attached a straightened coat hanger to the top of the door. He reached through a side window and hooked the other end of the wire around the top of the bag and moved it so the bag nearly teetered at the edge of the shelf. Bryan could not open the door without the glass crashing to the floor. Is that what he wanted? It was another silly ruse, he thought.

The only reason for Bryan to use the playhouse now would be as a temporary hideout. Otherwise, he would come directly to a window and want to come inside. Maybe he wanted to rape once more before he was caught or killed. Jack made the windows more inviting by not switching on the security lights.

He went through the house again, making sure every door and window was locked except the side window in Em's bedroom. He figured that Bryan would not likely come through the front one, so why keep it unlocked? He returned to her room. It was not quite dark. He took a penlight, lit it, and placed it on the windowsill. He sighted on it with the left camera, bringing the light sharply into focus. He repeated the process with the other camera as though this was a major photo assignment. He felt crazy doing it, yet he did it anyway. Everything was set. Soon, it was dark. He opened the blinds.

He went into his bedroom and packed. He hung his uniform on the doorframe and loaded a B-4 bag into the car. He considered whether or not to bring the car into the garage for the night. No. He would let Bryan know he was home. Besides, he usually kept the car outside the garage.

He grabbed a glass of ice water and returned to Em's room to sit in the darkness, listening, getting used to the night noises. Voices of frogs began to rise in unison from the bog at the edge of the canal two streets over. Crickets joined in. The crazy mockingbird stood atop the street lamp and went through its entire repertoire as though it were first light.

Perhaps it was the wine or the notion that Em and Bernice were out of harm's way, but he grew sleepy and dozed. When he awoke, he could not tell whether his eyes had closed for a second or several minutes, but he was startled by a tiny gnawing sound, like a rat chewing on hardwood. He opened his eyes with a start. A dark form loomed in the window. He looked indirectly at the movement, better able to catch the image through peripheral vision–a technique he learned in Nam.

A gloved hand was holding the corner of the window screen while the other worked with a tool at the metal screen above one of the screen locks. Jack caught his breath in time and took measured draughts of air, trying not to move or flinch. His stomach was churning. His chest was so tight it was difficult to breathe. He waited as the form reached in and flicked open the wire lock on the right side, then stretched around to unlock the second one. Jack's hand slid across his knee toward the remote camera switch. The intruder stepped back and removed the screen and placed it

Stalker

silently next to the window. Here he comes, Jack said to himself as his heart thumped and sweat poured down his face.

As Bryan's head and shoulders filled the window and he was peering with a steady gaze toward the wig that was half-buried in the bed clothes, Jack was suddenly seized with so much anger that he grabbed the softball bat with a rush and went at him.

"Have this, you raping, son-of-a-bitch," he shouted, closing the distance, getting a foot caught in camera cable, knocking cameras and tripods awry, winding up like he was going to hit a home run. Off balance and hardly able to see Bryan, Jack nevertheless struck at him with all his fury, landing one good hit on Bryan's shoulder, then grazing him across the neck, striking the window frame with the next blow, and swinging wildly as Bryan reeled back and banged against the fence behind him like a boxer on the ropes. Dogs barked.

"Come on," Jack screamed, shaking from head to toe. "Try me, you bastard!" Tears streamed down his face as he stood poised, waiting, shivering uncontrollably. Bryan, clutching his shoulder, looked at the window for a few seconds, then grunted and lunged toward the front yard.

"You're the bastard!" Bryan's voice shouted as he loped toward the corner of the house. There was a grating sound like pottery rubbing together. "You're the fucking bastard, Mr. Kaufman!"

Jack stood there gasping for breath, unable to move from the side window, when the front window exploded in a crash of sound and showering glass. He's thrown a damned rock, Jack thought, ducking. He rushed drunkenly through broken glass to the door, fumbling to turn on the hall light, then staggered to the studio and called 911. He could not be sure whether Bryan was coming at him through the front window or not. He was so out of breath that he could hardly whisper his address and tell what had happened to the operator. His hand was shaking so that he was forced to hold the phone in both hands as he watched the hallway, expecting Bryan's menacing hulk to fill the door frame any second.

He did not hear any movement inside the house. He put the phone down and held the bat ready for action. He stepped into the hall, braced to swing at any movement. Nothing. He walked down the hall and checked each room, then entered Em's bedroom and switched on the light. Glass and pieces of wood sash were everywhere. Much of the debris was on Em's bed, including the top of the birdbath. So that was what Bryan had pitched through the window: thirty-five pounds of concrete. Jack must not have wounded him too much, then.

By the time the police arrived, Bryan was long gone. The flashing blue lights of two cruisers turned the street into a grotesque scene.

Lt. Braggon put out an APB on his radio. Sgt. Hallsworth assured Jack they would keep the house under close surveillance. They examined everything.

Hallsworth made a few notes. Braggon called the station and gave a report. The operator contacted Chief Winters and patched him in. "Chief would like to speak with you, Mr. Kaufman."

He handed Jack his phone. "Hey, Bill."

"Are you okay?"

"Now I am."

"Think you hurt 'im?"

"Winged him on the shoulder. Hit him once across the neck, I think. All I know is I stopped him."

"What about the family? They okay?"

"Em and Bernice left earlier for Ft. Lauderdale. They'll be there all weekend."

"Good. We oughta catch him within the hour. We've got choppers, cruisers, K-9s, everybody we can muster. He won't be bothering you anymore. I can assure you of that."

"Appreciate your call, Bill."

"Put the lieutenant back on?"

"Sure."

The sergeant helped Jack clean up the larger pieces of destruction in Em's room. They threw the debris out the large hole in the window into the front yard. Neighbors stood in front of Wallace's house in bathrobes, watching, wondering what in hell was going on. Archie came by, brandishing his Smith & Wesson .38. Jack told him politely to put the thing away. No need to excite everybody at this time of night. Archie retreated home after Braggon assured him that Bryan Cutler was probably being arrested at that very minute.

Jack went to the garage and pulled down a piece of plywood from the rafters. He nailed it over the damaged window with the sergeant's help, waking more neighbors as he did so.

Old man Wallace ventured over in his bathrobe. He stood watching Jack, complaining about teenagers and their rowdy behavior. He was a man Jack had never liked. He always gave Em a hard time ever since she played with her first skateboard. It got away from her and ran up under Wallace's car. It made a lot of noise but caused no damage. After that, she couldn't do anything right so far as he was concerned. More than once Jack had wanted to take a poke at him, except he was too old.

"Some of yer daughter's friends are pretty wild," he said. "Didya know that, Jack? One of 'em hangs around here 'til all hours... Oughta put a stop to it."

Apparently Wallace was too dumb to connect the dots. It was two o'clock in the morning. He didn't need any lectures from a guy who disliked kids. "Why don't you get some sleep, Mr. Wallace? It's all over for tonight."

Jack continued pounding sixteen penny nails into the frame until he expended his anger. For certain, the patch was secure. The echoes from the hammering brought more lights on throughout the neighborhood. He would have waited until tomorrow to seal the window, except he had to leave the house early in the morning for Reserve duty. Wallace stood his ground, infecting the neighbors with his negative grumbling.

"Hope this doesn't go on..." mumbled Wallace as Jack thanked Braggon and Hallsworth for their help. They got in their cruisers and took off. Jack left Wallace standing in the middle of his front yard and went inside.

He shifted back to his regular bedroom, taking the softball bat and Colt .45 with him. He was pretty sure Bryan would not be back tonight. Not with police cruisers and those silent Nam choppers Chief Winters had scanning the neighborhood. Then he recalled he had said that to himself last night, too. He placed the Colt on the bedside table. If Cutler comes back, he's dead, Jack muttered.

Chapter 40

Saturday Morning, June 8.

Jack was worn out, although he had slept soundly and came awake automatically at five-thirty. He showered and dressed. He dusted off his spit-shined black shoes. He straightened the three rows of ribbons on his chest. It was not that he disliked them. He was damned proud. He had earned them. Still, were it not for the commander's insistence, he would have kept his ribbons in a drawer someplace. So many guys wore stuff they had not earned.

As he looked into the mirror, he was struck by the feeling that Bryan had left him a message. He just knew it. Bryan had avoided capture and written him again. He and Bryan were on the same wavelength, he thought.

He locked the house and turned the corner of the garage. His gut was right. A white envelope was tucked under the windshield wiper. His name was scrawled across the envelope: MR. KAUFMAN. Some police protection! They could have a dozen police cars patrolling the neighborhood, and Bryan would still find a way around them, he thought.

He put the envelope on the passenger seat. It would have to wait. He had miles to travel, if he wanted to report for duty on time. He would check the contents after he arrived.

As he drove up Interstate 95, watching the sky come to life with gray, then pink, then crimson light, gulls and pelicans flew in high echelon formations from lagoons east toward the sea. The envelope and its contents sat like an evil omen. He could not wait. He must open it.

He pulled off and parked at a Shoney's. His hand shook as he tore open the envelope and read the shaky, desperate printing.

MR. KAUFMAN

I MUST TALK WITH YOU. COM TO E. PRK WHERSAND BOX IS. BY 830 AM. KEEP COPS OUT OF THIS.

IT IS SO IMPORTNT WE TALK. I AM VERY SORY. I NEED YOR HELP. I'VE GOT BAD TRUBLE. PLEASE COME. IF YOU DON'T, I'L KILL MY SELF. PLESE, MR. KAFFMEN, I WON'T HURT YOU. I PROMIS TO GOD.

BRYAN

"God almighty," Jack said aloud. He ran to the pay phone in the lobby, dropped coins in and dialed Chief Winters. He glanced at his watch. Seven fifteen. Probably not in his office yet.

"Winters."

"Early riser, Bill. This is Jack."

"Yeah, Jack. I got a full report from the night duty officer. Unfortunately, we haven't caught Cutler yet."

"I had a letter on my windshield this morning. He wants me to meet him in Eisenhower Park at the sand boxes at eight thirty. He says if I don't come, he'll kill himself."

"Great. We'll throw a net around the park. Can you fax his message to me?"

"I'm half way up the Interstate to the Space Center. How 'bout I fax it from there?"

"Sure. You going to be away all weekend?"

"Yeah."

"Good. We'll keep an eye on your house."

"Very good."

He put the phone on the cradle. At least he thought it was very good. He visualized the house, sitting vacant, knowing Bryan could burn it down if he wanted to. Hell, he's got experience setting fires. He could get a good one going with all the chemicals in the studio. Jack climbed into the car and headed north again. Burning a house down is nothing compared to murdering people. How could he have missed Bryan's head when he swung the bat?

He went immediately to the Command Center and sent the fax. His friend Groves came over.

"Glad you could make it, Jack… General Selby really needs your expertise this weekend."

"You don't know the half of it, Bob. I feel lucky to be here."

Jack left the Command Center and headed toward the public affairs office. Five minutes after sitting down at his desk to look over photo assignments, his phone rang.

"Major Kaufman here."

"I believe we've got a document of yours, Major. You left it on the fax machine," said Groves. "General advises you to go home. Take care of your personal business."

His heart sank. The general? "How'd this get to the general? Which one? Hall or Selby?"

"Exercise commander, General Selby. He went to use the fax machine. Couldn't avoid reading the message. You okay?"

"Yeah, Bob... I'm okay. I'll be right over." As he got up from the desk, Colonel Mumford strolled in.

"Just had a call from Selby, Jack. He says you got serious problems. Something about a man is going to commit suicide this morning if you don't show up?"

Damn, he thought to himself. That's all he needed: a general spreading stuff about him causing a man to commit suicide. That would end his Reserve career for sure.

Mumford glanced at the clock. It was quarter to nine. Jack tried to play it cool. "No problem, Colonel. Ocean City police are handling it. The guy's the stalker I mentioned. He's been following my daughter around. He's the one who raped the coed in Seagate."

Mumford rested a hand on Jack's shoulder, looking at him like he was an alien. "General and I agree you ought to take this weekend off. Go home. I'll reassign your tasks to Captain Phillips. I've already put in a call. He's coming in."

"I assure you, Ed, it's all taken care of. There's nothing I can do at home. I'd much rather be here and get my mind off this character for a weekend."

The colonel shook his head.

"Uh, uh. No sir. Not on your life. General's orders. Come back next training assembly."

Ed was pushing him toward the door. There was no explaining. Jack drove over to headquarters. Chief Groves retrieved a manila envelope and handed it to him.

"Let us know if we can do anything," Groves said grimly.

"Thanks."

It was the usual, officious, big-buddy-offering-to-help-another-buddy-in-trouble thing. Only, in peacetime, it was so often more lip service than genuine. He nodded absently and went out through the swinging doors, glancing at the gantry tower. Everybody meant well when something happened. They were supportive at a polite distance. Only, they did not want you around.

Take your problems back home. Deal with them off base. Don't hang around headquarters, infecting everybody. That's how accidents happened. A guy with problems can't keep his mind on the job and, boom! The accident rate goes up, and the squadron gets a write-up when the next inspection comes along. Too many gigs and the commander is replaced. He knew it all by heart. And many of these weekend warriors with all their decorations and rank had never seen combat—especially in Nam.

He climbed into his car and headed out, thinking it could be the last time he would see the Space Center in uniform. He could imagine the notes scribbled on personal calendar books in the general's office. An incident involving Major Jack Kaufman, assigned to Public Affairs. He imagined his boss making similar notes. Mumford was sitting back, considering what he would tell General Selby about him at their next private briefing. Knowing tight-ass Ed Mumford, he would be figuring out the best strategies for covering his own ass at his expense. He could see him now.

"Well, General, I've been keeping an eye on Kaufman. He's conscientious and all..."

Then would come the but, the butt, the big BUT...

"But... I have concerns. He's got personal problems which are affecting his performance here at the Space Center, sir."

"Oh?"

"Yes, sir. Kaufman's wife is leaving him."

"Know why she's leaving him, Colonel?"

"No, sir... He never discusses it... But... I recall something about an alcohol thing... I don't remember exactly. Seems he binges or... she does? Don't remember, sir, but I vaguely recall..."

"Kaufman... Kaufman... Is he...?"

"I don't think so, General..."

"Well... Give me a full report, Ed. No bullshit. Tell it like it is... We can't afford one of your people–as highly visible as they are– with a drinking problem. Understand me?"

Jack thought back. Once he had shared with then First Lieutenant Ted Phillips that Bernice and he were having difficulties. He had told Ted he thought Bernice had a drinking problem. He was now Captain Phillips. The guy had been eyeing Jack's major slot for several months. He was slick, fast-talking. Owned an advertising agency. It suddenly dawned on Jack that Ted Phillips probably knew Bernice. Hell, they were in the same line of work. Both were in PR, probably competitors. It all fit. Ted and Mumford were big buddies. Ted had been doing free PR for Mumford's investment company. Jeez... He and Mumford had put him on the skids before he knew what was happening.

Even the best headquarters in peacetime was a quagmire of politics and conniving, he thought. You got into difficulties for the most amazing reasons. Innuendo mixed with calendar notes: a slight misunderstanding about instructions, a heated discussion about how to tackle an assignment, a bit of gossip about alcohol, a threat from some punk you did not even know, and a letter from him inadvertently left next to a fax machine. He could see Mumford building his paper case against him so he would be passed over for promotion. Yeah, Phillips wanted his job, and his absent-mindedness was helping him to get it.

Jack headed south, wondering whether Bryan had committed suicide. He saw him clearly, sprawled across the boarded edge of the sand box, face down, a pool of arterial blood spreading from beneath his body, turning the beige sand dark, sticky and warm.

As always, the police would get there just past the nick of time. They would be milling around, scratching themselves, calling for an ambulance or maybe a forensic investigator, fingering their guns and flashlights self-consciously. Others would be stretching yellow tape around the trunks of the pine trees, cordoning off the crime scene, doing the easy, mundane tasks.

Chief Winters would be there, too, in civilian clothes, hands on hips, wearing his orange tinted pilot's glasses, watching his chief of detectives as he went through Bryan's pockets. Is that how it was? Jack had to admit a certain satisfaction thinking Bryan was lying there dead and the turmoil was over. On the other hand, the whole thing was terribly sad and somehow unnecessary.

He dismissed the fantasy of Bryan's death and felt certain Bryan was very much alive. Bryan likely sensed the police were setting a net and got out of the park just in time. Bryan was expert at doing that. He was out there, looming very large, dark and menacing. Jack accelerated, pushing the BMW to a steady eighty miles an hour. He couldn't wait to get back and find out what had happened.

He turned on the radio and scanned for news. Nothing local. National news was not carrying any stories about Bryan. He switched to the jazz station and listened to an old classic by Red Norvo.

He could not get his stupidity out of his mind. Between that and Bryan's obsession, his career in the Air Force was probably over. Nineteen years. Nearly two of them in Vietnam. One more good year to go. What he had done for his country in the past didn't mean crap. And Bryan didn't have a clue about any of it. He couldn't care less.

Had he done a better job with the bat last night, all this would not be happening. Bryan would be in the morgue and he... he was sounding like Harvey.

He parked in front of Seagate police station. Hopefully, Sally would be in her office. He turned the corner. A police officer stood officiously at parade rest in front of Sally's door. Behind him, a squat, middle-aged woman with swollen red Basset hound eyes sat in a chair in front of Sally's desk bundled in a thick, dark dress. Sally saw him approaching. "He can come in, Corporal."

The cop moved aside, and Sally stood as he entered. Her eyes fastened momentarily on his uniform and ribbons. Her green eyes flashed him a warning and told him without words that this lady was Bryan's mother.

"Mrs. Cutler, this is Jack Kaufman, Emily's father."

The small lady removed her large black handbag from her lap and stood up, eyeing him scornfully. Her drooping cheeks and pursed mouth told him she'd like to slap him across the face. She did not offer her hand, nor did she speak.

"Hello, Mrs. Cutler." He said it gently, not knowing whether her son was alive or dead.

She gave the faintest nod and sat down, pulling her purse into her lap as though for protection. Her thick, fat hands appeared sunburned, probably from exposure to caustic substances she used at her job.

"Have a seat, Major." Sally motioned him to the other chair.

He stepped around Mrs. Cutler and sat down, hat in hand.

Sally sat down and leaned on her elbows, playing with the corner of what he believed was Bryan's file with her forefinger. She tilted her head toward him. "I don't know whether you heard... Ocean City police picked up Bryan this morning. He was at the park waiting for you."

He was strangely relieved Bryan had not killed himself nor gotten killed by police. How easily one's attitude changes when danger is past. Last night, his savage emotions took over. He was getting back for all the hell Bryan had caused. He was making him pay for Harvey, too: Harvey's anger and sadness and depression. Yes, he wanted to kill him last night, and would have... except for poor aim. Today, he was relieved Bryan was caught and alive. He felt Mrs. Cutler's eyes cutting through him. He avoided looking at her, concentrating on Sally's information.

"They're holding him at the city jail until they can make arrangements to have him transported down to Dade County. He will be in a psychiatric evaluation center for several days of observation and testing."

"I see," he said, thanking God he was behind bars.

Sally pulled her shoulders up and opened her hands like a preacher exhorting the flock. "What happens after that, I don't know."

From the corner of his eye, he saw large tears flowing down Mrs. Cutler's heavy cheeks. Sally nodded toward her.

"I was just explaining to Mrs. Cutler that Bryan will be tried as an adult. Once I file my report, I'll be out of the loop."

Mrs. Cutler opened her purse and pulled out a lacy handkerchief. She mopped her face and neck before stuffing it back in the purse. Her head turned towards Jack, her droopy eyes fierce.

"All this didn't hafta happen. I hope ya know that Mister... Mister..."

"Kaufman."

She pulled a red hand to her mouth as though wanting to hold the words in. Large pools formed again in the pockets beneath her eyes and overflowed their banks.

"If you'da let him date yer daughter like he ast ya ta do... Was that too much ta ask a body?"

He looked down at the spit shine on his military shoes. They reflected the leaves shaking on the sun-filled tree outside the window. Warm air wafted into the room, belying the tension and darkened thoughts.

"I had to protect Emily. Bryan would have raped her, just like he did this other woman. Don't you understand that?"

She seemed not to be listening. "My Bryan is all I have in the world." She sobbed. "He's been a good boy all his life. Now..." She wept and reached for the handkerchief. "Now... our lives are ruint... " She sniveled, "I hope ya know that... He'll be in jail the rest of his life."

She glared at Jack over her handkerchief. He made an attempt to console her. "I'm awfully sorry, Mrs. Cutler. I honestly tried to reach out to him. I sought help from counselors at the high school and at Ocean State. I tried to call you numerous times. I don't know what I could have done differently."

Mrs. Cutler took a deep breath, expanding and raising her chin defiantly like a puffed out bird. "Ya coulda not interfered, fer starters. That's whatcha coulda done. All he wanted ta do was ta date yer daughter. He loves her. And Bryan sez she loves him. They had fun tagether... 'til you barged in and spoilt it. And looka what's come of it. Ya caused Bryan to become hateful. Tha's watcha done. Ya can't blame him. He did the only nat'ral thing a boy would do..."

"And what is that," asked Sally, doubtfully.

"Why... Defend hisself! This man," she pointed toward Jack, "sent me a threaten'n letter... say'n if Bryan didn't stay clear of his daughter... What's a boy in love supposed ta do?"

She was pitiful. Sally's eyes connected with Jack's. Talk was futile. He rose and extended his hand to Mrs. Cutler.

"I'm sorry this happened, Mrs. Cutler."

She ignored his hand. Jack moved past her as Sally stood up.

"He meant no harm ta enybody..." Mrs. Cutler hissed.

"Call me later," Sally said and extended her hand. Her eyes dropped to the ribbons on his chest. She looked up again intently, speculatively.

"You in all day," he asked.

"'Until four."

"Now," whimpered Mrs. Cutler, "he's in jail an' I have nobody inna world ta help me..."

"I'll call you," Jack said, ignoring the woman.

He glanced at Mrs. Cutler who seemed lost behind her clenched fists, a wadded handkerchief, and a steady downpour of tears.

"Good-bye, Mrs. Cutler."

He escaped to his car as fast as he could.

Chapter 41

Saturday Afternoon, June 8.

Jack called Mike Breslin's number that Bernice had given him. He needed to let her and Em know they could relax, come home when they wanted to, and resume getting ready for Em's graduation. It took several minutes to be put through by marine telephone.

"Hello."

"Bernice?"

"Hi, Jack. Where are you?"

"Home. Bryan's been arrested. They caught him this morning."

"Oh my God! Are you all right?"

"Yeah. Anyway, I thought you might want to come home."

"We're on our way to Freeport. Would you mind if we came home Monday morning 'stead of tomorrow?"

"Em's going to miss school..."

"No problem. It's exam week. She's exempt from taking the English exam. That's the only one scheduled for Monday."

"I see... Em having a good time?"

"She loves Mike's boat. He's teaching her how to drive it or I'd put her on."

"No," he said, feeling like this rich jerk was stealing the affections of not only his wife but also his daughter. He tried to be light about it. "Don't interrupt her. Have fun. I'll see you Monday."

He put down the phone and tried to understand what was going on. Hey! He was free from worry. A free weekend! He did not have to worry about Bryan or Bernice or Em. He felt twenty pounds lighter! He unloaded the car, realizing he felt lighter with each bag and camera case he unpacked. Archie stopped by and asked whether he needed help with the window. No, he replied, wanting peace and quiet. He looked forward to being alone in the house, puttering around, feeling free to do whatever. He would normally have invited Archie to help, since he was a real handyman. But with Bryan, Bernice and Em out of the picture, he wanted to kick back. Still, Archie's offer made him realize he had to do something about repairing the damned window. He called his insurance agent. Gone for the weekend.

He reluctantly took hammer and wrecking bar and set about the task of removing the plywood from the smashed window. One look said it was not repairable. He took photos of it for insurance purposes, measured it, and drove down to Statler's Building Supply and bought a whole new window set. It was much heavier and larger than he had figured. He needed help getting it tied down on top of his car.

As he was attempting to remove it from the roof, Archie reappeared and gave him a hand. The installation took all afternoon. Thank heaven Archie persisted in his efforts to help. He insisted on doing the painting. He left and returned with a can of white primer and began applying it to the raw wood. Jack glanced at his watch. It was four-ten.

"Be back in a minute, Arch," he said, scrambling toward the door.

"No need to rush, Jack, this is a one-man job. I love to paint wood. Second thing in the world I most love to do."

He didn't need to ask what the first was. He'd heard it a dozen times before. He flipped open his pocket phone directory and dialed.

"Probation Department. Officer Brand here."

"You're staying overtime, Sally. It's Saturday."

She laughed lightly.

"I was waiting for your call."

"Oh?"

They were connecting again like this morning, only with voices instead of eyes. Amazing how emotional tensions can bring two people together. He waited for her to say something. Anything.

"Yeah. I couldn't talk in front of Mrs. Cutler. Police found monitoring devices in Bryan's room. Some were so powerful he could hear what you said in your living room from a hundred yards away."

"So that explains the absence of bugs."

"The computer is something else, too. He'd programmed maps of Seagate and Ocean City. They're so detailed he could use every alley and access space to elude police."

"How would he get maps like that?"

"Newspaper publisher. They have them for deliverymen. He used to deliver papers for the *Ocean County Herald* before he lost his license."

"That explains his ability to appear and disappear so fast."

"Yup. Another ugly surprise."

"What's that?"

"He's got an awesome address book."

"What's the ugly part?"

"White supremacy stuff. You know, skinheads, Ku Klux Klan, Aryan Nations..."

"It figures. Harvey got a crazy phone call from him. Bryan called him every anti-Semitic name he could think of. As bright as he is, I can't imagine Bryan falling for all that Hitler crap."

"True, but this guy's a loner. An outcast who obsesses and grabs onto people out of needs you and I can't imagine."

"But Harvey can't figure it. He's hurt to the core to know Bryan despises him because he's Jewish."

"But look what happened. They have a disagreement, right? Harvey fires him. Overnight, Bryan becomes a Jew hater. You love me, or you hate me. There's no gray with Bryan.... Except when he believes he's in love with a girl who refuses to go out with him. Then, he swings back and forth, between love and hate. You see what I mean?"

"I see."

"Harvey set himself up for the fire when he began playing watchman at the Civic Center."

"Yeah, I understand that part."

"Harvey's devastated, like you said. We had a long talk yesterday and another one this morning. He's terribly depressed."

"I'm really concerned. He feels personally responsible for Bryan's behavior."

"I know... I tried to reason with him, but nothing I could say made any difference. Oh! That reminds me. Could you believe Mrs. Cutler? Saying Em loves Bryan?"

"Pitiful. I really feel sorry for her. Is anybody looking after her?"

"Well, I've contacted the welfare department. Hopefully, a caseworker will check on her. She may qualify for some kind of treatment program."

"Probably... She's like Harvey described her."

"How?"

"Like a bagel without all the ingredients."

"It would be funny if it wasn't so sad..."

"Thanks for the info, Sally."

"By the way, you looked great in uniform."

"Thank you."

"Is that scar on your face a war wound?"

"No. I got it playing touch football."

"Take care."

"Bye."

He went outside. Archie had finished putting primer on the window. Jack looked at his watch. Four-twenty.

"I was going to check out my boat at the pier before supper, Archie."

"Go," he said, paint and brush in hand. "Have a drop cloth? I'd like to paint the inside if you don't mind. I'll only be a few minutes. Give me a key and I'll lock up."

"There's a roll of plastic in the garage. Leave the key on the hall cabinet and give the door a good slam when you leave. I won't need to fasten the dead bolts, Arch. Bryan's in jail."

"So I heard."

"Who told you?"

"Old man Wallace."

"Hm, figures. By the way, I want to pay you for the work."

Archie waved a brush at him. "Forget it! Besides, I'll need you to help when I put my boat in the water next month."

"Glad to do it."

He left him in the house and drove down East Seaview Boulevard. Masts loomed in the distance at the city pier.

He parked in the public lot next to where his boat was docked. How long had it been? He and Em used to take the boat out nearly every weekend. Since she got so busy, he had quit coming down very often.

He stepped aboard. The refinished deck looked great. He unlocked the hatch cover. He slid it aside and climbed into the hot interior. There was a rank smell of mildew. He opened ceiling and side ports in the semi darkness. The whole place needed airing. The image of Sally here working with him was strong. His fantasies shifted from working side-by-side to undressing each other in a furious rush of passion. He imagined her lying naked in the forward berth, waiting for him to join her. That time would come, he believed. Meanwhile, he wanted to get the boat half decent before he invited her aboard.

He hauled cushions and mattresses topside. He cleaned the hardware and wood sufaces, washed the vinyl pads, and worked up a good sweat. He listened to a baseball game on the radio: Braves against the Dodgers. Braves won seven to three with Ramirez hitting a home run with two aboard in the second inning.

He took a bag of sails from the locker to topside, stretching them loosely along the foredeck. Maybe when Bernice moved out and Emily went to Spain for the summer, he might just hop aboard this little baby and explore the Gulf to Mexico and back. Sounded like a plan. He could store his camera equipment. Arnold Baker could cover his photo assignments. He'd love it. His Technicolor fantasy of sailing in the Gulf all summer faded to black and white. If he were to save his Reserve position, he had better put in additional unit training assemblies and special assignments. He'd have to show old Mumford he was too valuable to be replaced by Ted Phillips.

Then he asked himself: 'why am I getting the boat cleaned up? Because,' he answered, you're going sailing tomorrow, dopey.' First chance to do it in months! Yeah. Except it's less fun by yourself. He gathered some change and walked across the parking lot to the pay phone in front of the Winn-Dixie Store. He punched in numbers.

"Bagel Shack."

"Mary, Jack Kaufman. How's Harvey?"

"Better, I guess. The probation lady came by. That raised his spirits."

"Good. Is he there?"

"He's in the kitchen."

"Could I speak with him, please?"

"Yes, sir. Just a minute..."

"...Harvey."

"Jack, Harvey. How'd you like to go sailing on my boat tomorrow?"

"Sailing? I'm afraid I would be a poor sailor..."

"Not true. You need to get out and enjoy some sea air for a change."

"With you I go sailing? I know nothing about sailing, and you want me to do it?"

"Sure. You'll love it."

"And how do I know you are a good sailor?" There was a touch of the old Harvey in his voice.

"You don't. We'll just go in the bay unless you want to chance it beyond the breakwater."

"I don't know about this sailing. Beyond breakwater is the ocean. When I come across the Atlantic in 1949, I get very seasick."

"Don't worry. The ocean's like glass. You won't get sick."

"Where would you take me on the ocean?"

"Anywhere. China. South America. Tahiti. You name it."

"Ha! What time?"

"Nine? Ten?"

"Do I wear bathing suit or what? I know nothing what you wear sailing."

"Bathing suit, shorts, long pants and t-shirt. Your call."

"I am not sure I can be good company, Jack…"

"Sure you will."

"Ach! How can I forget? I have date with Sally for lunch tomorrow. Can we make it at another time?"

"I guess so…"

"I tell you what. Suppose I call Sally and invite her along for the boat ride. Would you mind so much having another person… or is there not room?"

Harvey always seemed to catch him with some kind of surprise. Hell, the boat wasn't ready for her yet. It was not clean enough. Things weren't shipshape. He felt a rush. Could he get her tidy by nine? It was worth a try.

"Why, no. Sure. There's plenty of room." He threw in a dumb question. "Think she'd want to come?"

"Of course, Jack. And don't think about me and Sally like you are thinking… I am strictly father to her. Nothing more. I sit and admire her pretty freckles as she devours my cheesecake and says sweet things with her lovely mouth. We talk of Bryan and my friend Jack Kaufman. Nothing more, I assure you. Except, of course, the nothing more part is not of my own doing, you understand…"

"She talks about me?"

"Sometime I share what she tells me... Are you maybe a little bit in love with her?"

"No," he said, telling what Bernice would call a white lie. "Just curious is all."

"It is okay that I invite her?"

"Invite her."

"Don't busy yourself with food and drinks. I bring everything. Enough for five people!"

"Don't overdo it, Harvey. At least let me provide the drinks."

"I'll let you know in a few minutes whether it is okay with Sally, no?"

"You can't. I'm at a pay phone."

"You are not at home?"

"At the Winn-Dixie across from my boat, the Q-T-2."

"How's that?"

"You've heard of QE2? Queen Elizabeth the Second? Well, I kinda did a number on it. Name of my boat is QT2."

"You are a funny man, Jack. I suggest, however, you don't quit your photography."

"I'll call you back in ten minutes."

"Okay."

He put down the receiver and entered Winn-Dixie, randomly pulling items off the shelves and tossing them into the grocery cart. He was feeling very lucky and excited, like a teen-ager preparing for his first date.

Sally's face was constantly on his mind. Her pale skin above the swell of her breasts also had allure. He found himself at the Drug Department, eyeing packets of condoms. Maybe he should keep some on board for when Sally and he went sailing alone. There

Stalker

were too many options: regular or lubricated, textured or smooth? He paused. Why not? Be prepared for more surprises, he said to himself. He sheepishly bought some for the first time in years. Twenty minutes ago he was ready to go home. Now, he was full of expectations. He wheeled the grocery cart to the pay phone and called Harvey.

"Harvey, this is Jack."

"Sally says to tell you she'd love to sail with you... What does that tell you, my friend?"

An image of creamy skin with orange freckles barely covered with a bathing suit swam through his head. "You tell me, Harvey. Or better, don't tell me. I'm still married."

"I will see you nine o'clock tomorrow. Do you mind that Sally drives herself over? She has other business until nine-thirty."

"Not at all. You can help me set the new halyards."

"You will have to teach me halyards. How do I tell Sally directions to your boat?"

"Easy. Seaview Boulevard east to the public docks. You can park next to my BMW across the street from Winn-Dixie. Mine's the fifty-foot, two-mast ketch–blue and white–with QT2 in bold black paint on the bow. Berth number sixty-four. You can't miss it."

"Good. I tell her."

He hung up and removed the bags of groceries from the cart, wondering what other extraordinary thing might happen. He crossed the street and went aboard QT2. He checked the storage locker in the forward cabin for fresh clothes and toilet articles. He returned to the galley and cleaned out the refrigerator. He put all the old staple items from the fridge and food locker into a plastic bag to toss and wiped the interiors clean. He filled the refrigerator with the new groceries and stowed the dry foods. He checked the stove. He didn't need to go home tonight. He would work until the major tasks were finished. He had the whole night to get her ship-shape, if he needed it. He hadn't felt this happy in a long time.

He worked furiously, dousing the interior with a lemon-scented anti-mildew spray and applying wood wax to the teak. He stowed all the gear from topside.

He showered, washing the head at the same time, and wiping the Plexiglas surfaces as he toweled off. A pair of white shorts, no underwear, a T-shirt, and boat moccasins felt, as Em would say, 'really cool.'

He carried a tray loaded with a wine glass, Winn-Dixie Deli pastrami sandwich, potato salad, *The Times*, and a bottle of wine topside. He sat in the stern cockpit and leaned back on the soft cushions. A gull hovered overhead. Don't drop anything on me, he pleaded silently. The gull inspected the chow, and tilted, causing wind to luff from its wings, and swooped down and away like a Huey to visit a more promising boat. Jack supposed the gull was looking for shrimp. The gulls were spoiled by fishermen dumping their extra bait shrimp overboard after returning from fishing. And they weren't doing the gulls any favor, either.

He opened the wine using a Swiss knife opener and poured some Chardonnay into the glass. He propped his legs on the cushions. This was the most relaxed he had been in months. He would sleep well tonight after staying up the better part of the last three nights. He raised the glass to his lips and held the wine in his mouth, savoring its flavors of grape, butter and oak. He swallowed, feeling the liquid evaporating into a lovely, clean, dry apricot finish.

He scanned the headlines of *The Times*. There were five photographs of Josef Mengele, the Auschwitz death doctor, on the front page: some with him clean shaven, others with a moustache. The story alleged that Mengele's son visited him in Brazil back in the 1970's. Harvey was bound to see the spread, which could take him over the brink. He folded the paper and threw it aside. Tomorrow, he would get Harvey into sailing by letting him handle the tiller. Yes, that would be a tonic. Forget about Cutler for a while.

Did Sally really want to know how to sail? He could see her moving about, setting lines, hauling sheets, adjusting the tiller. How pretty her legs would look in shorts as she sat back and braced her feet against the cabin. She'd become adept. She'd sit next to him, browning in the sun, and he would watch her freckles change and blend in her tan, making her more exotic each day. How did he know it would happen, he asked himself: I know, he answered, because I want it so...

Chapter 42

Sunday Morning, June 9.

A rowdy flock of gulls awakened Jack. He'd had another nightmare about Nam. He rose slowly from the berth, aware that his body was moist and hot. He glanced out a bow porthole. Everything was slate gray in first light, wet, silent, except for the hollow slap of tide against hull. A mist was rising off the water, promising a hot day. The shrill cries of gulls moving across a cloudless sky echoed down the channel, a definite wake-up call.

He showered, remembering the nightmare and the sounds of two Hueys... It was daybreak and they were moving fast and low over muddy delta rice paddies. Coming upon the target, a village of seven huts where Viet Cong were supposed to be holed up, the choppers opened fire on the huts and people rushed out and began running everywhere in little circles, trying to escape. No return fire. Just a bunch of peasants: women, old men, and children, running, looking up, waving fists, crying, shouting, and dying.

The side gunner next to Jack was screaming obscenities and crying as he fired randomly at point blank range. A huge black water buffalo that was tethered to a post had broken free and bolted toward the lagoon. The machine gun followed, bullets pock-marking the dirt; small bursts of skin and flesh and blood appeared as the bullets moved up the buffalo's back. The creature slowed, moved erratically for a few seconds, falling on its side in shallow water. The buffalo looked back, kicking with useless hind legs, eyes wide, then dulling as the head and great horns turned back and fell, dead weight into the water.

"No Cong! No Cong!" Jack screamed. The gunner continued to pump bullets into the writhing carcass. Blood from the buffalo's mouth formed a dark pool in the brown water. Jack punched the gunner in the shoulder and shouted over his own raging cries, "No Cong, God damn it! No Cong!" The gunner continued firing, bawling aloud.

There were no Cong or else they'd have returned fire. A voice on the intercom said something. The copter pilot shouted back something unintelligible. The gunner stopped firing, hunched over the machine gun, exhausted, still bawling like a baby.

And like two satiated birds of prey, the Hueys tilted, swung around in formation, and headed toward the rising sun. Jack looked back through the open bay and watched the pandemonium of the living and the wounded moving about, checking the dead and the dying. A small boy rested his arm about the neck of the buffalo, his head down next to its ear, seeming to be talking to it, perhaps begging it not to be dead, not to be dying, coaxing it to come alive again.

Another mission accomplished. They were headed back to base for a post-mission briefing, a shower, a fresh uniform, a good breakfast, some sleep, a game of volleyball or poker. Later on, they would go to some bar and try to drown the mission in alcohol. And when that did not work, they would seek out and bed the prostitutes. In the dream, Jack had fired the camera continuously, knowing that it contained no film. He was going through the motions, doing his duty... for God and country, for the folks back home... He was burned out and knew it.

Jack puzzled over why there was no film in the camera and concluded that in his dream he must have wanted to protect himself against having to record the atrocities. The image of the great water buffalo trying to escape to the water lingered... along with the second image of the young boy tending to it.

He tried to shake off the dream, yet it lingered: the first part in black and white, and then changing to full, brilliant, terrible color. He dressed and put on running shoes and a Braves cap. He went topside. Good air was stirring and already warming. A great day for sailing. He tried to forget the dream by imagining Sally coming aboard, wearing a light sundress or a tank top and cut-offs. He smiled. Sally would be on the boat within a few hours.

He jogged down the quay, crossing the bridge to Spyglass Lane and running along the beach for a mile before returning the same way. After his shower, he put on a fresh T-shirt and shorts, and crossed the boulevard to the Mariner Cafe. There were hardly any customers yet. He waited at an outdoor table that was beaded with moisture. Jason, the owner's son, came out with a towel and wiped the chair and table top dry and returned with his order: orange juice, coffee, and a bowl of cereal with sliced banana. He ate quickly, thinking about the several tasks to be completed before Harvey and Sally arrived. Then, he headed back.

A final safety check was in order. The gas tank was full, but he needed to refill the water tank. He removed the cover to the inboard engine and inspected the wiring, checked the battery, wiped the distributor cap clean and replaced it. He pushed the starter. It squealed twice before the motor chugged, fired, and rumbled in a steady, warbling voice. He loved the sound. She was good. Ought to be. Only had twenty-six hours on her since the last overhaul. He replaced the engine cover and let the motor run several minutes, goosing the accelerator now and then, recalling the rapid fire of the machine gun in the Huey. He switched off the engine and began setting the new halyards. He tied them to the old ones, ran them aloft, then untied the old ones and put them in a grocery bag to be thrown away. It was not even seven thirty. He had time on his hands. He tied off the halyards and checked the stays fore and aft.

After the rigging was finished, he used the dinghy to swab the sides of the vessel from stem to stern above the water line. He replaced the hose, bucket and brush in the locker on the pier.

Bilge pump. He always forgot to check it. He entered the aft cockpit and switched the pump on, still obsessed with the image of the poor water buffalo being slaughtered. He went below and opened the compartment. There was a slight leak around one coupling. He switched the pump off and retrieved a Stillson pipe wrench and a new gasket from the tool locker. He detached the coupling, removed the worn gasket, inserted the new one, and tightened the fitting with the wrench. He laid the wrench on a seat in the salon and switched on the pump. No leak. He switched off the pump and closed the compartment. It was eight-forty. He was sweaty. He had time for another shower before Harvey arrived.

It was the third shower of the day already. He toweled off and put on a pair of briefs and khaki shorts. He was slipping a white T-shirt over his head when he felt the slight but sudden list of QT2's deck that told him somebody had stepped aboard.

"Be right up, Harvey." he called out, reaching for his moccasins. He slipped one on, leaning against the bulkhead as he did so.

A shadow fell across the cabin. There was heavy breathing. He heard a whizzing sound. Something crashed against his skull. He fell back against a bulwark, head swirling dizzily, hurting as if he had been whacked with a concrete block. Something was striking his ribs, his legs, his back. He heard noises like ice cracking. He slumped to the deck. His body thumped against a bulkhead again and again. He couldn't open his eyes, yet saw millions of dots of light swarming this way and that like newborn shrimp in a dark lagoon. His head was growing numb. He tried to bring his left arm up so he could feel his head, but something smacked his elbow and he could hear more ice cracking. Part of him was so numb he could only feel sensations of thumping that moved his body this way and that as though he were a giant rag doll.

Above the ringing in his ears and din of something hitting him was a voice. It was shouting obscenities and seemed out of breath, trying to shout while hammering his body.

Then, there was a hollow sounding thump like the impact of a boxer's hook to the ribs. A great weight fell on him, pushing all his breath out so he gasped and choked under the mass. It began squirming like a huge octopus with many tentacles, shifting on him at different places, causing great pain in his legs there, his ribs here, grinding his head into the deck.

Far off was a hollow plop, like a skull hitting concrete, and he felt a jolt above him as the massive weight shifted and covered him, smothering him again at a different angle. And then, blessedly, a lightness as the mass shifted, lifting off his body, and he felt feather-light.

A voice very close to his head called so that he heard and felt the pressure of the air with each syllable upon his burning ear. The voice came from far away.

"Can you hear me, Jack?" the voice seemed to ask, yet it was so far away, like it was coming from the bottom of a well. There was a tapping on his shoulder. The tapping was excruciating. He grimaced and yelled, "Stop!" yet he could not hear his own voice.

The tapping stopped followed by shuffling, something sliding on the deck, causing strange sounds in his right ear. Someone must have broken a jar of syrup. It was thick and warm beneath his head. That is what he must have heard, the plopping sound and glass breaking was the Peter Rabbit brand of syrup he liked on pancakes.

"Yes…" the voice came from the old Victrola in his grandfather's house. "I need an ambulance immediately at city pier…" came a voice. Was it John McCormack or Caruso? He could not tell because of scratchy surface noises. A new needle. We need a new needle. "Berth number? Yes. Berth sixty-four, across from Winn-Dixie." John McCormack, the Irish tenor. Grandpop's favorite. He ought to be singing, though.

"Ah, I'm not sure. Two men. Both unconscious. Hurry, please." John McCormack's voice is more nasal. Squawking sounds, like the volume of the Victrola was too loud. 'Turn it down, Grandpop. Get him to sing something.' The voice and noise ran down together. He could hear nothing now except a ringing in his left ear. Then, the needle skipping at the end of the record began, making a poking little noise: Ka-poke, ka-poke, ka-poke. 'Fix it, Grandpop.' He tried to lift the silver arm with the needle off the record and return it to the beginning. He could not. He tried to wind the Victrola using the crank, but his left arm felt like three pieces of broken wood, and he could not lift it to the Victrola.

A heavy shuffling next to his ear. Scent of Old Spice. Grandpop. Something moist and cool rested against his throbbing head, just above the ear. The scent drew closer, stronger. There was light pressure at the side of his throat, shaking slightly. Grandpop was breathing heavily, shifting, touching his throat. He wanted to tell him the Victrola's stopped. That he wanted to hear John McCormack sing *In the Gloaming* again... Yes... There it was, he said, smiling to himself... the song he wanted, yet different, like a siren approaching. He thought it was the fanfare to Rossini's *William Tell*.

Voices. Is it the three part harmony from... something Bizet wrote? There were men's voices, deep, sonorous. The deck listed beneath his ear in the syrup.

"Down here," John McCormack said, probably to Grandpop. Shuffling, shifting.

"Afraid he's gone," said Caruso. "Let's check this one out..."

More shuffling. Wintergreen breath cascaded over his face as a cool hand lifted an eyelid. He saw dark forms before a light blinded and sent spears of glistening diamonds into the center of his head, going black again when the cool hand shifted to his neck. Pressure along his side, too. Grandpop likes to tickle, but it doesn't feel tickly.

"He's still breathing," Caruso told Grandpop and John McCormack. "Bring in the stretcher."

'Yes,' he said. 'Put on the record and wind up the Victrola. I want to hear the rest of it...'

He felt himself shifted, pulled, lifted. Something was pushed under him, catching one of the pieces of wood next to him, wracking him with pain.

"Make way, here he comes," said a voice. He thought it must be Grandpop's.

The air was not stuffy, yet he could hardly breathe. Someone had lashed him to the Victrola and it was being carried out of Grandpop's barn and into fresh air. Sun struck his face, warming his eyelids, turning the background of the dancing lights inside his head from white to red. The Victrola's cabinet doors burst open like bomb bay doors, and the large, black, red-labeled RCA Victor records fell everywhere around him.

There went Grandpop's favorite–the tan colored one, an Oriole Record, *The March of the Toy Soldiers*. Some of them were breaking, some were rolling across the stones in front of the barn, spinning, rolling in circles, colliding, as with a final lurch, his body jarred against the Victrola and the lid of it came down with a slam just above him...

'Thank God,' he said to John McCormack, 'that the Victrola lid did not strike my head. It could've killed me...' A slight, distant sound of ice cracking, and he fell gently through the well in the orchard behind Grandpop's garden. He tumbled endlessly into blackness...

Chapter 43

Thursday, June 13.

Something was brushing his fingers. He attempted to open his eyes, but only his right one opened. It was difficult to focus. A ghost form appeared next to him and grasped his fingers lightly.

"Hello, there! Welcome back," said Em gently.

He could see her only peripherally out of his right eye, and could not move his head to look at her. He must be inside the Victrola because he felt totally enclosed.

Many moments later, holding Em's hand and listening to her saying things he did not understand, he realized he was in a hospital room. His cocoon was made of plaster and bandages. The television was on, but muted. His body throbbed terribly. Tubes filled his nose and throat. He felt imprisoned, nearly suffocating.

"Hey!" was all he could get out. One breath of effort before contact between lungs and ribs brought a thousand darts of pain to his chest. He gasped for breath, trying not to expand his lungs yet needing air.

"Don't try to talk, Dad... You're going to be all right. Just rest, okay?"

Em reached for something. A distant bell rang. A woman in white entered.

"He's awake finally, thank God," said Em.

"Wonderful!" The nurse touched his right wrist, taking his pulse. "Glad to see your eyes open. You gave us a good scare, Mr. Kaufman..."

He tried to nod, but it was impossible. He could hear thunder. Bursts of lightning lit the room. Someone drew the curtains.

The nurse leaned down so he could see her face.

"Do you know how long you've been unconscious?"

A stupid question, he thought. How would he know? He could feel her breath on his face as she leaned closer. His eye focused upon the bright red lipstick that moved sensuously to form words, showing worn teeth. Too much lipstick for the size of her mouth, he concluded. She must use it to distract attention from the little brown wart eyeing him like a tiny clitoris from the crease at the corner of her mouth.

"Four days... Mr. Kaufman. You've been out of it four days..."

Out of what? He tried to remember. A Victrola. He was being carried under a Victrola. Grandpop. It happened at Grandpop's. He had fallen into the well.

Em and Bernice took turns staying with him. Both of them looked worn out and sad. He could do nothing about their sadness. They made him sad, too, and that was confusing because he had nothing to be sad about. Falling into the well was an accident. He didn't mean to do it. It was he who was hurt, not they. And he had nothing to do with all the phonograph records breaking either. 'Tell Grandpop it wasn't me,' he tried to say.

He knew little about the time of day or when night came. He dozed fitfully, often catching his breath on sharp needles that brought him instantly awake with a groan or muffled shout. He often heard Em and Bernice nearby. A nurse appeared and disappeared frequently in and out of fog. Dismembered arms with hands touched him here and there. Deep male voices said unintelligible things.

Now and then, he was given sedatives, he suspected, in the IV in his right arm. At intervals, a team of young men came in and lifted him, moving his body to what he recognized from Nam as a Stryker frame. Doctors came in to check this and that, remove plaster, adjust plastic splints, take X-rays, discuss another surgery. He glided in and out of consciousness in a limbo of medicines and injuries. Yet, gradually, he awakened to a rhythm of activity and routine that slowly he even looked forward to.

At some point, they removed the heaviest bandages from his head and neck, and he saw with both eyes. Except, he could not see as well with his left eye.

Gradually, he could speak with limitations: a whispered yes or no, and brief sentences without verbs or adjectives.

Bernice and Em seemed perplexed when he tried to explain about the well and the Victrola. Naturally, he was worried that all of Grandpop's records were gone. That was why they were so sad, he surmised. They did not want to tell him all the wonderful music was gone forever. He feared Grandpop was cross with them about it. And, too, the Victrola did need a new needle. Needles cost money.

One day, Chief Winters came by. He asked Jack what he remembered.

"I remember the Victrola was scratchy and needed a new needle. John McCormack and Enrico Caruso talked about an accident. And three guys sang a trio from Bizet."

Winters scratched his face and nodded officiously. He understood, Jack thought. The chief went away before he could tell him about the records being destroyed.

Another day, Bernice brought in a uniformed woman. Bernice had never looked happier than when she said, "See who's here! Your friend Sally's been very worried about you."

It was Sally. She leaned in, freckled face soft and warm. She brushed back her hair. Her scent was heavenly. "You owe me a sail, fella!"

He smiled and discovered it did not hurt to do it. "I do?"

"Soon's you're outta here." She took his hand and gave it a light squeeze. "I'll stop by again soon."

She turned away. She smelled like his shirts used to smell when Grandmom dried them on the clothesline: sunshine and spring air. He wanted to keep her here, but realized she was probably working today.

"Thanks," he managed to mumble.

And as though by magic, Sally's visit brought him a memory. They had planned a sail. The three of them: Harvey, Sally and him.

"Where's Harvey," he asked Bernice.

"Um," said Bernice, eyes fluttering. "He's around. You just concentrate on getting better now."

"Harvey should be here." He raised his voice. "I want Harvey."

"Not now, honey," said Bernice. She pushed a button.

The nurse with the heavy lipstick came and gawked at him, as though trying to decipher his latest problem.

"You think you can give him another tranquilizer, Sue? He's getting agitated again."

"I don't need any," he protested. "I want Harvey... Tell Harvey to come by... and bring cheesecake. All I need is Harvey's cheesecake."

He hurt like hell, but suddenly he was more worried about why Harvey hadn't come by.

Chapter 44

Tuesday, July 2.

It was nearly three weeks before Jack learned the truth. Chief Winters and Sally put it together for him.

"Bryan caught you by surprise in the forward berth," Winters explained. "He struck you across the side of your head with a tire iron. That one blow must have taken you down. Lucky it didn't strike any lower. You would have died instantly."

"He's in jail," Jack protested. "He's south of here... In Dade..."

"Well," said Winters, smoothing his slicked hair back, "Something happened when they were taking four guys down to Dade County in the hospital van. One of the prisoners managed to overpower the guy riding shotgun. We don't think it was Bryan. Anyway, they forced the driver off the road, knocked him and the guard unconscious, and then commandeered a vehicle in Harbor Town. Bryan was loose and back in town shortly after midnight of the day we took him into custody."

"Jesus..."

"We got word of their escape around two in the morning, after the van failed to arrive at the Psychiatric Center. We put out an

APB and had cruisers swarming your place and Bryan's apartment. No luck. You were gone. No sign of Bryan."

"How'd he find me? Your officers checked the entire house for bugs. Everything was clean, including the phones."

"We never thought to check your car. He'd bugged it using a silent beeper, just like the ones we use in our cruisers. God knows where he got it. He was able to use a computer monitoring program similar to ours. Whenever he wanted to know your whereabouts, he'd check the computer. He had sectional maps of the city. The computer screen gave him your location within a few hundred feet."

Jack lifted himself up and hauled the cast on his left arm onto the extension table. He understood now. "So all those times when we saw Bryan sitting at a bus stop, watching his computer, he wasn't playing chess–at least not the kind normal people play."

"For sure," said Winters, smoothing his hair.

"But how could he use his computer? You arrested him. Sally said his computers were confiscated."

Winters shook his head. "We never found his bike or his portable computer. When we arrested him, my guys searched the park high and low, thinking the bike would be close by. He musta stashed it and his knapsack, maybe at his new hangout. Seagate PD had his apartment under surveillance. After being served to appear in court, he never went back there."

"So when Bryan escaped, he came back and got his bike and computer."

"Correct. He knew your car was at the dock."

"Funny why he didn't attack me in the middle of the night."

"He had to get high first. He musta spent the night with his drug buddies. Probably slept a while 'til he could navigate his bike. The coroner's report shows he was on speed."

"Bryan's dead?"

"Uh, yes, Jack. He's dead. Hasn't Sally told you?"

"No," he replied, thinking there was plenty more nobody had told him.

Winters bent down and examined Jack's partially closed left eye. "Were you conscious after the first blow?"

"I remember the thuds. Seems I leaned against the hull and tried to stay on my feet. Then, I remember going down, feeling my body jumping this way and that."

"He kicked the hell out of you. You looked like you'd fallen off a ten story building."

He grinned faintly. "I felt like it, too."

"Cutler worked you over from head to toes. It's a wonder you survived..."

Yes, he thought. Why did Bryan spare him? It didn't jibe. Another blow to his head with the tire iron... "How come I did?"

"What?"

"Survive."

Winters smoothed his hair with both hands and wiped them together. "You wouldn't have, except Harvey got there in time."

"Harvey saved my life?"

"Yes..."

"What about Harvey?"

Winters looked down at the floor. He grimaced. "Well, let me take you through the whole scenario. The Coroner places Bryan's death at approximately three minutes after nine. Harvey told the medics that when he arrived at the boat, he heard cursing and stomping. He sneaked down the hatch and found Bryan kicking you and had a tire iron in his hand.

Stalker

"Harvey grabbed a pipe wrench from the galley and struck Bryan with it between the shoulder blades. That took him out. For good measure, he delivered an upward blow to the base of Bryan's skull, severing the spinal cord. Bryan died instantly. Apparently, Harvey pulled Bryan off you and dragged him into the galley where the medics found him."

"So... Where's Harvey?"

Winters held out his hand flat. "I'm coming to that. After he dialed 911 and the medics loaded you up, Harvey said he'd wait for crime scene investigators to show. Last the medics know, Harvey was standing on the deck of your boat."

"And?"

"When our guys arrive, Harvey's gone. They do their thing. Check Bryan out, locate the weapons he and Harvey used, and discover the computer in a knapsack on Bryan's bike. They search your car and find the beeper. Sally arrives. She says she had a date with you guys at nine-thirty. She actually arrived closer to ten. She asks where Harvey is. Our investigators don't know. They get Harvey's description from Sally and call the medics who picked you up. It matches. An APB is put out for Harvey."

"Yeah?"

"Two patrolmen locate Harvey's car behind his shop, break in the door to his upstairs apartment, and find he's shot himself in the temple with his own gun."

A wave of heat flashed into Jack's cheeks. He remembered the morning they had sat together in his office, Jack holding Harvey's hand, consoling, doing everything he could think of to get him out of his depression. He had seen guys in Nam look like that. And soon after, they would take one on purpose. Put themselves out of their misery. He felt overcome with sadness and loss. Harvey was so honest. He was like a conscience to him, explaining how to behave and how to do the right thing by people. Tears streamed down Jack's face.

"I'm sorry," said Winters. "I knew he was special to you. There was a suicide note... Addressed to Sally. He musta suffered extreme depression for a long time. We've learned he was a Holocaust victim. Sally says Harvey once told her he saw his entire family being marched to the gas chambers."

"Yeah. He told me. I can't believe it. He told me one night my life would change forever... And it has... And at what cost?"

"Harvey also wrote up a will. Your daughter is in it."

"Em?"

"A gift to both of you. He told me one time he admired how close you and Emily are. And Sally says Harvey worried that Bryan would hurt her. You probably didn't know it, but Harvey spent hours keeping a watch on Bryan. Even staked out Emily's boyfriend's car at play practice after that rat incident."

"I did know."

"Probably explains why Cutler turned on Harvey."

"What's his will say about Emily?"

"He wants the shop to be sold and half the proceeds divided between Emily and Bryan's mother. He specifies Emily is to use the money for education. Mrs. Cutler's is to be used for expenses at Wellspring Center. It seems Harvey had set up some arrangements at Wellspring for when he became infirm."

"What about the other half?"

"Divided among his employees with the hope they'll use the money for college. Apparently, he had no family left. No heirs."

"Yeah. True."

Tears continued to stream down Jack's face. He was at a loss to know his own feelings. He had so looked forward to having

Stalker

Harvey Gold as a lasting friend. Chief Winters stepped aside. Sally appeared. She took a tissue and wiped his eyes.

"I'll leave you two alone," said Winters.

Sally bit her lip and sat on the edge of the bed.

"Horrible, isn't it," she whispered. Tears filled her eyes. She brushed them aside. She was wearing light, frilly civilian clothes, a teal blouse open at the neck, revealing freckled cleavage, and small gold earrings and bracelets that shone brightly. She took his hand and bent closer.

"Harvey wrote a letter to me. Would you like to hear it?"

"Sure," he said, still numb from Winters' revelations.

Dear Sally:

I want to thank you for being my friend. You and I know Bryan as nobody else in the world, maybe even more than God. Once, when I looked upon him as my son, I made him sole heir to my store and the little real estate I own. After his car accident, I decide I cannot overlook facts any longer. I change my will from Bryan to the high school across the street, which brought me so good livelihood. Now, I change the will again.

Bryan is beyond help, much in the same way as I experience madness. And during worst nights, I've imagined I confronted Bryan doing a bad thing and found myself killing him. I've imagined doing it many places. At your office, trying to protect you from him. At Jack's home, catching Bryan in the act of climbing through a window. In my shop, keeping him from someone's throat. Somehow, I felt God knew I would kill Bryan and that it wouldn't be a very bad thing.

When I actually found Bryan hurting Jack, I had no second thoughts. I'd rehearsed it so often in my mind like actor in a play. When I arrive on the boat, God provided me with the proper tool. A wrench waited for me to take it and strike a death blow cleanly so that Bryan would not suffer. He would merely be dead. He would hurt no one again forever. And that is what happened, as God willed.

After the ambulance left, I went back and sat down next to Bryan's body and felt deepest sadness of my life, far deeper than when I watched my family die. For I had killed the final hope I had in myself. Bryan and I shared tormented souls. With Bryan's death, my soul is gone. I want to embrace Bryan in death as I wanted to in life--a gift God would not grant me until now.

I drive home to where I sit, rewriting my will and sharing with you my last minutes on earth. I seek only to join Bryan in death and peace. I cannot believe a just God will punish Bryan and me anymore– unless he has a Jewish sense of humor.

If Jack should be alive still, and I pray to God he lives, tell him I have best New York cheese cake and cherry blintz for him in the refrigerator. I make sure they are fresh for him last night. You tell him to share them with you. A last gift of food from Harvey Gold to you.

And another thing. Jack does not know it yet, but he is in love with you. Do you know that? I think you are in love with him, too, true? You both would do well to see what is so clear to me. You would be a perfect match made in heaven. And God doesn't often make perfection, except perhaps when he guides my hand in making bagels and pastries...Masel Tov to you both!

Please don't be sad at my passing, Sally. I will be at peace, after so long a life of torment and suffering.

With deep affection and love,
Harvey.

"I've read it over and over so often I can't cry about it anymore," Sally said, wiping Jack's tears with a tissue. She pursed her lips and ran her hand lightly over his cheek. "Maybe this isn't the time or place, but I need to tell you I'm in love with you, Jack."

She began to weep and he did too. He wished he could pull her hand to his lips, but he did not have the strength.

"Me, too, Sally," he managed to whisper.

Sally leaned over and kissed him on the forehead. Her perfume was light and willowy, like she was. She moved off the bed to take a tissue from a box on the table and dabbed her eyes.

Em came up next to Sally and put her arm around her. Jack watched them standing close together, smiling at him and at each other.

"So... are you guys coming out or what?" Em asked mischievously.

"How'd you know, Em," Jack asked.

Em looked at Sally. They laughed and squeezed each other. "Oh, we've had lots of hours together here over the past three weeks. It was Mom who spotted it."

"Spotted what?"

"The look in your eye when Sally came to visit. And the same was true when Sally talked about you. Mom put two and two together. Mom says you're both like two lovesick puppies. She's very happy for you. And so am I."

"Well, Em," he said, trying to be the decorous father, "Sally and I hardly know each other."

"Sure, sure, I've heard that line before. At least wait until I come back from Spain."

"Em and I were talking about it," Sally said, coming up and grasping his hand in hers. "We can have a small wedding with a few friends. Could we have it on the boat?"

"Why not," he said, thinking women were always about ten steps ahead of men when it came to making plans.

Em clutched Sally around the waist. "Can I be the flower girl or something? Maybe I'd be good as the ring bearer. Or best girl? Would you mind if I give you away, Dad? Yeah, best girl suits me. Whaddya think?"

A Personal Epilogue
by Jack Kaufman

September 26, 1990.

It has taken me over five years to heal emotionally and physically following those tragic days in 1985. At the time, I wasn't sure I would survive. I must thank all my loved ones—Em, Bernice, Sally, Bill, and a whole host of others–for their support and help during the darkest times. And I think Harvey Gold's sacrifice was, ironically, a mainstay in my recovery. I felt like Harvey had given his life so I could live to tell our story, since Harvey, Bryan, and I are in a strange way forever kindred spirits.

Looking back, all of us involved became better people because Bryan Cutler threatened our lives. It made us realize how destructive emotional trauma can be. All of us are making renewed efforts to identify people in our community who are suffering post traumatic stress and to direct them to the agencies that are available to help them. I am, for the first time, able to talk about my experiences in Vietnam without feeling extreme guilt or rage. I've come a long way in overcoming the demons that once haunted me to near-suicide.

But there are other positive things that resulted from those nightmarish days of 1985. I'd like to recount some for you. Here's a brief summary.

There was enough money in Harvey's real estate holdings to build a new theatre wing at Ocean High School. It is called Gold Theater in his honor. A plaque at the front tells Harvey's story and lists the 32 extended family members who died in concentration camps between 1942 and 1945. The black leather tefillin Harvey wore on his arm when he read the Torah was found among his belongings. It still has verses of scripture in it. The tefillin is in a glass case in my studio. It reminds me every day to think about God and things of the spirit, and this always brings back the voice, the laughter, the taste of pastries, and the wonderful admonitions of Harvey Gold.

Em? What can I say? She's resilient. She won the Best Actor award for her performance in the senior play and graduated with honors. She ended up spending a whole year in Madrid, thanks to Harvey's generosity, studying Spanish culture, dance and acting. When she returned, she obtained a scholarship to Colgate and is currently a senior with many theater credits to her name. She is destined for Broadway. At least Mr. Enright assures me she has what it takes to get there.

Bernice did leave in June of 1985 as planned. She recanted and removed most of the yellow stickers from furniture and other items. We're on amicable terms. She and Em communicate regularly. Bernie is living happily with her new husband, Mike Breslin, in a penthouse suite overlooking the yacht basin in Fort Lauderdale. I hear she's quit smoking and has cut down her wine consumption, too.

Chief Bill Winters retired under pressure from the mayor less than a month after I got out of the hospital. It seems the mayor accused Bill of favoring a few friends over the majority of other citizens when it came to police protection. The extra squad cars and foot soldiers in my neighborhood were a matter of record. The mayor said he would take the evidence of cronyism to the newspapers unless Bill resigned. No contest. Bill and I have since become close buddies. We fish and sail together at least once a week.

Chuck (Goliath) Hampton and David Welch went west after graduation. Chuck studied at Cal Arts and became a set designer and drama instructor for a small college in the California wine country. Dave stayed in Los Angeles where he is now a journeyman lighting specialist for a major movie studio.

Jean Weston, the young woman Bryan Cutler raped, spent considerable time in psychotherapy before resuming a relatively normal life. She has since graduated from a beauty school and works in a salon in Clearwater. She recently married and hopes to have some children soon.

Mrs. Cutler, by the way, lives in a really nice high-rise apartment overlooking the ocean at Wellspring Center. She's on medication and is a different person from the woman I met, according to Sally. Sally goes to see her occasionally, takes her presents, and makes sure she is okay.

And Sally? She's my dearest love. We got married after Em returned from Spain. Sold both our houses and bought a larger boat and a condo. She now heads the probation department for Ocean County and is lobbying the state for earlier intervention in stalking cases. She's considered an expert witness in stalking-related court cases. She's become an excellent sailor and has fulfilled a childhood dream: acting with a local community theater group.

Me? Well, I've had to make adjustments, as I mentioned previously. I've finally learned the meaning of what we all said we'd do when we came back from Vietnam: Don't sweat the small stuff. I have only partial sight in my left eye and about fifty percent use of my left arm. I have a permanent limp. I never was able to finish my twenty good years in the military. And I no longer do freelance photography. My new thing is portraiture. I have a dynamite studio on Seaview Boulevard near the Winn-Dixie across from our boat. I'm doing a growing number of racing crew portraits, plus regular families and individuals. It won't make me rich, but it's fun. Besides, I have a lot more time for sailing now. We also have a new family member: a black mongrel bitch named Chloe who just turned two. She keeps me company every day at the studio and loves to sail.

Life's good. Visit, if you're in the neighborhood.

Jack

Made in the USA
Charleston, SC
07 November 2012